Savarona

J. Patrick Hart

PublishAmerica
Baltimore

First printing

ISBN: 1-4137-1446-3
PUBLISHED BY PUBLISHAMERICA, LLLP
www.publishamerica.com
Baltimore

Printed in the United States of America

To my girls.

Author's Notes

This is an attempt at fiction. Yet there are also some inescapable references to fact, including the existence of a place called Istanbul and a terrorist group known as the PKK, as well as certain background events that did take place, though not necessarily in the order or timeframe presented here. The main elements of the plot, however, are purely and absolutely imaginary, as are the characters, at least to the extent it's possible to imagine characters without borrowing bits and pieces from the people we've known.

The passages that Vram's father reads aloud in Part Three of this novel are from the official dispatches of Leslie A. Davis, an American diplomat posted in eastern Turkey in 1915, a time when the Armenian population was being decimated by massacres and deportations. These reports are available in U.S. government archives and in *The Slaughterhouse Province*, edited by Susan Blair; Melissa Media, 1989. Two other books that served as especially useful and enjoyable background reading for this novel were *Ataturk* by Lord Kinross; Quill, William Morrow, New York, 1964; and *Touched with Fire* by Kay Redfield Jamison, Free Press, Reissue Edition, 1996. I thank Michael D. Crawford for granting me permission to use his manic poem in Part Two, recited by the narrator as he goes to pieces in his Beyoğlu hotel room. I am especially grateful to Elmira Bayrasli and Edwin Latter for generously giving their time to edit this novel as it took shape.

The Turkish alphabet is like its English counterpart, but with a few differences: To simplify pronunciation, the Turkish ç and ş appear in these pages as "ch" and "sh." The Turkish ö and ü appear as they are. C in Turkish is pronounced as "j" and the ğ is silent.

PART ONE

Look me in the eyes and tell me
that I'm satisfied.
Now, are you satisfied?

—*Paul Westerberg*

* * *

It is said that the Bosphorous Straits, the mighty waters that cut through Istanbul, flow at once in two directions. On the surface, the current is strong and true, spilling from the Black Sea south, driving untold tons of sewage first to the Sea of Marmara then on to the Aegean, where it clings to the bodies of unsuspecting bathers. But farther below, in the depths beneath the white caps, scouring the mud which holds the secrets of a millennium, a hidden current doubles back and flows north, ensuring that the city will taste its refuse twice.

"Not much of a metaphor, is it?" asks a young American through a graveyard of empty Efes bottles. He draws pensively from his cigarette, and adds a smoke ring to the already hazy Sultan "Pub." Outside the window, the red walls of Aya Sofya, Church of Divine Wisdom, are barely visible in the darkness. Now that the Muslims run Constantinople, the bubbled contours of the nearby Blue Mosque are forever flooded with dazzling white light—a vain attempt to surpass the grandeur of its Christian neighbor, yet the glory of Aya Sofya, even from the shadows, is undiminished.

"What I mean is," continues the young man. He has bright red hair and pasty freckled skin that might seem comical on someone half his age, but in his case looks slightly odd and unpleasant. "Everything in Turkey is about east versus west, not north versus south. You know, the only country to sit astride two continents. The bridge. The crossroads. Occident and Orient. The clash of civilizations. So, you see, a north-south current in the Bosphorous isn't much of a metaphor. Not for this country."

In lieu of an answer, his drinking partner, an Australian, lifts a fresh beer to his lips then sets it down with a thump, as if the table had just risen without his noticing. He is taller than the red-haired one, and better looking with angular features, baked blonde hair and muscles that show through his shirt. Safely drunk, he no longer feigns interest in the conversation; too much talk about politics and what's all this about metaphors? For the first time in weeks, he's ready to pass on a round, maybe even stop before he throws up.

A long pause, then the red-haired one lolls his head. "You don't think the aborigines have a right to complain after the way they've been treated?" It's the second time he's asked. He picks the last shreds of label from his beer bottle and rolls the moist paper between his fingers.

"Look mate, if you'd ever been to my country—if you'd ever been to an abo town—you'd see for yourself they live like animals. All that money we give them? You reckon it goes anywhere but for grog?"

"I reckon..." says the American. He stops on the word, tastes it, finds it sour. "You probably vote for, what, the most right-wing party?"

"I reckon. Yih. But voting's compulsory. I couldn't really give a stuff. Left-wing, right wing; they're all a bunch of crims. You's gotta vote for someone is the way it is. Who am I going to vote for? Labor? There's no more country party, so I reckon the Nats is as good as the next."

This brings a look of satisfaction to the red-haired one. He is quiet for a moment, then his expression breaks to show a decision's been made. "You smoke hash?" he asks.

The Australian sits up as sharply as his buzz allows. "Why do you ask?"

"Why do you think I ask?"

"Good on you. Let's go then." The sight of them rising stirs a table across the room, where three darker young men have been nursing single glasses of raki for most of the night. They call themselves Kurds, these three, though they barely speak the language and regard those who do as reactionary peasants, mere foot soldiers in the movement. For days, they've waited in frustration for their red-headed American comrade to select his prey; Red Halabja, that's what they call him, in tribute to the village of Halabja in Northern Iraq that Saddam Hussein laid waste with nerve gas and cyanide. And because of his crazy-colored hair.

Zakho, one of the three, is also named after a village in Kurdistan. He is the leader of their cell and the one who persuaded Red to make tonight his rite of passage, his trial by fire. "If they're not for us they're against us," Zakho had reminded him as they drove into the heart of Istanbul's tourist district. Then he'd pulled the car over so that Red could empty his stomach onto the sidewalk. Amidst the standard sludge, it had scarcely made a difference. "You'll feel better when it's over," Zakho had said—

and it was true. The action itself is never the hard part. The agony is in the waiting, in the anticipation leading up to the event, when planning is laced with bitter debate and, with debate, doubt. Pulling the trigger is the easy part; nothing feels more certain than that. And the rush that follows makes up for it all.

Will he go through with it? Perhaps, for now he has paid the bill and is leading the drunk Australian to the door. The Kurds follow them outside. "Durun," says Zakho. Stop. He lights a cigarette and takes a seat in the darkness. "Let them be."

They stroll beneath Aya Sofya, one quiet and sullen, the other joking loudly, past the street hawkers who cry "Yes please" even at this late hour. Beyond the tour buses, the street drops downhill then curves gently into a gully of late Ottoman era homes, converted into shops next to slums in a neighborhood half-gentrified. They take an alley that darkens as it splits a cluster of broken shacks on pavement that turns to potholes, cobblestone and, finally, dirt. Beyond screenless windows, shuttered tight, the sound of family chatter is heard, ever so faintly. It sounds warm inside, comfortable despite the poverty. In the alleyway, all is quiet.

"Where you taking me, mate? I reckon this is far enough."

"Have you ever seen the inside of a Turkish jail?" snaps Red. "I for one am taking no chances." The Australian shrugs and keeps walking. They come to a stop, at last, behind a stone wall, ageless and sturdy beneath a tangle of scruffy bushes. The house opposite has a hollow, forlorn look; it seems a thousand years empty. How many times through the ages has this place been used for this purpose? Red moves his hand beneath his jacket. It's leather, from the Grand Bazaar, and it's falling apart though only a few months old. Even now, as he steadies himself to cross the threshold, to take that step from which there is no turning back, the trivial thought that the leather salesman ripped him off intrudes: A lousy one hundred dollars. But he should have known better, shouldn't he? Why was he such a sucker?

"Okay, mate. Let's have a look, shall we?" The Australian takes a step forward, stumbles, then steadies himself on the wall. "I reckon this is the first thing I need," he laughs.

Red stiffens. "You're not much interested in politics are you?"

"Ah, there you go again." His hands are imploring. "C'mon, c'mon."

"I reckon," Red says with disdain, "a person of integrity should be willing to die for his politics. For his cause."

"Ah, you and your—Die for politics? Nah, footy maybe. But never ..." He seems to lose his train of thought. Only now does it occur to him that something is wrong.

Red pulls a handgun from his pocket, a relic from the late seventies—a time when the streets of Istanbul echoed at night with gunfire, months of chaos before the military stepped in to restore order. Once owned by a Bulgarian border guard, the gun was traded back to the Soviets when the new models arrived, and eventually spirited across the Turkish border beneath the floorboards of a horse-drawn cart. It's a small caliber weapon, old and a little rusty, the kind of weapon best fired at close range and with accuracy to avoid the need for a second shot.

Red aims it carefully.

* * *

One morning George McCall—*Vice Consul* George McCall, according to his commission from the U.S. Congress—awoke with a sense of deep foreboding, a suspicion that something was wrong, the tip of a nightmare. He felt it in a physical way, not in the pit of his stomach but right up near the forehead. He felt it during breakfast and he felt it during lunch—a little edge on his laugh, a distant wound to his *authenticity*. Outside, wind chimes jangled in the breeze. It was an astonishingly sunny day.

One year later, the feeling is still there.

George is not as pear-shaped as his older colleagues, but the mirror says he is dangerously on his way. Language class was an excellent place to put on weight; food never tasted so good as in the present tense. But that was six months ago and still he is growing. He recalls a Paul Simon song and says the words aloud: "Why am I so soft in the middle when the rest of my life is so hard?"

He ties a Windsor, the only knot he knows. There was a time in his life, not so long ago, when his next stop would have been the bathroom, for a washcloth to scrub the spit-up stains from his shirt. Never quite succeeding, it seemed he always wore the faint shadow of his daughter's colic—until it all came to an end six months ago. How old does that make her now? Two plus six equals eight months. The mirror is cruel; he retreats and scratches his arm; the skin is red and raw.

He holds a coffee cup, but the contents are cold. The apartment is large and appallingly expensive, filled with government-issued furniture and little else, a place where not everything works but still looks like it does. From the window he can see the Bosphorous cutting through the continents, separating Asia from Europe, east from west. Down below, the doormen are hard at work, scrubbing other people's cars. The neighborhood is waking up. For the moment it's all business. But once the residents have left to trade in steel and textiles, the courtyard will take on the rhythms of the Anatolian countryside: The doormen will drop their hoses for backgammon boards; maids will gather to chat; children will play with half-inflated balls or just rocks while their head-scarved mothers hover with smiles of crooked teeth. In the windows above, soap operas will flicker. Once in a while, a door will open and a smartly-dressed woman will leave an overbred animal with her doorman, then catch a taxi downtown to join her friends in brushing her roots blonde and discussing her *gelin*. In Turkish, "gelin" means "daughter-in-law." It also means "Come!"

The guard springs from his chair when George arrives downstairs, then stands by with a worried look as George checks the underbelly of his car, climbs in and starts the engine. The guard directs him backward, standing two feet off his bumper, earning his eighty-five dollars a month. "Gelin!" he shouts.

George makes his way downhill to the shore road, his mind on breakfast and his insurgent bowels. The simits sold on the side of the road, baked rings sprinkled with deep-fried sesame seeds, have been exposed to lead fumes since the night before. Now they'll be served in hands blackened by soot. Disgusting, but what the hell, they're delicious and, anyway, he's up on his hepatitis series.

George glances at the water, just off the left shoulder. A Ukrainian cargo ship drifts serenely by, as long as a football field. It looks diseased and rusted, desperate to rest on the ocean floor in a blanket of barnacles.

This is a route he has driven every day for six months, amazingly without a single mishap. What a contrast with the rest of his life, which in retrospect seems nothing more than an accumulation of accidents. By far the youngest in his family, there is little doubt George wasn't planned. As for his career, it was no more than a sign in the hallway that led him to take the Foreign Service Exam. If he hadn't seen it, and if the test hadn't been free, God knows what he'd be doing now. Certainly his parents hadn't pointed him in any particular direction, unless one counts the impact of their perpetual migration; until the day they died they had always been on the road, from one shabby half-furnished house to another, in cities that must have been selected for their utter inconsequence. Chula Vista, Akron, Syracuse.

Rootlessness. This seemed to be the key. Margaret had never understood the clock that went off in his head every few years, the alarm that rang incessantly until he woke up and again moved on. To her, Monrovia, their first and only assignment together, was an adventure, a dangerous escape from the reality of normal life. But to George it was as real as reality could be, minus the hot water and electricity.

And so they had separated, opting for a temporary solution that was meant to last weeks—certainly not for six months. She was supposed to join him later.

Later. But of course she never did. Perhaps he'd known all along that this would happen. Perhaps they'd both conspired to kid each other, and to kid themselves. Even though it was she who should have come, what kind of father was he—to leave? With a wife and infant daughter in his wake?

The simit salesman wears at least three sweaters, piled one on top of the other. His hands are black indeed. He has no change, so tells George to pay tomorrow.

Back on the road, George scans the Bosphorous for his friend, Truman, one of several political officers at the consulate. Three months ago, after his third fender-bender, Truman traded his car for a motorboat. Now he commutes by water, parking his dinghy at the foot of the Galata bridge where an old man keeps watch for a handful of lira.

George considers the high road, shrugs it off, and continues along the water, beneath the consul general's cliff-top residence where the Ortaköy bridge comes into sight. He shouldn't be driving the same route as yesterday, and the day before that. *Vary your routes*, is what he was taught. Terrorists are compulsive planners and prefer soft targets, seldom attacking unless they know when and where their victims will be. George has heard the story a half- dozen times: An American military attaché was in the habit of looking under his car each morning before starting it up. When the police broke up a terrorist cell, they learned the American had been targeted but not attacked thanks to his *counter-terrorist precautions*. The attaché was commended for his attention to personal security, at which point he explained his car had been leaking oil, and he'd been checking every morning to see if the problem was solved.

American Consulate General Istanbul sits on a back street in Beyoğlu, the neighborhood once called Pera. This was the European quarter in the age of the sultans, where Italians, Jews and other infidels practiced their infidelities away from the city's Muslims. A century later, the fine buildings of Istiklal Street have been converted into banks, boutiques and fast- food franchises. Turkish shoppers and a few foreign tourists make it an up-scale place by day, but by night it retains a new sort of licentiousness. When darkness falls the neon lights flicker on, advertising alcohol and dancing girls. Blonde Russians, *Natashas* as they are known, scurry between bars and brothels, calling Moscow from the pay phones and enduring stares from mustached young men whose jokes they don't understand.

Opposite high gray walls on nearby Mesrutiyet Street, stands the consulate in the Palazzo Corpi, yet another monument in a city exhausted by history. The

Palazzo was built by a Genoese ship owner, a few years after the end of the American civil war. When the Genoan died, the building was leased to the U.S. Government as its embassy to the Sublime Porte. The American Ambassador in Constantinople purchased it outright with his own money in 1907, only to subsequently regain the sum from a tight-fisted congressional appropriations committee in an all-night poker game.

The interior is elegantly detailed but sparsely furnished, the rooms remarkable for their frescoes, which had to be restored after the prudish wife of a former ambassador objected to the nudes and had them plastered over. The hush of the reception area is broken only by occasional passers- by, who swiftly retreat into rooms where access is limited. A wrought- iron banister leads visitors up a marble staircase to the political section, where spacious rooms swallow what little sound is generated by the tap-tap-tapping of word processors. At every turn there is a windowless wall, a door that won't open.

But the Palazzo is not George McCall's destination. After popping the hood to reveal to the guards the presence or absence of car bombs, he is off to the annex, a slightly smaller, vastly uglier box on the opposite end of the parking lot.

He wants to be there early, for this is the day that Winston Craine, his new boss, will arrive. Otherwise, it's a day more or less like any other. On the sidewalk across the street, a hundred visa applicants gather in a clumpy line that disappears around the corner and continues another fifty feet up mud alley. Inside, it's all file cabinets and government manuals and old visa machines beneath a layer of dust, in a space smaller than George's apartment. Most of the staff are Turkish, mainly women, gossiping in a collective sing-song voice about the need for a cost of living adjustment, a recent article on the "Kurdish problem," and the perennial question of who is sleeping with whom, in Turkish that most of the Americans, with their formal language training, can't hope to understand.

George turns on his word processor. Interviews begin in an hour, barely time to draft a report from yesterday's visit to Bayrampasha prison. Looking after troubled Americans is his favorite part of the job. In this case, the prisoner complained of being tortured—of being punched in the face, of having his testicles shocked and squeezed, of having his feet beaten in the style known as *falaka*. It was a caricature list, reflecting sound research but little imagination; no doubt he'd concocted the story with the help of his attorney or his less fortunate Kurdish or African roommates. These days, the Turks knew better than to torture westerners.

George stalls on the portion of the cable that calls for "remarks." While he is confident the American is lying, the allegations are too grave to dismiss out of hand. With some dissatisfaction, he decides the right word is "skeptical."

He looks up to find Truman Vasser standing near, looking exhilarated from his ride down the Bosphorous. Truman's navy blue jacket is rumpled and his hair—more hair than anyone in his mid-thirties is entitled to have—falls over his eyes. He brings news of last night's boy party at the Austrian consulate.

"You mean Gustov's a member of the tribe?" asks George. This is out of sync with his image of the husky kraut.

Truman rolls his eyes. "Yorgo, turn your gaydar on. What a party. Most of the Turkish ballet was there. Just to die for."

"There's a Turkish ballet?"

Until now, Zeynep, George's Turkish assistant, has shown no reaction. Now she looks up. "There's something from the department, George Bey, you must read."

"This?" It's a *Welfare and Whereabouts* cable, the kind that comes when an American goes missing and a friend or relative calls the state department for help. George gets one almost every week, usually from the parent of a backpacking son who has forgotten to call home. Lack of money will invariably force him to surface, usually from some flea-bitten hotel in the boondocks. George can't remember a Welfare and Whereabouts case that ended in tragedy. But this is about to change.

George reads the cable aloud. "According to subject's parents, Taylor Moore is studying at Bosphorous University...his welfare a matter of strong congressional interest...Zeynep, can I ask you to call the University? There are names..."

"Yaptim. Done. I spoke to Professor Yilmaz. He says he is happy to meet with you. He says come with yourself alone because he is knowing too many things but will not say them by the telephone. When you are ready I will make the time."

George glances at the visa windows; the shades conceal a dozen hopeful faces. "What is so secret that he can't talk on an open line? Tell him..." He pauses. "When does our new boss get here?"

"He's here," says Truman. "I met him at Priscilla's last night. For dinner. Before Gustov's party. Winston..."

"Craine," says George. "Shit. Where was I?" Priscilla is the Consul General. An invitation to her home—or the lack of one—is a good indication of one's standing at the consulate.

Truman shrugs. "I would have happily given you my seat."

It's a lie, but George lets it pass. "So? What's this Craine guy like?" He scratches his left arm; the skin is tender, and quickly turns painful.

Truman shrugs again. Discretion is out of character for him; it gives George a sinking feeling.

"What?" George insists.

Now Zeynep is interested too; she keeps typing, but her pace slows to around forty words a minute.

They drift toward the visa windows. Behind them, Zeynep staples something a little too loudly. "What's wrong?" asks George.

"Let's just say your next two years should be interesting," says Truman. The belly of a visa applicant is momentarily visible through the bulletproof glass. George snaps the shade taut, cutting him off.

"Where do I start…" Truman counts his fingers. "Hasn't been promoted for a decade. Can't speak an intelligible word of Turkish after eleven months at the Foreign Service Institute. For that matter, doesn't speak much English either. Won't talk unless you talk to him. Was drunk before the entree came. Had a mysterious departure from his last post, which I'm guessing was some kind of psychevac…"

Zeynep joins them. "Professor Yilmaz is holding. Do you want to be speaking to him?"

"Tell him…tell him eight thirty tomorrow. I'll go straight from my house"

"Tamam." Okay.

"I have to go," says Truman. "I do have work to do. We'll talk later."

"C'mon, what else?"

"You know I'm not a gossip."

George smiles but avoids his eyes. "Of course not." Truman is a stereotype in so many ways, with his faint lisp and rigid walk and his collection of Barbara Streisand records. But he's also incongruously sloppy, too poorly arranged to be convincingly gay. His drooping collar and lolling stare, his five o'clock shadow at eight in the morning—all converge to give him a look of perpetual drunkenness. Any hint of boyishness is gone, perhaps drummed out by the daily battles of life beyond the closet, by the funerals of a dozen friends cut down by the plague.

"Anyway," says Truman. "I have to finish telling you about Gustov's party!"

But George doesn't hear. His thoughts have moved on, apropos of nothing, to his wife and daughter in America. The image makes him wobbly, wrecks his mood. How did he ever come to such a spot? It is a long story—too long, really, with so many visa applicants in the waiting room.

Like everything else on his mind, his story, and Margaret's, would have to wait until the visa interviews were over.

* * *

Interesting, no?

Well, there's plenty more where that came from. It's all here, in these hundreds of pages of state department memoranda piled high in my room, authored by the aforementioned Winston Craine, Consul, Foreign Service of the United States of America. Memoranda bursting with tales of espionage and terrorism and the private life of George McCall, all set in exotic Istanbul, the city that teeters between East and West, that sits astride two continents. The bridge, as the memo says. The crossroads.

Though I'd expected to find deep, dark secrets in Craine's file, earth-shaking revelations, it never occurred to me that I'd find something akin to literature, or at least pulp fiction. After all, I was the one who was supposed to be the writer, not Winston. And aren't government memos required to be boring? Boring, according to the regulations that would stretch to the very cosmos if stacked one on top of the other?

But Craine's memos aren't boring at all. Why, just take a look at this passage:

The line from the bulletproof glass to the grime of mud alley is mainly Turks and Iranians, with the occasional Iraqi, Bosnian, Chechen, Russian, Arab, and African thrown in for color. What they seek is permission to travel temporarily to America—for business, study or pleasure—as opposed to the fifty more who will line up in the afternoon for permanent immigration visas. But since most intending immigrants don't qualify for afternoon appointments, they show up in the morning instead, armed with clever stories and false documents, to try for tourist visas to get past immigration at JFK. It's safe to assume there are at least a dozen such cases today. Once in the United States, it scarcely matters how long they've been told they can stay; they will simply disappear, becoming an anonymous face in a Brooklyn restaurant, a Los Angeles grocery, a New Jersey gas station. No one will find them, and few will look very hard. If they commit crimes, they may be caught. But even then, deportation is a hassle. The truth is that once they have their visas there's no stopping them; only the vice consul stands between them and a better life.

You see? These pages stamped CONFIDENTIAL are not boring at all. When I first went through them, I swear to you I would have laughed; I would have cried; I would have run through the whole gamut of emotions had I not been sedated precisely against such contingencies. Even now, just lifting the piles of paper, feeling their heft, setting them down again in some other part of the room, satisfies me to no end. The entire file must weigh a good five pounds, more if you count the accompanying hand-scrawled notes.

But enough about the memos—let me tell you something about your other narrator, which is I, or me, whatever the case may be (grammar has never been my strong suit). Because make no mistake about it, this is as much my story as Winston Craine's, or George McCall's for that matter, as will become crystal clear in time.

You may be wondering how I came to be in possession of diplomatic correspondence, especially papers marked CONFIDENTIAL, or how it was that I even came to be rubbing shoulders with such a hoity-toity crowd—me, failed writer and only marginally more successful seller of retail golf equipment, writing to you now from a desk of discarded milk crates and an old door that I found down the block, in a basement apartment smelling of unwashed socks. Let it be known that I am not a wealthy man. Apart from my camera and my Smith-Corona typewriter, and of course this manuscript, which is borrowed at best, the only items I have of any value are my books, mainly novels by Graham Greene. In their vertical accumulation they obscure the only window in the room, partially blocking my view of the dumpsters next door, which are already fuzzy thanks to the rain that falls with alarming frequency here in Gresham, Oregon.

Or are the dumpsters fuzzy because of my medication?

Listen up, and I'll explain. It was in Australia that I first met Winston Craine. This was before his transfer to Istanbul, that is to say, before he became George's boss. At first glance, Craine seemed not very diplomatic looking to me, standing as he did no more than five- feet- five inches tall, with a sharp paunch and a bald, flaky scalp that fell apart and got stuck in his ears. Beads of sweat anchored the few strands of hair that remained on his head which, unfortunately, he'd permitted to grow long, then combed sideways in a vain attempt to cover his baldness.

Or am I remembering our second meeting, which was more dramatic than our first? I am jumping ahead now to Istanbul, when the same bald head loomed above me like a ceiling lamp. But, no, that's not right. His head was exactly *not* like a ceiling lamp since it shaded me from the bright lights of Bakirköy Hospital where I lay with my ankles fastened tightly to the bed posts. Whatever. Moments before Craine's pendulous head swung into view, I had awoken to find myself inspected by doctors who looked not the least bit friendly and spoke in all too strange tongues. I suppose I would have screamed—or at least I would have gone on screaming—if not for Winston, who at that moment stepped between the white gowns, placed his hand on my shoulder, and asked in a clear and kind American voice whether I had any money to pay the bill.

I was happy to see him, yes. But I was still angry at what he'd put me through in the many months since our first meeting in Melbourne. And I was angrier still when he failed to recognize me. Was I mad enough to shoot him? I don't know. Perhaps. How else to explain that one day I would find myself on a ship in the Bosphorous named *Savarona*, standing between Europe and Asia, pointing a pistol at Craine's head, and applying gentle pressure to the trigger? Only God knows for sure.

It was such a long way there. Of course, it has been an even longer way here, to this place—no, not place—to this situation, where I can finally write with objectivity and clarity, though perhaps with all the spontaneity of stale bread. That's lithium for you. If you've ever dreamed the sun was so bright you couldn't open your eyes, or you needed to run away from something but your legs wouldn't move—*wouldn't move*—then you'll know what I mean. But then I suppose that sanity has its price.

But I'm sorry, I've gotten ahead of myself. I should explain how I came to be committed to a psychiatric ward in Istanbul, where Craine came to see me, the same hospital where Billy Hayes of *Midnight Express* fame was once in residence, and how I came to be so angry with the man to whom this story owes its origin. Let me start at the beginning.

As I said, the first time I met Winston Craine, in Australia, I was struck by his undiplomatic appearance. Beads of sweat anchored the few strands of hair that remained on his head—well, you've heard all that—and he wore a tattered backpack that seemed horribly out of place against his pinstriped suit, though his outfit was rumpled anyway and his tie was not tied at all, but rather strangled like a hose that won't give water. I was happy to see him, yes, but the sight of him also gave me a feeling of dread, not because I was disappointed to see my country represented by such a diminished figure, but because it occurred to me that, should he invite me for dinner, I might very well have to foot my half of the bill. This was a concern because my Aunt Sally had not yet passed away, and I was counting on more free meals like the one I'd received at the hands of the British consul, who'd been so pleased to hear about my article on the Royal Family's visit that he'd reciprocated with a plate of linguini and several Chivas and sodas, which gave me such joy that I'd hummed "*God Save the Queen*" while he paid the tab, which amounted to my entire weekly budget.

Of course, I had never intended to write any nonsense about the Queen of England or any other queens for that matter. In fact, sadly, I'd pretty much forgotten what I'd come to Australia to write about. That's why I was selling golf equipment again, something else I'd lost my talent for, though occasionally I could still break forty in nine holes. Ironically, or perhaps not ironically, for I must take seriously the past accusation that I have no idea what irony is, the story I was working on down under was an allegory of the CIA's plot against Fidel Castro using characters on a golf course much as Orwell brought the Bolshevik revolution to life using animals on a farm. Unfortunately, that's where the similarities ended, since Orwell was never, so far as I know, called "sophomoric," "pretentious," or "so lacking in subtlety that Oliver Stone would gag."

My wife, before she left me, was more supportive than the critics. But once her car was loaded up and the key beyond my grasp, she confessed that she'd always found my work ridiculous. I'm sure she was just lashing out at me in revenge for years of neglect, because when I wrote, and drank, and forgot to take my pills, I would disappear into a cerebral world that nobody, least of all she, could penetrate. I'm sure it was this and not the lack of money, because I never made much money selling golf equipment either, but we were happy as all get-out, as clams even, in those pre-literary days.

Don't get the wrong idea. There was a time before the troubles began when I was considered good. *Bill Bigelow, promising young writer*, that's what they said. I still have the clippings to prove it.

No, the problems came later, after my diagnosis and the assorted medical *interventions*, when thinking things up and writing them down became less fun, less a pleasure than an obsession, a chore that was never complete. The problems began when nothing I wrote was good anymore. When the pages came slowly, and all were destroyed in disgust.

And so I would stop, and for a while I'd put up with the monotony and melancholy, until the thoughts in my head would start to build and build again, demanding that I put them on paper where they could be cheapened and degraded. And that would start me writing again, miserable, miserable, only slightly less so than when I did not.

And then, you see, without warning, it would happen—a shotgun blast of thoughts to my head! I remember once I wrote four hundred and ninety pages on the International Monetary Fund's enslavement of the third world through compulsory borrowing and blind devotion to free-flowing capital, which I entitled "The International Monetary Fund's Enslavement of the Third World through Compulsory Borrowing and Blind Devotion to Free-Flowing Capital." Like one of those Desk Jet printers I admired through windows, my brain simply printed the paper and, at the end of the week, I threw it away. If memory serves, that was some two weeks after I flushed my prescription down a toilet in Budapest, and right before I got deported to Madrid, which was okay in the end because a Spanish doctor started me on Serzone, replacing Zoloft which had tended to leave me limp. If you know what I mean. Soon my head was screwed on right again. I was fully sane, a new man, and as wise and frisky as Bob Dole.

But back to Winston Craine. Like I was saying, my first meeting with Winston was less dramatic than my second. It was in Australia, as I may or may not have explained already, when I was finishing some research at the consulate and heard him in the next room, speaking loudly in an unsteady voice to a swarthy fellow who sounded not at all Australian, as he explained that his brother in Brooklyn was dying. *Since your brother went to America illegally, he can die there illegally for all I care*, was the thrust of Craine's response, leaving me wondering if it might indeed be illegal to die. At this point the applicant began to cry in his strange foreign accent, which only prompted Craine to raise his voice and threaten to call the marines. Though there were no marines in sight, the man slinked sheepishly away, his eyes suddenly dry, and the room again grew quiet.

"You have a very difficult job," I told him. A diet of sausage rolls had sharpened my skills at flattery, and soon enough I was able to draw him out from behind the bulletproof glass. He sat down heavily in a government-issued waiting room chair and sighed. "The world as we know it is burning." Unable to think of a fitting response, I sat there quietly, until he said, "What can I do you for?" I informed him that I was a travelling writer, with many books and articles in the works, and that I wanted to register my name. By way of conversation, I asked if he'd read my account of life with the aborigines. After some hesitation he replied that he had not, which must have been true since I'd never published anything of the sort. The news that I was a writer, though, seemed to cheer him up. "The abo situation is a mess," he said with sudden severity. "The Aussies haven't done nearly enough to *ah-sewage* the situation." It took me a moment to recognize the mangled word, but by the time I did I had already agreed with him, as I am bound to do when out of money. He told me then that he'd heard of my book, that good things were being said about it, and that he hoped to read it; and I watched his pupils take flight, until they were tiny pinpricks floating in pools of green.

When we met for dinner that evening, Craine informed me that he, too, would like to be a writer, since ordinary people—that was the term he used—would no doubt be fascinated by the exotic lives that diplomats lead, and by the great trouble that ordinary people were in the habit of causing them. Absentmindedly, for I was busy interrogating the waiter on my top-shelf options, I asked him why he had never written a novel. In lieu of an answer, he propped his briefcase on his lap, opened it with a flourish, and leaned it my way. It virtually overflowed with pages stamped CONFIDENTIAL in inks of different hues. The effect was hypnotic. "If anything should happen to me, I would like you to have this," he said in a sinister tone, then slammed the briefcase shut. When I said it seemed unlikely that anything would happen to him in Melbourne, except perchance a freak gardening accident or a scalding from the barbie, he wagged a finger at me and said he needn't remind me that radicals had recently burned to the ground the French consulate in Perth—some to-do about nuclear testing. This event rang no bells with me, but before I could say so he went on.

"The diplomat's life," he said gravely, "is filled with uncertainty." As if to underscore his point, he stole a long, furtive look at the shadows, then pinned me down with his eyes. "It's a house of cards," he said. "All of it." He lifted the briefcase with obvious strain. "To bring it down all I have to do is exhale."

For what seemed an eternity neither of us spoke. *It.* I wasn't certain what *It* was, but I knew very well what *It* did. *It* brought down governments. *It* wire-tapped phones. *It* sent satellites into the stratosphere that could read our very menus. *It* made the CIA look like the Sunday papers. I knew that much about *It. It* was *The Power.*

Was it possible? Could Winston Craine be a fellow traveler?

Then the moment was lost; Craine fell back in his chair and cried out in laughter and his body was wracked with spasms, sending dry, flaky bits of scalp into his Hanoi grilled pork, which would be less delicious now, but still edible, as Melbourne has some of the finest Vietnamese food in the world.

In the weeks that followed our strange dinner, I neither saw nor heard from

Craine again, though this was his choice and not mine since it was he who had paid the bill. From our meeting I had just one souvenir: A memorandum from Winston Craine "To the File" in rigid government format, filled with typos, which he'd given me after dinner. It was the entire Old Testament Book of Jonah, word for word, the one with the guy who gets swallowed by the whale, a short book as the Old Testament goes, but plenty long if you're a poor typist since it's filled with words like Amittai, Ninevah, and sackcloth.

I guess I should have been more curious why the consul would turn a chapter of the Bible into an unclassified memo. But at the time, my only thought was that I wanted the classified ones.

Indeed, I couldn't get them out of my mind. Perhaps it was because my Fidel Castro CIA golf course allegory was going nowhere. I was selling a sufficient number of PING irons and switching long distance services enough to keep food on the table; but the pages of my book continued to collect, without resolution, in yellowing heaps on my Brunswick flat desk. When I read them back they made no sense. I was floundering, and I knew it, but my dinner with Craine had given me the germ of an idea—*It*. I could ignore *It* no longer. *It* was what I had to write about. But I couldn't do that here. Australia did not inspire. The country was the most powerful sedative I'd ever consumed. Its citizens, if you can call them that, ran about in track suits, chatting with Bruces and Sheilas on mobile phones. Politics took a back seat to whatever sport was in season—footy, cricket, swimming, even three-wheel bouncy dirt bike racing. "Collingwood over Footscray," the newspapers proclaimed. Then, somewhere off the front page, perhaps near the classifieds: "Prime Minister assassinated. Indonesia invades."

And then there were the flies, flies that swarmed in the heat, flies that flung themselves at every moist orifice, at the ears, the eyes, the nostrils, the mouth. Tiny little flies that barely buzzed, that hung around stupidly, begging to be slapped, suicidal, happy for others to take the place of their remains. Flies that had me forever exhaling, blowing wind from my mouth, starving my brain of much-needed oxygen.

Then one day the letter came, from the attorney of my dear old Aunt Sally. In an undertaker's tone, it said in so many words that the old lady had died and that I was the sole heir to her estate, my brothers and sisters be damned. Suddenly, a woman I hadn't considered in nearly a decade was fresh in my mind. "In the olden days," I remembered her telling my unlucky siblings, "artists were supported by society so that they could focus on creating. The rest of you kids will do just fine without my money." And she was right; all of them were stock- brokers now, or real estate agents, or married to the same, with sit-on lawn mowers and double-doored fridges and TVs and stereos and DVD players running on single remotes perpetually lost between the couch cushions.

That night, I drank to the memory of my Aunt Sally and flushed my prescription down the toilet, an impulsive act I know, but I just couldn't help myself. First went the Serzone, my favorite anti-depressant, then the Xanax, which curbed my anxiety but tended to make me drowsy. I flushed the little red ones, then the big white ones, then the yellows whose job it was to counter the side effects of the reds. The Lithium I tossed in from three-point range, bringing splashes up over the rim. Then came the Tegratol, in such quantities that I had to flush twice. Finally, I dumped the horsepills that helped me sleep. Sleep was no longer in my plans; I felt energized, as alive as I'd been in many months. Aunt Sally had inspired me. It was Budapest all over again, only this time the toilet water swirled in the other direction.

Then I sat down to write. *It.* What was *It*? *It* was the Power. *Fight the Power*, I wrote. I sat back and studied my work. Now I had a title. I wrote it again, changing the period to an exclamation mark. Better.

When I awoke the next day from erotic dreams I could hear the birds, for the first time in months it seemed; I watched the baskers on Swanborne Street, ate Thai food, then slept elated in the sun on the banks of the Yarra, the river that flows through the city upside down. So sharp were my senses that I could read the Herald Sun from forty yards; in England, a train had crashed in a fiery inferno and half the survivors had made for the airport and boarded flights to who-knows-where, playing dead so that they could begin life again from scratch, anonymous. Here was my proof that all men live lives of quiet desperation—not just me.

And then I read the important news—an American diplomat fond of snorkeling had been half-eaten by a shark near Wilson's Promontory, and was dead as a result. Without hesitation I recalled the memo that Winston had left me, and my sadness at his death was tempered by the awe I felt at the premonition he'd constructed, notwithstanding that Jonah was consumed whole by his fish—actually, a whale is a mammal and not a fish at all, but let's not quibble—while the diplomat in question had been chewed up pretty good, his torso left to bob in the waves until its discovery by a band of drunken surfers.

I raced to the consulate, preparing answers to questions I was sure to receive. There would be a briefcase waiting for me, I supposed, to be claimed by presenting the memo, Jonah 1:4-17. After all, hadn't Winston willed it to me from his watery grave? Now I know that this wasn't the case, but at the time

I was blinded by the thought of writing in great sweeping strokes, day and night, with eyes propped open by toothpicks.

When I reached the waiting room, I found an unfamiliar officer speaking in familiar tones to a visa applicant, and my heart skipped a beat. After waiting my turn, I asked coyly if I could see Mr. Craine, not letting on that I knew. The young man said this would not be possible—and here I drew a breath—since he had left for his new assignment in Istanbul only a week ago. When I wondered aloud if he was speaking in euphemisms, the young man replied that Istanbul was the largest city in Turkey. Then, obviously pleased to provide a lesson in geography, the young wonk produced a map of the world and pointed to Asia Minor, which I saw resembled the head of a horse, nostrils flaring, charging west into the very heart of Europe.

With a mixture of apprehension and relief—for though I wanted the consul's file I didn't really want him dead—I thanked the man and left.

There was only one book I carried wherever I went. This was partly because I related to its theme—that man is doomed to live either in the convulsions of distress or in the lethargy of boredom—but also because, unlike the Warren Commission report, the book, *Candide,* fit nicely in my pocket. "We must cultivate our garden," was Voltaire's advice, spoken through the character of an old Turk. A Turk! Oh, the synergy! And then a further thought: My landlord once mentioned friends in the shipping business offering paid positions on freighters bound for Bangkok. Since this was more or less in the right direction, I resolved to speak with him at the earliest opportunity.

Fight the Power! I had my title. Now it was only the briefcase I needed. The certainty that I should have it grew within me until it was as familiar as my own heartbeat.

When I arrived back at my apartment, I took a seat and wrote until the morning sun streamed in. With the air still reeking of the fresh Australian morning, I dusted off my suitcase and began to pack.

* * *

The line from the bulletproof glass to the grime of mud alley is mainly Turks and Iranians, with the occasional Iraqi, Bosnian, Chechen, Russian, Arab, and African thrown in for color. What they seek is permission to travel temporarily to America—for business, study and pleasure—as opposed to the dozens more who will line up in the afternoon for permanent immigration visas. But since most intending immigrants don't qualify for afternoon appointments, they show up in the morning instead, armed with clever stories and false documents, to try for tourist visas to get past immigration at JFK. It's safe to assume there are at least a dozen such cases today. Once in the United States, it scarcely matters how long they've been told they can stay; they will simply disappear, becoming an anonymous face in a Brooklyn restaurant, a Los Angeles grocery, a New Jersey gas station. No one will find them, and few will look very hard. If they commit crimes, they may be caught. But even then, deportation is a hassle. The truth is once they have their visas there's no stopping them; only the vice consul stands between them and a better life.

George takes his seat at window three. When the shutter lifts, the window fills with hopeful faces. First in line is an Iranian; George sends him to wait in the back while he deals with the easier Turks. A messenger steps forward with passports of plump Turks, their pages cluttered with European visas. George circles *issued* and motions to the next in line.

A middle-aged woman makes way for her son, a gaunt young man with circles beneath his eyes, aged beyond his years. If his dirty fingernails are any indication, his fluorescent green suit is a loaner—perhaps from an uncle who hit the big city first. His Turkish comes in mumbles. "I will travel with my father. He is sick," he says. "He will have treatment in Houston." In Turkish, the sentence runs backwards: *Houston, in, treatment his, it will be*. George studies the papers. The diagnosis is throat cancer. The medical documents look real enough, but the property deeds are from the wrong neighborhood and the family accounts show barely enough for a tonsillectomy.

"Where do you work?"

"With my father." The tax statement is for a shop in Kasimpasha; George pictures stacks of mop buckets, rubber stoppers, used batteries in containers sealed by scotch tape. Every shop there looks the same. George asks more questions, too many; the line presses forward. He hesitates, then finds a solution that satisfies him.

"I can issue visas to your mother and father but, I'm sorry, not you."

"Please," says the young man. "Lütfen," repeats his mother.

George directs them to a Turkish employee to argue in their native language. Two windows away, he can hear the old lady's lütfens growing louder. "Tell her it's not too late for me to refuse her husband!" As soon as he says it, he regrets it; it's too early in the morning to lose his temper.

Nor is it the right time to interview the Iranian, but George calls him forward anyway and slips comfortably into Farsi. George knows he's not the brightest of foreign service officers in the same way that he understands intrinsically, deep in his gut, that he will never have a washboard stomach. But his gift for languages is undeniable. Spanish he learned in high school, German in college, and Arabic while studying toward his unfinished Masters. French he learned on the side, taking courses at the U.S. Department of Agriculture; his accent was so good that even the French understood him. Turkish was his first formal language in the Service. Farsi was just something he picked up at post.

"May I tell you about my situation?" asks the Iranian.

"Please do," says George. But there is really no need. The man has no previous travel and several siblings in America. The odds of his returning to Iran after a visit to The Great Satan are perhaps one in three. The interview is over; only the refusal remains.

The Iranian speaks quickly, mixing flattery with promises. George tries to look interested. He shuffles through the papers, reads a few words and pretends to read more, confirms he has no hope for a visa and promptly tells him so. There are more promises, which turn to pleas, and five minutes pass before George persuades him to go away, doing so, finally, by surrendering his name which will surely return to haunt him on congressional letterhead.

"Mr. George, I can come tomorrow and make an application?" asks the man.

"Well, yes, you can come anytime but it won't..."

"And I will ask for you."

"Fine," says George. The man smiles gratefully and is gone.

A Turkish family of five with a summer home in Bodrum and kids in private school pass quickly by, followed by stock brokers with cover letters on fancy letterhead and an elderly Sephardic Jewess visiting her American citizen daughter. George slows to interview a young man with a crooked nose and oddly pallid skin. *Vram* is not a Turkish name; *Hurtuoğlu* might be, but the *oğ lu*, is probably a replacement for *yan*. George glances at his female companion, and wonders if she's Armenian too.

"May I say something please?" The woman speaks in British-accented English, as correct as any newscaster on the BBC. The effect is jarring.

"Why not," says George, allowing his glance to rest on her a moment too long. She has heavy-set eyes, and a face disrupted by gravity. In truth she's homely, but there's more—a vague something that both attracts and repels, a blend of nausea and delight, more arousing than mere beauty.

"My friend would like to attend university in the United States. We brought all the necessary—."

"Why are you speaking for him?"

"He is a friend of my family's, and as I speak English..."

"Are you romantically involved?"

"No," she says quickly. Too quickly. "Vram's uncle is my father's business partner. He has a home in Los Angeles in addition to his home in Turkey. That's where Vram will stay whilst he attends university. His uncle is quite successful. Honestly. He owns a splendid jewelry business. Quality jewelry." She pauses, and seems to catch herself. "But his father has his own company here as well, a travel agency. Oh, I rather wish I'd brought a brochure. Vram must come back and manage it because his father is getting old. Oh, I hope I haven't said anything wrong."

The documents show Vram accepted into UCLA. There are signature circulars, tax statements and property deeds in several good Istanbul neighborhoods; the family is doing alright. George can't remember interviewing an Armenian doctor, or a lawyer, not even a bureaucrat. In Turkey, business is the field for Christians.

"When did you graduate from high school?"

"Oh, you speak Turkish," says the young woman. "And chok güzel!" Very good! George ignores the compliment.

"Two years after," Vram answers slowly in English.

"Have you been to university here?"

"I worked all of the times for my father."

George frowns. Surely this young man's life would be better if he lived in America. But maybe not, if his family is as rich as the documents suggest. Then again, wealth can always be moved, and his uncle can help him with that. But is it necessarily a bad sign that he wants to study where he has connections?

No, but it does mean less reason to return. But this isn't some community college he's been accepted to; it's UCLA, which suggests he's a serious student and a smart kid. Or maybe it's his uncle who's the smart one. At any rate he's rich, and the education would help him here. Sure, but it'd help him even more in the U.S., wouldn't it? Maybe, but who can say what will happen in four years? Is it really possible to predict what any college student will do, where he'll go to work, four years from now? Why single out this poor Armenian?

Back and forth he goes, running his fingers through his hair; when he pulls them out they're moist. *When in doubt keep them out,* George thinks. It's a line he's heard many times as a consular officer, and one he follows about half the time.

"Tough case?" asks Dawn.

"Borderline," he says.

Dawn is the other junior officer on the visa line, twenty-five- years- old and also on her second assignment, having spent her first tour at the Vatican picking up phrases like ciao and buon giorno which she continues to use with distressing frequency. She takes a seat at window two, late as always. No matter, today she'll plough through twice as many cases as George, and still take an hour for lunch.

"What do you think?" George shows her the application form. Whatever else he thinks of her, he trusts her judgement and respects her decisiveness.

"PPM?" she asks. PPM stands for *possibly persecuted minority. Armenian* would be more to the point, but since visa applications are obtainable through the Freedom of Information Act, it's wise to be discreet.

"Young. No travel. No university. PPM. Uncle in L.A.," Dawn reads the notes aloud. "Well, if it were me, I'd tell him arrivederci." She waves in her first applicant.

George nods; of course she's right. "I'm sorry," he tells the two. "Every applicant has to show strong ties to a country outside of the United States. According to U.S. law, which is very strict, the burden of proof is on the applicant. Unless I am convinced that you intend to return to Turkey, I am unable to issue the visa."

Guilty until proven innocent. The young woman looks perplexed. "But as an American citizen, surely Vram's uncle has the right to take him to the United States for a visit," she says.

"No. Actually he doesn't," says George. "And neither do I." He stamps "application received" in Vram's passport and slides it under the glass. "I'm sorry."

The woman opens her mouth to speak, but the words fall away. For a moment her eyes fix on his, intelligent and intense. The pause grows awkward; George wants to fill it but feels he's being tested. When he finally speaks, to inform her the window is needed by the next in line, he is troubled by the sound of his own voice—tight, nasal, with the faintest of tremors. He glances at Dawn, finds her occupied with a pair of Bosnians. Slowly, painfully, the woman's voice gains in volume while his own recedes. He takes a long, deep breath, then another. At last he is able to explain to the young man, softly but firmly, that the time has come for him to leave.

"Tamam," says the young woman simply, suddenly light-hearted. "Okay. Thank you very much." With a whisper in the young man's ear, they go.

A hand on his shoulder makes him jump. It's Truman. "Any gene pool visas today?"

"Not sure we'd agree who qualifies," says George. He tries to laugh, but can't shake his unease.

"My turn," says Truman. George sits back as Truman takes over the interview, navigating the standard questions—where are you going, what will you do, where do you work, how much do you make—with impressive speed. George is satisfied with the answers, and signs off on the form.

Less placid sounds emanate from window two, where Dawn is finished with the Bosnians and has now taken the offensive against some unfortunate Iranian. "*Sir*, did you or did you not just say that you told the consular officer three years ago—I'm not talking about today—that you were going on a tourist trip? And then you stayed three years!"

His lips carve the same pattern as hers, one word at a time. "But I had come back, last week, because of my mother sick."

"And now you expect me to issue you another visa? So that you can stay another three years?" Dawn waves off the interpreter, determined to complete the interview in English.

"Not three years. Just give me one time visa. For one month. Even just one day."

Dawn shakes her head, so hard it looks painful. "Were you lying then, *sir*, or are you lying now? *Sir*, I want you to write down what you told the consular officer three years ago." Her fingers grope for a pen, knocking a stapler to the floor.

"Here we go," says Truman. "The screaming shrew." George raises a finger to his lips, but it's unclear who it's meant for. The Turks in line begin to stir.

"You're lying," says Dawn, raising her voice. "You were lying then and you're lying now and I want you to admit it."

"Not to understand. Pardon me?"

"You know perfectly well what I'm saying."

"Of course he's lying," Truman mutters, loud enough for Dawn to hear. "Who wouldn't lie? To get out of Iran. Where a woman can get arrested just for smiling? You'd lie too. We'd all lie 'til we were blue in the face."

This is too much for Dawn. She turns on Truman, trapping George in the middle. "I would never lie," she says. "Not like they do."

"Oh, bullshit," Truman replies. George is startled by how quickly this has turned ugly. He sympathizes with Truman, of course, but knows that in a sense he is wrong. As sure as the applicant is lying now, Dawn is not. Nor would she under the same circumstances, guided as she is by an ethic too twisted to bend.

"Not lie," says the Iranian, pulling himself up to his full height and raising his right hand. Truman's intervention seems to buck him up. "By Allah, not lie."

"Allah will damn you because you *are* lying!" cries Dawn. If anyone in line wasn't listening before, they are now.

Truman looks at George. "Damning to hell. Are we qualified to do that?"

Dawn stares away, makes her case to an invisible third party. "It's the lying! Do you hear how he's lying to me?"

"Not to you," says Truman. "How can he be lying to you if he doesn't even know who you are? It's the U.S. government he's lying to, not to you!" George is startled to find the trace of a smile on his friend's face; he's enjoying this. "Why don't you—."

"Why don't *you* go back to whatever you were doing before you came down here which probably wasn't much…"

"Oh sit down, Dawn."

"You—to be lecturing me! On how to conduct myself. You of all people! I know what you do." Dawn takes a step back, her lips pinched. She is suddenly deflated. Wheeling about, she is gone from the room.

The Iranian barely misses a beat; sensing an ally he starts making his case to Truman. The men have arrived, he must be thinking, the responsible, rational men. George belatedly pulls down the shade, cutting him off.

Truman Vasser nods his head. "Uh huh," he says, nodding again. It seems that something important has been confirmed.

George looks at his watch. It reads nine thirty-three. The day is young, but he no longer misses the visa line.

"He is coming," says Zeynep. "He is coming."

"Who?"

"The new patron. He is coming here now." She sets down the telephone and in her haughtiest tone adds, "So all of you must behave."

Dawn throws her a hateful glance. Two hours have passed since her little scene, and no one has mentioned it until now. Truman has long since gone back upstairs.

Zeynep makes herself busy, but keeps an eye to the door. In her career at the consulate, she has worked for no less than five consuls. At stake is her morale for the next three years. So it is at U.S. missions around the world—the American officers come, serve for a time then go, yielding to others who will one day be memories themselves. And of course it is the local employees who remember. Is there a single American who heard the thump of the rocket that bounced off the consulate in '93, fired by Dev Sol terrorists? Who recalls the romance between a previous consul general and her chauffeur? Who knows what the visa section looked like without carpeting? The consulate might be an outpost of the United States, but it is permanent only to the Turks. The Americans are transitory—their friendships, cliques and dysfunctions doomed to be erased by time, broken and scattered by onward assignments to Bangkok, Lima, and Ouagadougou. And since the same collection of people never takes shape twice, for the Americans there is no going home again. Not ever.

The front door opens to reveal a stocky bald man, with large furry hands that grope a hairless head in great swooping strokes. Zeynep stands stiffly at attention, the self-appointed welcoming committee. The other Turks rise from their desks. But their attempts at eye contact fail. Deftly, as if he's walked this route a thousand times, the new consul moves forward with tiny steps and surprising speed, shriveling up as he goes, barely touching even the clothes on his back.

The eyes of the consular section follow Winston Craine to the door of his new office. When he reaches it, he pauses as if seized by the thought that he should say something—and of course he should—but instead he only turns and smiles wanly, then opens the door, falsely casual, and disappears inside.

The click of the lock is like a gunshot in the quiet room.

Zeynep is at her desk, making passports with short, sharp shots to the typewriter. "I will not call him again," she says. "He does not answer his telephone."

"How long has it been since the consul general called?" asks George. He studies the office door; there's been no sign of life for hours.

"Fifteen minutes. And now she called again. You listen. He is typing."

George approaches the door. Distantly, a single finger taps an old keyboard, followed by the unmistakable sound of a carriage snapping back into place. How much old equipment do they keep in that office?

"Mr. Craine, can I speak to you a second?" George knocks twice, half-heartedly, then a third time, more firmly; it's for Winston's own good. "Priscilla wants us in her office. It sounds important."

One, two, three taps on the typewriter; George waits for the fourth, but it fails to come. Is that Craine rustling inches away, on the opposite side of the door? "Winston…"

"Please tell the Cee-Gee I'm engaged at this juncture," is all he says. A moment later the typing resumes. George goes away.

Priscilla sits in what was once an Italian's bedroom, overlooking the garden where the consulate hosts its social functions—modest events, thanks to the pathetic budget which supports, at best, Budweiser and Turkish wine. Spouses often provide the catering; there is no money for anything more. As the highest ranking official in Istanbul of the world's sole remaining superpower, Priscilla sometimes has trouble swallowing scotch and caviar at functions hosted by, say, the Slovak Republic.

In Priscilla's office, George is surprised to find Phil, the CIA's chief of station. Phil sits up with a start as George enters the room, then smiles blandly and makes space on the couch. The silence smacks of a conversation broken off in mid-stream.

Priscilla is extraordinarily tall, nearly six-foot-one, a very dark-skinned African-American, impossible not to notice. Phil is White and not so tall, as nondescript as Priscilla is striking. George knows little about him, just rumors of rugged operations in Colombia, fighting narco-traffickers and leftist rebels. On the couch, he seems more at home than he would in some jungle, surrounded by grubby men with M-16s.

"Winston asked me to tell you…" George pauses; he hasn't given his explanation much thought. "He's tied up at the moment," An awkward silence. "I can brief him later."

Phil shoots a sideways look at Priscilla, who shows a poker face. George wonders why Phil is here, and whether he intends to stay. He lets his eyes roam the spacious room. The vaulted ceiling adds some grandeur, but the furniture is circa 1965.

"Is Truman in today?" asks Phil. "I called this morning about eight- thirty. The Turks said he hadn't come in yet."

"Sure he's here. Just saw him in the consular section. He's probably…"

"In by now," says Phil. "I just wondered. Another late night?" The smile doesn't leave his face.

George shrugs. "He takes that little boat to work. Must be a rough ride." He pauses, feels the need to choose his words carefully. "I don't know how he navigates upstream…"

"In the dark? Yes, I know. He's quite the late-nighter." Phil has the unnerving habit of finishing other peoples' sentences.

George glances at Priscilla, who looks away. Odd, she's usually loathe to waste time on idle chat. George knows her style well; it just so happened that Priscilla had been his consul general in Monrovia too, for the first six months anyway. Of course, it hadn't *just so happened.* It was Priscilla who had arranged this job for George to follow that one. The service is like that; if you don't have powerful superiors promoting you behind the scenes, someone else is going to get the job.

Less clear was how Priscilla had made it to Istanbul. Most had assumed that her follow-on assignment from Monrovia would be as ambassador in some small, African backwater. And why not? She must have known that in the Bureau of European Affairs, the state department's waspiest, she would be suspected of advancing on the basis of her skin. No shrinking violet, perhaps she was here to shoot that notion down. Or maybe she just felt a special connection to Turkey, a country that fit no less awkwardly into the European Bureau, and into Europe itself.

Priscilla's expression offers no clues. Why has she given the floor to Phil? Is this the meeting?

Phil laughs; it sounds forced. "Truman probably has more fun in this town than the rest of us put together. We could all learn something from him. He's…" Here, Phil seems to pick his words carefully. "Quite a personality. Damn good diplomat, though," as if the two didn't mix.

"Good guy to work with," George replies. He returns Phil's frozen smile. The office is immensely quiet with the door closed, a silence which begs to be broken.

"Well, Phil," says Priscilla. "I need to discuss a small consular matter with George before my three o'clock. You're welcome to stay but…"

"But I should go," Phil replies. And with that he is gone.

George settles back in his chair.

Priscilla doesn't trouble herself with a segue. "I got a call from Art Zimmerman this morning." She raises her eyes to drive the point home. "Not from a staffer. From the Congressman himself. You know Zimmerman?"

"Chair of the House Foreign Relations Committee?"

"Appropriations. Zimmerman's not in the habit of operating the telephone himself." She says it with more bitterness than humor. "One of his constituents is worried about his son, a student at Bosphorous University...So you know about this case."

"We got a Welfare and Whereabouts cable this morning. Zeynep called the university, talked to a professor who knows the kid. But he wouldn't say anything over the phone. Insisted I come in person."

"When?"

"Tomorrow morning, if I can break away."

"You can," says Priscilla. "Please solve it before Zimmerman gets to Istanbul."

"He's coming here? For this?"

Priscilla shakes her head. "They say he's going to lead a congressional delegation, a Codel, to Ankara to look at foreign military sales, that sort of thing. But I'm sure he'll do us the honor as well."

George nods. Istanbul, with its history, its charm, its unparalleled shopping, is a preferred destination for senators and congressmen travelling on the taxpayer's dime. To conduct official government business, one must travel to dismal Ankara on the Anatolian steppe. Yet somehow, congressional delegations keep finding their way to the shores of the Bosphorous. What's generally needed is a pretense, however flimsy—breakfast with the marines, for example, or lunch with a couple of businessmen—then it's off to Topkapi Palace and the Covered Bazaar and a ride on the Bosphorous on the consulate's boat, the Hiawatha.

A running joke in the consulate is the "five hundred mile rule": Any congressman within five hundred miles of Istanbul on a Friday will be in the city for the weekend. No one laughs anymore.

"Have you been a control officer yet?"

George remembers carrying luggage for the one congressman brave enough to visit Monrovia. The thought reminds him of the little problem he picked up there—not the *disease*, or the *illness*, but the *condition*, as the regional medical officer insisted on calling it, with its unpronounceable name but straightforward symptoms: A subtle itch in his left forearm beneath the surface of the skin that is, more or less, always there. The doctors gave him cream and pills, and candidly told him it might or might not go away. It hasn't. He has learned to live with it, and to ignore it as best he can. Scratching it does no good, but he scratches it anyway as Priscilla goes on.

"You'll have more responsibility this time," she says. "In fact..." she pauses. "I'm going to ask you to take on a little more responsibility in the consular section too, with Winston's supervision of course. For starters I'd like you to handle American citizens' services so that Winston can focus on..." she pauses. "Broader management issues." Start with this missing American." She pauses again. "We should try to arrange for regular meetings, you and I. Once a week would be best." Priscilla checks her watch again. "I'm running late. We'll talk more later."

"Oh, and George?" He is almost to the door.

"Did you know that I worked with Winston before?"

He shakes his head, no.

"Almost fifteen years ago, when we were both mid-level officers in Beijing. He was good, talented. That was before he met Felicitas, when he was still with his first wife. A long time ago," she sighs. "He...they...had a daughter. Pretty little girl." Priscilla stares at the wall, suddenly preoccupied, as if there's something she's forgotten to do. "In Beijing we all had gas heaters, they weren't very safe. One night when Winston and his first wife—what was her name? Lois maybe. Yes, that's it, Lois. They were at a function and their little girl was with a baby sitter—.Well, to make a long story short the heater had a leak and the little girl died in her sleep. God—." A long pause. "Not sure whatever became of Lois..." Priscilla takes a seat at her desk and absently shuffles some papers. "I've been to posts where they're still using those things. Stop and see Helen, will you George? She can put you on my schedule for next week."

"George?"

He stops again.

"Is Winston still locked in his office?" Priscilla tries to smile, but succeeds only in looking a little less sad.

George nods. The sound of the consul general shaking her head is almost audible as he heads downstairs.

* * *

Standing at the stone-framed window in the office of Dr. Yavuz Yilmaz, Professor of Psychology at Bosphorous University, George finds it hard not to stare. Where the garden ends the trees begin, a late-fall canopy as beautiful as a red sumak carpet, plunging over the hillside toward the chaos of Bebek. So this is what air looks like, thinks George. The beauty of the place is too much for his system to cope—like drinking a good Pinot Noir after Miller Lite. All is quiet but for the giggling co-eds who pass through Yilmaz's office, depositing their homework, collecting their grades. George listens to their high-pitched squeals, lilting and buoyant, absurdly sing-songy: "Bee-bee-bee-bee-bee." Could this be natural? A genetic mistake? Or just a feminine pose?

Outside, young Turks parade with a lack of purpose that only students can manage. They are good looking kids. Their clothes are western, but conformity betrays them—the young men in tight jeans and T-shirts, the women in retro clogs and bell bottoms. Apparently the seventies are back in style, but it's a fashion that time has not improved. Black roots aside, they are still fairer than their Anatolian cousins, for whom Bosphorous University might as well be the Sorbonne. Their grandparents could not have come from Diyarbakir, Konya or Erzerum, but from Greece or Bulgaria or Bosnia, in the bad years when Ottoman rule collapsed and the fez gave way to the cross. For these youngsters Anatolia is a fuzzy dream, a bad one, a backwards place without seafood or discos, a war-zone they will visit only if, Allah forbid, the army sends them there.

George feels himself slipping away. For a half hour, Yilmaz has talked of everything but the missing American, from U.S.-Turkish relations to the threat of Islam to his multiple-indefinite visa, which George assures him is still valid. The professor looks perpetually ill at ease. He is slight and spindly, and moves as if jerked by strings. Absurdly, his name means "ferocious."

"Yavuz Bey, I don't want to take too much of your time. My boss doesn't let me out of the office too often. If I don't return soon, I'll turn into a kabak." His own memory amazes him; where did he learn the word, *pumpkin*?

The joke is lost on Yilmaz, who continues his oration until a young woman appears at the door. "Nazan," he says to her. "I am sorry I can't speak at you today. The consul of the United States is with me for important matters. You will return later?" But his visitor won't be denied; she squeezes past Yilmaz and extends her hand.

"Vice consul," George says, enjoying the discomfort that this small revelation causes his host. He takes her hand and shakes it, then hesitates before letting go. Where has he seen her before? She is older than the other students, wrinkled about the eyes and oddly assured. Vague, pathetic guilt is George's first sensation; he has to remind himself that he's been nothing but faithful to Margaret. The woman's hair is very short, unusual for a Turk, but her hair is as black as her genes intended, too serious for dye.

"It's my pleasure to meet you," she says simply, in upper-crust British English, a voice that doesn't seem hers. George feels the moment calls for something more, but then she is gone from the room, without looking back.

Puzzled, Yilmaz watches her go. "You will have tea," he says at last. George agrees, but his mind is elsewhere. Her accent, so odd from the mouth of a Turk, tells him that they have met before, no doubt on the visa line, his second home. He can't remember if hers was a good case or a bad one, an issuance or a denial. The tea comes quickly, in the hands of a young man who regards him blankly—the ubiquitous sheep-herder's stare. George is disappointed to find it's apple, sickly sweet and sugary. It gives Yilmaz something new to talk about: "So you like our Turkish tea."

"Very much. Yavuz Bey, you said you could help me find one of your old students…Taylor Moore."

Yilmaz clicks his tongue and nods his head, a gesture that means, no. "I did not say you will find him. I think you will not. I think he is not wanting to be found." Yilmaz makes the moment count; he leans in closely, as if sharing a conspiracy. "I am sorry you must come to my office to discuss this subject. But in Turkey some matters must be treated…" he pauses for effect. "Sensitively. On the telephone, it is usually a party line, no?"

True, thinks George. Wire-tapping is the preferred method of surveillance for MIT, Turkey's intelligence service. For diplomats in Istanbul, having a third person on the line is commonplace, a fact of life, as mundane as diarrhea or the din of bleating traffic.

"Always better to be safe," says George.

"What do you know about this student?" Yilmaz asks with sudden severity. "What he has done to make the Americans so much interested?" George is surprised by the swift change in mood. Yilmaz is out of his seat and pacing.

"I was hoping you could..."

"America is never far from the problems of Turkey," says Yilmaz with a wink. His voice grows seductive, as if he's touched on something of profound importance. "Where there is smoke there is usually something burning." He stops at the window. "Do you know that I am being partly a Kurd? My father from the Sanjak, but my mother from Mersin. When I was a child she spoke Kürtche. You are surprised?"

George shrugs, but in truth he is a little. Kurdishness is hardly something to boast about in good company. At best, it implies lowly village roots, a certain country bumpkinness—at worst, the specter of disloyalty to the Turkish Republic.

Yilmaz goes on. "She met my father like a fairy tale, and today I am being a Turk. Why? Because I choose it. Atatürk dreamed a free, secular nation. Today Turkey is a democracy, a part of the West, fully European."

Here we go again, thinks George. Atatürk, the hero of Gallipoli, savior of the Turkish nation, founder of the Republic. Atatürk, the all powerful and all knowing. If not for Atatürk would the sun even rise in the morning? For the Turks he is George Washington, Thomas Jefferson and Abraham Lincoln all rolled into one, the man who resurrected Turkey from the ashes of the first world war, then dragged it kicking and screaming westward into the twentieth century—replacing the sultan with a president, Shariah law with a European civil code, Arabic with latin script.

But now, at the other end of the century, with female university students clamoring for the right to wear headscarves to class, Turkey's European identity seems as pretentious as the bowler hat that Atatürk hoped would replace the fez. How long can the artifice of Kemalism survive before Turkey's true nature rises and sweeps it away?

George suppresses a yawn.

Yilmaz is still talking. "The Kurdish problem does not exist. Many of us are Kurds. In Turkey, a Kurd can be even the Prime Minister. This is true. The problem for me is the Islamists. If they have power it will be like Iran. No, even more worse. Like Algeria. They will not stop until the woman is wearing the chador. Until there is Shariah law."

George nods lamely and stirs his tea. It was a refusal, wasn't it? Now he remembers. What was her name? Nazan. She was there making a case for a young Armenian fellow, probably her boyfriend. Didn't put up much of a fight, no shrill pleas or angry tears, just her ridiculous tea-time voice. And dignity, the kind that makes you wonder if you decided wrong. Did he?

"Yes, I remember this Taylor," says Yilmaz. "He was not for long one of my students, but I remember him. Never. The. Less." Yilmaz dissects the word as he says it, much the same way that George might pronounce *yapabilirmelerinde*—not quite rolling off his tongue. "He was not so interested in studying, more interested in narkotik."

"Narcotics? You're saying Taylor was taking drugs?"

"Not taking. Selling. Okay, maybe he takes too. He sell the hashish to other students."

George is not surprised. It all fits; another spoiled rich kid with parents in denial. He pictures the congressional letters that will come, demanding that the consulate rush to Taylor's aid while the kid cuts class and sells dope.

Yilmaz misinterprets his silence. "Do not say you are surprised…A young man who is all the time making trouble…" He pauses. When he turns to face George, his expression has changed. "You may check his file if you think I am making the mistake." By this he means the CIA computer which contains information on every individual on the planet, and which exists only in his mind.

George has more questions, but now the professor keeps his answers short. Yes, Taylor had friends, but he doesn't know any of them by name. No, Taylor hasn't been seen for several weeks. Yes, he has an idea why he left; the police came asking questions and Taylor disappeared soon after. No, the police haven't returned; maybe the jails should be checked. No, he hasn't heard anything else. Yes, he will call if he does. No, it wasn't any trouble to speak with him. Yes, he enjoyed meeting him too.

Outside, George contemplates searching for another professor, maybe a roommate—someone, anyone—who knows Taylor. But this would take time, and he suspects there's already a pile-up on his desk. He decides to let Zeynep inquire by phone. The sky is dismal now, a gray overcast of infinite depth. The November wind blows cold. He is irritated by Yilmaz's paranoia, but can't fully blame him. In Turkey, just because you're paranoid doesn't mean they're *not* out to get you.

A voice from behind him interrupts his thoughts.

"Hello, we met before," says Nazan. She must have approached quietly, and now stands before him unabashed. "Before, before," she corrects herself. "I met you when I came to the consulate. Do you remember?"

"Yes. You were with a young man. I'm sorry. I don't remember his situation exactly…"

"He applied for a visa. You were very cross. You thought he might stay in America and work."

"Yes. Well."

"Well," she says, making a face like she's forgotten what she wanted to say. "I guess there's nothing more to be said about that." But still she stands there. "May I ask you something?"

George nods. He doesn't like running into refusals outside the office, but it's hard not to like this young woman with her ludicrous BBC accent.

"Would you like to go for tea and speak privately? I know a restaurant that makes brilliant *meze* if you have the time. Chok Hosh," she says. Very pleasant.

George smiles and excuses himself politely.

In the parking lot she catches up, slightly breathless. "Did you think I want to discuss my friend's visa?" She has her hands on her hips. "Well, really. I just thought you might want to hear more about your American friend, Taylor. Taylor Moore?"

They settle on a fish restaurant in Emirgan, on the cheap side of the street, away from the water. She is adamant he try the eggplant. George has had it dozens of times—fried, oiled, battered, mashed, whipped, stewed, stuffed and pureed—but agrees anyway and resolves early on to pick up the check. The late lunch crowd streams out to the tune of "*My Way*," strained through speakers in the ceiling. The old cassette drops to half-speed then lurches forward before lagging again, transforming Old Blue Eyes into a wailing muezzin. The waiters hover close, as Turks are bound to do, poised to leap on the first plate that empties. George has had glasses, half-full, virtually seized from his grip; now he watches his mineral water closely.

Nazan is less circumspect than the professor. She met Moore through the international students group, she explains; he was a little tuhaf—strange—but intelligent. He was interested in politics. He asked the other students what they thought about the Kurdish problem, and even asked again and again if they were Kurds themselves. Of course, this troubled them. He was disliked by many, but also had a way of drawing others close, a special charisma. He could be very cold, or very charming; very loud or very private. He challenged his professors openly, often, and with outrageous audacity, about Kurds, human rights, Armenians. He had nothing but horrible things to say about America, which confused his fellow students. Everyone at the university knew Taylor; really, he was quite famous.

"What about his drug use? Did you know about that?"

Nazan takes a calculated spoonful of mercümek soup, and follows it with a sip of raki. She has ordered a bottle too large even for two, and seems disappointed to be drinking alone, though it doesn't slow her down. For a second time she fills her glass, then douses the clear liquid with water. Soon it's a milky froth. George has heard that raki tastes something like ouzo, only thinner and more potent. Though he never cared for ouzo, he can't suppress the desire it spawns in him now. The urge to knock her aside and consume the contents of her glass in one almighty heave.

"I've never met a diplomat who didn't drink," she reproaches him.

"Have you met many diplomats?" George asks, steering clear of the subject.

She shrugs. "My friend's father is the honorary consul for Pakistan. But I suppose that's not quite the same thing. To be a real diplomat; how very glamorous it must be."

Sure, glamorous. In the morning, he works on an assembly line doing quality control, separating good travelers from bad; and in the afternoon he's a social worker for his own countrymen, most of whom will never reconcile what they see here with their preconceived notions of diplomacy as a world of top hats and limousines—a world that exists only in the movies and in the minds of certain senators.

How glamorous was it to live for two years out of a suitcase? He remembers the way Margaret cried when in Monrovia they learned that their personal belongings would not arrive for many months—that the ship carrying their furniture, their stereo, their TV set, most of their clothing, their crystal and china wedding gifts, had not even made it to Antwerp! Many months later, when the ship finally did arrive, there were no longer any able-bodied Monrovians to unload it, most having taken to the streets with guns. So on the docks it sat. When Margaret was evacuated, the embassy ordered the effects transferred to a ship bound for America, but when it finally set sail it went to Hong Kong instead. Eventually the department caught up with it and the goods got off-loaded and pointed in the right direction. But by then Margaret, who was well into her second trimester, had made it clear that she would never return to Liberia, not even if the fighting ceased. She had already bought new furniture for her one-bedroom apartment in Arlington, which softened the blow a little when George informed her the ship had inexplicably stopped in Israel, well off its scheduled course. The department's lawyers were still trying to find out why. Would they ever get their stuff? George wondered. Margaret had cried hardest over the photo albums, especially the wedding pictures. But as time passed she had stopped crying, even seemed to accept their loss as permanent. Her fatalism was troubling; it was if their marriage had gone the way of their household effects, suspended in international limbo, terminally missing, perhaps equally doomed.

"Yeah it's..." He lets it drop, then finishes his eggplant in silence. His left arm itches, but he resists the urge to scratch.

"Are you quite sure?" She dangles the bottle of raki. "This is too much for me to drink." He shakes his head as she tops off her glass. "Maintenance or binge?" she says suddenly.

"Pardon me?"

Her look is penetrating. "A maintenance drinker, I think. Like most diplomats. You're all so bottled up." She shakes her head sadly. "Now what is this nonsense about Taylor being some kind of common criminal?"

George recovers. "Yilmaz says he's a regular Al Capone. Al Capone...never mind. He said Taylor's been dealing hashish, all sorts of drugs."

She laughs. "That is an interesting red herring."

"What do you mean?"

"Taylor is many things, but a criminal, hardly. He's too pure..."

"Pure."

"Pure is the wrong word. I don't mean good. No, of course he's quite a bad hat. But idealistic. Uncompromising. Drugs are always a compromise. He would never get involved with that. Of course, that is why Yilmaz envies him so. Yilmaz is a fool, like all Marxists. Like all those who refuse to believe the Cold War has ended. Living in the past. Really, he is just pathetic."

"A Marxist? Yilmaz? All he did was carry on about Atatürk. He's a regular poster child for the Turkish Republic." No better than the Islamists, thinks George, though he doesn't say so.

"Poster I don't know, but not a child. He's such an old..." Nazan shivers theatrically. "George...may I call you George?" She dips a chunk of bread in haydari and passes it to him, then licks her fingertips. "Don't chase wild geese. If you want to find Taylor, go to the Euphrates Center for Human Rights."

"The what?"

"Near Istiklal. Not far from your consulate." She slurs faintly. "They sell Kurdish books and music to finance the terrorists. Taylor goes there frequently. Perhaps it was because of his American passport that the police didn't capture him along with the others. Though perhaps now they have."

"Terrorists? What are you saying? That Taylor is involved with the PKK? This guy sure gets around." George takes a scoop of haydari, ignoring Nazan's frown. PKK is *Partia Karkaris Kurdistan*, the Kurdish Worker's Party, a violent terrorist organization which purports to represent Turkey's Kurdish population, an ethnic minority that has long been a *cause celebre* in the West but a more complicated picture back home. For the Kurds there is no discrimination in Turkey—so long as they behave as Turks first and Kurds a distant second. Those who politicize their Kurdishness suffer the wrath of the State. In the early 1980s, the more desperate among them discovered Marxism and joined the PKK. They have been fighting ever since.

Their commander-in-chief is Apo, a man whose real name no longer matters. As a young man, Apo wanted nothing more than to enter Turkey's army to defend Atatürk's Republic. Instead, he entered university and wound up a student militant, in the turbulent years before the 1980 coup. When the military restored order, Apo fled to Damascus, where the Syrians readily turned him into a freedom fighter for the Kurdish cause or, more to the point, a thorn in Ankara's side.

From Syria, Apo appealed to those Kurds in Turkey who identified Ankara as the enemy, who wanted Kurdish education, Kurdish broadcasts, Kurdish holidays. Never mind that he spoke barely a word of Kurdish himself.

Apo aimed the armed struggle at local administrators, government engineers, local mayors, teachers. In response, the State deployed a quarter of a million soldiers to the southeast to keep the peace. By day they succeeded, but at night the land belonged to the PKK. Atrocities from both sides drove millions of refugees to the slums of Diyarbakir, Adana, Malatya, Istanbul. Every year, the government claimed victory, and every year the war grew larger—until now. For the first time in a decade, violence is down. The rebels are on the run. Even the human rights situation has started to improve, with so few villages left for the army to raze.

Now Apo is running too. No one knows his whereabouts, not even the CIA. Until recently he was untouchable, commanding his troops from the safety of the Bekaa Valley in Lebanon, which the Syrians controlled. For years the Turks pressed Damascus to stop sheltering him, but their diplomacy was fruitless. Finally they shrugged and did what they should have done long ago—sent tanks to the border. Finally threatened by war, the Syrians buckled, and Apo left Damascus on a flight to who knows where. Since then, there have been Apo sightings from Holland to Moscow to Azerbaijan. Dozens of intelligence organizations are on his trail, first and foremost Turkey's MIT, which will stop at nothing to bring him to justice.

"You're having fun at my expense," says Nazan, wearing a mock expression of hurt. "Well, that was chok hosh." She begins to stand, reconsiders, and sits down heavily. With a glance at the waiters huddled by the door, she locates the cap to the raki bottle, screws it on, and drops it in her oversized purse. The way she zips it up makes it clear George won't have to argue for the bill. "You needn't listen to me," she says. "I will give you the address and you may do with it as you wish." She writes on a napkin, hesitates, then adds her own telephone number. When she stands up again, there's the slightest hint she won't stay upright. Her English suffers. "Do you know? I never ask you. What makes you interested in this boy? You know so little about him."

"His father," says George. "He wants us to find him."

"His father? In that case I don't think that you will."

"Why's that?"

"Because, in my opinion. And now I speak to you as a student of psychology…" She steadies herself on a chair that threatens to tip. "It's because of Taylor's father that he has gone missing."

George takes a detour on his way back to the consulate, content to be alone with his thoughts. Drugs. Kurds. What was Taylor into? He thinks of Nazan, and decides he would like to see her again. He feels a sense of disquiet—something he did wrong, maybe. Or just something he didn't do right enough.

At the main intersection in Kasimpasha, a gypsy child throws an oily rag across his windshield and an open hand at his window. There's something wrong with these scruffy kids, all wide-eyed and manic, that makes locking the door seem wise. Even the eight-year-old girls look threatening.

George checks the address on a note he scribbled to himself some weeks back; it belongs to an old visa applicant. A bad case.

George finds the tiny street, parks, then starts to make his way around the holes in the sidewalk. The shopkeepers stare at him quizzically. He wanders back and forth, then finds his bearings: one- twelve, one- ten, one- eight. He burrows his chin in his overcoat and curses. The shop is closed.

Two, three weeks ago, he refused a visa to the owner of this shop—a man claiming to need treatment for throat cancer, but with no evidence whatsoever. George studies the door and the windows for some hint of why the place is closed. A passerby stops, offers to help, but George turns him away. Goddamn it. Nothing. But what did he expect to find? If the shop was open and the old man inside, selling watch bands and batteries, would that prove anything? Maybe if he'd found a party in full swing, raki flowing and the old man plucking a *saz* and crooning Anatolian folk songs, then he'd have his proof. But no, he would never get that kind of closure. Not with visa work. Perhaps not with anything.

George lingers, debating whether to question the neighbors; the thought only depresses him further. He curses again and, with a last glance at the storefront, abandons the place for good.

He decides he has to stop doing this.

A pile of paperwork is George's punishment for being absent half the day. A note from Zeynep says the consul general wants an update on six American sailors from the destroyer USS something-or-other, jailed for brawling the night before. According to the sailors, the trouble started after a night of bar-hopping when they'd asked a cabby to take them to their ship; instead he took them to a house of ill repute. When they emerged from the taxi, disoriented and wondering where the ship was, some pimps tried to force them inside, and that's when the fight broke out. The sailors were remarkably consistent in telling their stories, but none could explain what led them to search for their destroyer in the heart of Istanbul's red-light district, high on a hill above the Bosphorous.

George takes a call from an Iranian-American whose brother has failed again to qualify for *his* visa. "We've sent all the medical documents," she argues. "You have everything you need!"

George remembers the case—another young man with an unpronounceable disease meaning certain death if not treated by an American doctor. "I'm happy to check the case, ma'am," he says. He covers the phone. "Dawn, you refused that kid, Hashemi, didn't you? This morning? The one with the supposed weird disease? Anything you want to add?"

"Is that his sister on the phone? She called ten minutes ago! You tell her…" She starts his way. "The case is, like, *so* bad. If you wanna issue, go ahead. But the case stinks. He's lying his…"

"Fine, Dawn, fine…" He waves her off then, back on the phone, recites the standard refusal language. By the time he ends the call the Iranian is sobbing hysterically, Truman is at his desk, and Dawn is nowhere in sight.

"Iranians," says George, replacing the receiver. "Is there any other race so prone to obscure, deadly diseases? What a load of bull."

"Her problem is that she takes it personally," says Truman, glancing at Dawn's empty desk. "If she can't stomach being lied to, she should find other work."

"Sometimes it's hard to stay detached."

"She has no right to let her personal feelings influence her adjudications. She's a commissioned law enforcement officer. She has to follow the law. My God, some of the lowlifes I've issued in my day..."

George nods. His friend speaks from experience, having served in Santo Domingo and Seoul—two of the world's biggest visa mills. But was true objectivity really possible? Dawn had her angry spells, but at least she wasn't haunted, as he was, by the inevitability of being wrong at least some of the time. At least she didn't obsess over visa decisions which destroyed vacations, university studies, business deals, even life-saving medical care. At least she didn't second-guess herself with fruitless visits to closed-up shops in bad neighborhoods, checking her work. Did she honestly believe that her decisions were always right? Whatever the case, she continued to judge, day after day, without hesitation, in a way that George could not. And despite Truman's prompting, he could not so easily judge her now.

"What's wrong? You seem down."

George shrugs. "Nothing. My stomach's funny."

"What are you doing this weekend?"

Probably driving to Umraniye to see if that Kurdish family I issued last month ever came back, he thinks to himself, but only shrugs.

"I'm making the Thanksgiving run to Izmir. "Turkeys and Cranberry sauce for the breeders, and booze for my happy hours. Why don't we go together?" He glances at Craine's door. It was closed before, but now is open a crack.

When George looks too, it slams shut.

Truman laughs. "C'mon, join me. Winston obviously has this place under control."

"Two days on those insane roads? Tempting, but I should pass."

"Maybe it's not such a good idea."

"Hmm?"

"You don't want people to talk. You have a reputation to protect. Especially with the spooks."

George thinks of Phil, and his odd comments about Truman in Priscilla's office, but says nothing.

"You know they've been stealing the GLIFA newsletter," says Truman. GLIFA is *Gays and Lesbians in Foreign Affairs*, an organization with many members at state. Truman has made a practice of posting their newsletter in the foyer, to the chagrin of a conservative few; lately the newsletters have been disappearing.

"Maybe Phil wants to read them in private," says George. Though he won't admit it, ever since Truman started posting the newsletters, he feels ill at ease himself loitering too long at the bulletin board.

"The lady doth protest too much?" Truman smiles. I doubt it. Phil's a perfect zero on the McKenzie scale. You on the other hand..."

George doesn't smile.

"Oh, come on," says Truman. "Lighten up." He lets out a sigh. "I'll just find someone else to go with me." Absently, he lets his hand drift to his hip; it's a dead giveaway.

"Alright, look..." says George.

"Yes?"

"We're not going to do any of your bars in Izmir, are we?" He means it as a question, but it sounds like a warning.

"Oh, God," says Truman. "Don't worry. We don't even have to have fun. We can both get in touch with our inner old ladies."

They agree to leave on Saturday morning.

* * *

Listen up. There's a story that you won't find in any of Winston Markey's memos, and it happened in a place called Doğubeyazit in Turkey's far east, not far from the Iranian border, which I had crossed to get there just a few days earlier.

Why Iran, you might ask? I suppose that I could have traveled to Turkey from the other direction, from the west, that is, and in doing so spared myself stops in Calcutta and Qatar, but when you're trying to leave Australia, any direction seems more or less as good as the next.

Doğubeyazit I remember well for the Hotel Isfahan and its most prized possession—a western toilet, probably the only one in town. The last time I saw it, it was filled with gratuitously spinning waste, unwilling to navigate the drain no matter how hard I flushed. But at least this time the water was spinning in the right direction.

I was dizzy and my temples ached; sweat poured down my face; my skull felt on the verge of sprouting horns. When I flushed again, the room spun faster than the water. Air, I needed air. A moment later I had found the door and I was looking at the sky. Then, I was looking at nothing at all.

But more on that later.

To the Hotel Isfahan in Doğubeyazit, Turkey from Melbourne, Australia, takes precisely 87 days door-to-door, for those of you planning a trip. The most arduous part was the first hundred miles, as our cargo ship, El Destino, pounded its way out of Port Phillip Bay, buffetted by strong Antarctic winds.

Even after a week on dry land, I still felt the sway of the sea. The cold memory of seasickness sent shivers down my spine and filled my mouth with brine. My ears still rang from the roar of the ship's engines, which were deafening in the kitchen which was my job to clean, and in the adjacent compartment that I shared with a novice Philippino more sea-sick than myself. To make matters worse, the height of the storm coincided with my first psychic downturn; as the waves tossed, black kelp boiled in my head. The churning of the sea was like a never-ending flush, a daily reminder of my fateful decision to ditch my medication. At the height of my despair, I gave serious thought to throwing myself into the sea, to descend beneath the turmoil; but then my roommate produced a bottle of something called lumbanog which, foul as it was, placated my demons, though it didn't stop either of us from throwing up. And so it was that I arrived in Bangkok drained and many pounds lighter; but by then I was back on the upswing, my mind as lucid as a candle.

Aboard the ship, I had managed to finish *Chapter One*, all about JFK's assassination. Never mind the grassy knoll; a photograph shows Oswald standing on the street the very moment that shots were fired from the fifth floor of the Book Depository building. Lee never used his middle name; the *Harvey* looked strange to him when he saw it in print. David Ferrie really was one, a fairy.

In Doğubeyazit I started on Chapter Two. Logically enough, I planned to write about the Kurds who, like me, were out *fighting the power*. Could it be that the CIA was working to transform the Kurdish resistance into a narco-trafficking mafia, as they had in Central America, harnessing Marxism to the cause of black genocide by ensuring the supply of cheap cocaine? I'd seen no evidence to the contrary. Obviously there were American secrets here that only a hungry journalist could unveil.

My goal was to expose the links between these conspiracies—to reveal the web, the single fabric, the comprehensive whole. *It*, I knew, was bigger than the CIA, bigger than the NSA, and far more powerful than the sum of its parts. And *It* was right in front of me—I knew that much—like an impressionist painting that must be viewed from afar, like invisible ink exposed under light. This was my quest, my Holy Grail, to shine a spotlight on this tapestry, to prove to the world that *It* was there.

Every day my mind raced on, spitting out loads of questions, fewer answers. How did one win the Pulitzer? Was it all political? Power coursed through my arms, my legs, every ortifice and artery. My body was as clean, as toxin-free, as an alpine stream. I heard my own laughter, which made me laugh again. Life and death were wonderful things. Had anyone on earth, I wondered, ever felt so alive?

Those who have never seen Mount Ararat don't know what they're missing. Like Kilamanjaro, it rises from a plain, every one of its seventeen thousand feet visible, unobscured by adjacent peaks or hills. The top third of the mountain is snowy all year around, but where the slopes turn flat the fields are splashed with color. Thousands of animals graze in the shadow of the great volcano, painting a picture of Eden.

At least that's what I'm told; when I arrived in December the mountain was submerged in clouds, and the streets of Doğubeyazit buried in slush that soaked the cash in my sock and kept me indoors. When I wasn't writing, I passed the time playing tavla, backgammon, with Haluk, the Isfahan's front desk clerk. Haluk boasted of being the only Doğubeyazit resident who knew more than ten words of English, having once overstayed a visa in England by many months.

In the course of a long and sleepless night my book had taken an unexpected autobiographical turn. I found myself struggling to describe my beginnings as Bill Bigelow, son of Frank "Blister" Bigelow, first lieutenant in the U.S. Army, stationed in Frankfurt. My first encounter with the U.S. government came early in life—a slap on the ass after a messy c-section, which left my mother in a coma. Things went downhill from there. When I was a year old, I went under the knife myself, to correct a minor *encephalomyeloneuropathy*, as the doctors called it. My Aunt Sally said it was *nothing with which one should be unduly concerned*—the wires in my brain were slightly tangled but the doctors had straightened them out. Sadly, she was mistaken. Whatever it was that the doctors did in there—and for all I know they planted rhododendrons—the result was a time bomb set for my eighteenth birthday and my first suicide attempt, a "cry for help," as everyone insisted on calling it just because I ate children's chewables instead of adult aspirin, which I despised swallowing. Little did I know how much swallowing was in store for me in the years ahead.

From that day on, I was officially categorized as bipolar. My shrinking number of friends assumed this meant that I swung neatly from euphoria one day to depression the next, as if my brain was a track with stations at both ends. But in fact, for me, the trains were always moving in both directions at once and often crashing in the middle, where the debris from one became indistinguishable from the other.

Indistinguishable from the other, I wrote, then lay my pen down. I put my face in my hands. Nearly two months had passed since I mailed my query letters from El Destino to Doubleday, and Random House, and Dell and Warner, and Scribners, and Penguin Books, and Simon and Schuster—and still no response. Nor had Paul Thoreaux, Janet Reno, or the Sultan of Brunei written me back. At the cyber cafe in Tehran, my Hotmail account had been utterly void. Yet I was undaunted, teflon-coated, impermeable to discouragement, even as I felt more and more strongly the darkness at the edge of my being, still banished to the extremities but clawing ever closer to my heart. The trains had left their stations and location, location, location, was everything.

I picked a book out of Haluk's private collection—*Moments of Doubt, the Mountaineers*, by a man named David Roberts, who I imagined to be impressively fit and tan. The cover was of snowy peaks and men in parkas. Holiday Inns had Bibles at bedside; the Hotel Isfahan, it seemed, had books on climbing mountains. I opened it to a random page, and began to read.

How much of the appeal of mountaineering lies in its simplification of interpersonal relationships, its reduction of friendship to smooth interaction (like war), its substitution of an Other (the mountain, the challenge) for the relationship itself? Behind a mystique of adventure, toughness, footloose vagabondage—all much needed antidotes to our culture's built-in comfort and convenience—may lie a kind of adolescent refusal to take seriously aging, the frailty of others, interpersonal responsibility, weakness of all kinds, the slow and unspectacular course of life itself.

I put the book down and took pen in hand again and drew a line down the middle of the page. I wrote *Meaning, Faith, Certainty* in capital letters in the left column, then the words *nihilism, agnosticism, doubt*, in lower- case on the right. When I was done, I stared at my work and wondered what it meant.

Haluk played tavla, backgammon, like the Turks fought their wars, straight ahead with no thought for defense. Again and again I landed on his pieces, and again and again he leapt back onto the board and left them exposed. I won every third game.

"What are you thinking?" he asked, stealing the dice from my hand to expedite his roll. The air was smoky and warm; I should have felt cozy amid the fluffy kilim pillows, but I had a bad case of the jitters. It was hard to sit still. There were signs on the wall that said *Hotel Toors to Noah's Ark* with yellowing photos of past expeditions and newspaper clippings indicating that the Ark had long since been stolen by aliens. Everything on the wall was many years old, giving the place a bygone feel; how long had it been since a westerner came to town?

"I'm wasting my time here," I told Haluk. "I didn't come to Doggy-beyazit to drink tea."

"Tours are finished," he said. "Come in summer. Then we start again. Unless there is more fighting." He lit a cigarette and frowned. "You roll, please. Not too much thinking now."

Tired of tavla, I put on my coat and went outside where I found a taxi stuck in the snow. I helped him dig out the wheels, then asked for a ride to the fortress known as Ishak Pasha, several miles out of town. By Turkish standards, it was new construction, dating only to the time of the U.S. Declaration of Independence. I'd seen it in pictures, a walled city that could be ancient Jericho if not for the minaret. Slabs of solid gold served as the front doors until 1917, when marauding Russians hauled them off to Moscow. Last year, workmen doing renovations found skeletons strewn about the subterranean corridors. *Turks killed by Armenian invaders*, was what they told the tourists, tidying up their history. The bones were gathered in sacks and tossed into a corner, where they remained long after the workers went home.

I gave the cabbie a generous tip from my sock and sent him away, then sat beneath an archway in the courtyard of the fortress with my jacket drawn tight. The high walls of the fortress shielded me from the wind. There was no one around. From my protected spot, I could see very little, only tools and scraps randomly discarded as if a sudden blizzard had interrupted work in full swing. Beneath a virgin layer of snow, the courtyard was quiet. Only my head seemed to hum. I shivered, feeling the familiar cycle take hold. My thoughts were building to a climax; soon I would be there, and afterward I would have nothing whatsoever to write. The clouds of interference would descend, rendering all impossible. I told myself to wait it out, let the fever pass, as it always did. In the meantime, stay out of trouble.

Maybe I could solve my problem with a little strenuous activity; I strained my eyes to see the mountain, the fabled resting place of Noah's Ark, and discovered that I was not alone after all.

"Aleman?"

"American." I said.

"Ah, good, my English is more better than my German." There were three of them, not Turks, but tourists like me, or so they said. The tallest introduced himself as Lahcen. He had a *savoir faire*, a *je ne sais quoi*, that made me like him immediately. His black eyes twinkled as he spoke. The others were quieter, shuffling from foot to foot in clothes that made no sense for the weather. It was cold, much too cold it seemed, for the light rain that was beginning to fall. As we strolled together, the clouds parted to reveal barren hills—what the PKK and its supporters would call Kurdistan—then just as quickly they were gone. I agreed to join them in their car.

With Lahcen driving, we started north along the highway in the direction of Kars, where my plane had landed the week before on a sheet of ice, the passengers breaking into cheers as if landing intact had been for all a pleasant surprise.

Lahcen wanted to know why an American had come all this way. I told him about my book, and all but narrated the first two chapters. He was a good listener, and his friends too, insofar as they understood.

"What's all this?" I asked when we had driven almost an hour. We were surrounded by ancient lava fields poking through the snow. Tents littered the moonscape.

"Kürtler. Before, they lived on the mountain. The army says they help the freedom fighters so they evacuate them."

Lahcen pointed to the villages from which they'd come, clusters of empty stone houses high in the distant hills. If the PKK wanted help from the villagers now, they'd have to cross the highway, a treacherous divide. Tanks passed us by, followed by trucks full of soldiers with blank stares and helmets too big for their heads. The refugee kids hollered as we passed. When I photographed a machine gunner lying in a pit, Lahcen swatted the camera from my hands. "Uf!" Stop it! "Does a murderer sit for his picture?"

When he winked a moment later, and flashed that wicked Lachen smile, I forgave him, though my lip still stung. In fact, I was too fuzzy to do anything else. The word repeated in my head like a dripping faucet, rote and relentless. Uf. Uf. Uf. With all my might, I couldn't make it go away. As we made our way back to Doğubeyazit, I loaned him my camera to admire; he inspected it carefully, turning it over and over in his hands and asking how each piece worked. I suppose that should have been my first clue.

That evening, we went to the nearest restaurant. Omnipresent Atatürk watched us eat. I told Lachen my plan. "Tomorrow I will go up on the mountain to photograph Noah's Ark. Haluk says the road is clear up to here…" As I spread the map I felt my juices stir. "And then it's only a four-mile hike to the Ark, taking the most direct route. Once there, of course, we'll find shelter in the ship's hold. The trip shouldn't be too difficult. The snow was wet today; after it freezes tonight, it will be firm and easy to walk on. It should only take a day to get there; if it takes longer, of course we'll have a tent. And I've already shopped for food and supplies."

"There are soldiers on the mountain."

"They shouldn't object to a scientific expedition. Anyway, they won't see us." Uf, uf, uf, went my head.

"And wolves."

"Aha!"

"It not is a thing you should do alone."

I nodded with enthusiasm. Besides Lachen, I anticipated the company of his two sidekicks, though they were such nonentities I often forgot they were there. Always they lingered about, filling their mouths with whatever we ordered or scratching themselves as we talked.

Lahcen nodded in agreement, and I felt a flickering sense of well-being. I ordered a bottle of raki and insisted he share a toast. After apologizing to his God, Lahcen gave in and took a tepid swig. Feeling energized, I announced sarcastic admiration for the art on the walls—velvet unicorns, puppies and kittens, and cheesy landscapes with bright sunsets—but stopped when his friends agreed that they were fine art indeed. That's about all I remember. Lahcen ordered a second bottle of raki, which made me listless after the third glass. Since when had I been such a lightweight? I asked Lahcen and his friends if the food had upset their stomachs, and they told me no. What else? The cook took an interest in my condition and stood by our table for what seemed an eternity. I was grateful for his concern, but the dirt beneath his nails only made me more ill. I don't recall if I made it back to the hotel under my own power, or whether Lahcen and the others helped me there. I do know, though, that I insisted on being left alone in my room. I don't like others around when I'm going to be sick.

I heard a buzzing in my ear and slapped without effect. Damn Australian flies, were my last words, I think.

Then there was the toilet, and the spinning, and the flush that did no good, and my long stagger down the steps and the blast of cold air that almost bowled me over. When I next opened my eyes, it was to fill them with grit and slush which, conspiring with the roadside, politely declined to lower me down to that non-living side of the earth.

The walls of the Doğubeyazit jail were as bland as the eyes of the cop who sat working his pen with methodic precision, as if it were a calligrapher's tool. "Isminiz ne?" He asked, not looking up. When I said nothing his pen went still.

"Nem?"

"Bill," I said, which was true enough.

"Bil," said the cop. "Bil." He smiled pleasantly and returned to his task, moving the pen slowly. I watched his single eyebrow furrow in concentration.

Lahcen and I sat across from the policeman's desk. A portrait of Atatürk hung on the gray, unpainted wall—not the young Colonel who repelled the Anzacs at Gallipoli, replete with mustache and fez, nor the pot-bellied alcoholic nearing death. This was Atatürk the teacher, traversing Anatolia in his Model-T with chalkboard and pointy stick, stopping here and there to hold forth with the peasants on the wonders of latin letters and bowler hats.

When the cop had finished his forms, he let out a heavy sigh and lit a cigarette, then switched on the TV and fiddled with the rabbit ears until *Wheel of Fortune* came on. A foreign Vanna White turned the boxes and formed words, but they were no more intelligible than the random letters had been. The cop, it was obvious, found the game difficult. I looked at Lahcen; he was gazing laconically at the TV, or perhaps it was the door beside the TV that held his attention. It was not how they had brought us in. But now, quite suddenly, it opened and a heavy-set officer stepped in. The cop stumbled to his feet and ran his hands over his uniform.

"Hallo," said the officer who had entered.

"Hello."

"No problem?"

I shrugged.

"No problem?" he asked again, gently tapping me on the forehead. "Okay?"

"No problem," I agreed. But in fact there was a problem. I was in a foreign police station and couldn't remember how I'd come to be there. I had no idea what I'd done. The air in the windowless room stank of coal dust, sweat, and ammonia. A dictator was watching us from a frame on the wall, a benevolent one, but a dictator nonetheless. Time had stopped. It could have been snowing outside, or sweltering hot, or pouring monsoon rains; it was irrelevant now. My heart pounded; I felt dizzy; it seemed possible that I might soon throw up.

In my stupor, I didn't notice the officer moving behind me until his hands were on my shoulders, half-lifting me from the chair and forcing me against the wall. Instinctively, as if I knew this drill, I went spread-eagle as my shirt was pulled over my head. His hands were like sand and I flinched at the touch. "Good," said the officer when I was back in my chair. He grinned. My face was cupped lovingly in his hands; he gave me a fatherly pat on the cheek and smiled again. Then he released me and went to Lahcen.

The first hot splat of skin on skin cleared my head a little; the second turned me numb. Lahcen dropped his chin to his chest, as if counting on his body to somehow swallow his head, but the cop just gave his hair a tug and again his cheek was exposed. The third slap brought a sick, gurgling cry, and a strand of spit that swung crazily before settling on Lahcen's shoulder.

"Boo-y-roon," said the policeman, cupping Lahcen's jaw less tenderly than he had mine, and turning it sharply toward me. *Buyrun* was a catch-all word. From a grocer it might mean "buy this pear." Or from a doorman, "come in." But from the officer, it clearly meant "your turn."

"No, thank you," I said politely. It was one of just two expressions I knew. The other, *does this train stop in Yeshilyurt*, I was still waiting for a chance to use.

I suppose I expected gratitude in Lahcen's eyes, but instead I saw only disdain. Does he think I can't throw a punch, I wondered, chafing at the insult. Our eye contact was broken by a foot placed squarely in Lahcen's groin, then a box to his ear that sent him reeling to the floor. The chair went with him, cuffed to one hand. For a moment, Lahcen seemed to debate whether or not to cry. He gave in, and his free hand stretched upward, coming to rest on the officer's belt. This was too much for the other cop, who took a break from *Wheel of Fortune* to drive a nightstick into the small of Lahcen's back, sending him back to the floor where he curled up like a fetus.

After that the violence stopped for a while. Lahcen lay on the floor, face down, unnaturally still. I scanned the room. There was nothing to keep me from getting up and bolting through the door; it was unlocked and, unlike Lahcen, I wasn't cuffed to a chair. I would be out the door before the cops even gave chase. Then I'd sprint down the hall and... Yes, that's what I would do. But first I just needed to rest.

The officer took a seat to my left. He lit a cigarette, a local brand, and gave it to me; the tobacco was like manure. While we smoked, tea was served by a little man who came in and bowed courteously; even Lahcen got a glass, sipping slowly to make the most of the break. When the tea guy came back for the empties, he had some new things on his tray—something that looked like a potato peeler, a miniature ice-pick, and a thingamajig that more or less resembled a dental probe.

The officer took the tools, and Lahcen, behind the mystery door. For several minutes there was pleading, then only the faint mewing of a frightened animal. Suddenly the door thrust open and Lahcen came stumbling in, his hands grasping his crotch; a stain ran from his groin to his knee. The officer seemed to find this hilarious; he laughed aloud and jabbed me good-naturedly. When the laughter had died down and Lahcen had returned to his fetal position on the floor, I requested permission to visit the toilet. More laughter. The cop escorted me upstairs, to the edge of a tiny stall that had a single hole in the floor. I would not suffer the same humiliation if I could help it; when my turn came I wanted my organs dry. But as I stood uneventfully at the hole, I realized that they already were; my body was a desert, my mouth so arid that I couldn't find spit; my lips were chapped to the point of cracking.

"You," said the officer when we were back in the room. He lolled his head and exhibited deep concentration, his eyes clenched shut. "You like," he said at last. "You like Kurdistan?"

"Yes. Yes." I said. The officer raised his eyebrows and I recognized my error. "I like Turkey very much. A whole bunch," I almost gasped.

The officer smiled a deep smile; he seemed relieved. "Türkiye güzel, değ il mi?" He said. Turkey's nice, isn't it? I recognized the word and repeated it twice.

"Goozel. Goozel."

"Chok," the officer confirmed. He smiled broadly and pinched his thumb and forefinger together so that the back of his fingers showed. They had thick calluses where none should have been.

From where we sat, we could just reach Lahcen by extending our legs straight. The officer tapped him gently with the toe of his boot. He asked questions, and I identified the word "camera," then "passport."

Lahcen answered quietly, but the answers must have been wrong. In time the taps became bumps, which soon turned to kicks. I stared into space, trying to recall what I was doing here. Uf, uf, went my head not unhelpfully. Oh, yes, I remembered now; I was drugged and robbed. I had done nothing wrong. I should have been relieved, but panic gripped me instead. Where was my manuscript? Oh, here in my hands. My fingers were sore from gripping it with such force. Thank God they hadn't taken that. Anger welled within me. And my camera? The cash in my socks? And my passport? I hope they catch the thief. I noticed the pathetic creature on the floor. Oh, they have.

Lahcen was crying again. His voice had grown loud and shrill, and with every kick I felt my head pound. The first cop was still at the TV, slumped back with dreamy, half-closed eyes. "Bodrum!" he shouted out suddenly. And Bodrum it was when Turkey's version of Vanna dispatched with the letters.

When *Wheel of Fortune* was over, the cops announced a change of venue and soon enough I was in the passenger seat of a police car, racing through the narrow streets of Doğubeyazit. The cop who'd been behind the desk was now behind the wheel, and Lahcen sat behind us, flanked by the chief and a scrawny little policeman who dug deeply into his nose as we drove. The vinyl seat was like ice.

"Turn right at the mosque." At least this is what I guessed was said, for it was at the mosque that we turned.

The door to Lahcen's hideaway came loose with one kick. There were colorful blankets on the floor and a tea kettle still warm. The junior cop took up the chase but returned a short time later, breathing hard and clicking his tongue. My camera sat on the floor, tipped carelessly on its side but undamaged; there was no cash in sight.

As I made to leave, certain I would never see my money again, but grateful for my photos and, more importantly, my book, the chief suggested a picture of us together, squatting amid the boxes of stolen goods. I had never used the timer before, and wasn't sure I could make it work.

But it did. I still have the picture, one of my personal favorites. In it, the cop squats between Lahcen and me, his arms draped over our shoulders. He is a father figure, urging his sons to forgive and forget. And I am a deer in the headlights. For the camera, Lahcen has summoned all his remaining dignity, forcing an expression akin to the cocky arrogance I recall from our drive up Mount Ararat. The junior cop cuts an earnest figure, his expression proud and haughty, like a hunter displaying his kill.

But there is a flaw in the photo, one that makes me feel guilty when I mail it, some months later, to the *Emniyet Polis Istasyonu, Doğubeyazit, Turkiye*, zip code unknown. Two fingers protrude from behind the cop's head like rabbit ears—the age-old adolescent gag. And for a moment I marvel at Lahcen's balls for mocking the cop before heading back to the police station for another round of beatings. But then I look more closely and I realize; those fingers are mine.

* * *

Taylor Moore is a good-looking young man, tall and broad-shouldered and difficult to squeeze into the shower stall. Several days' growth of beard can't conceal his youth, though one could hardly call him fresh. His lips, though cracked and powder-blue, still hold the trace of a smile, oddly serene. His fingernails have grown to an obscene length. Tiny holes, needle tracks, speckle both arms. His shoulder-length hair—too long, really, for a kid who arouses such interest in the U.S. House of Representatives—runs dark against the porcelain, which is not white at all but semi-gray, having not been washed with enthusiasm for a very long time.

Slowly, the basin fills with water and the ice cubes turn to bergs, bobbing gently against the ship-wrecked young man.

"Truman," says George.

"Yes?"

"How long, do you think, before a body starts to decompose?"

No response. Truman is busy laying out the contents of the young man's wallet on the coffee table: There's a MasterCard co-signed by a Peggy Moore, a photograph of a pretty young woman in a cocktail apron, and an organ-donor's card that's of little use here. The only photo ID is his passport, which shows the wear of hard travel. It contains an address and telephone number, scrawled in ink that has started to run. Three million, six hundred and fifty-six thousand Turkish lira, the equivalent of seventy U.S. dollars, lies stacked and divided in neat little piles, and of course the inevitable scraps of paper scrawled with Turkish names and street numbers. The villagers are always handing their addresses to foreigners, eager to test this thing called mail; there's no easier country to find pen-pals.

George looks at his watch. At two in the morning the air still stifles in Gelibolu, a dusty town off highway twenty-four between Thrace and the Aegean Sea, crammed with state-of-the-art brown and gray slab buildings. To see anything worthwhile, one has to drive another hour south, to the killing fields of Gallipoli, where Turkish farmers still run their hoes over helmets and bayonets. But for all the tourists who visit, there are no decent hotels anywhere on the peninsula, no rooms with air conditioning unless one follows Lord Byron's example and crosses the Hellespont.

Gelibolu's chief of police is snoring loudly on the couch, his mouth wide open.

George eyes his roommates—one cop, one gay, one dead—and wishes for rain. In the truck outside are dozens of Thanksgiving hams and turkeys and a shrinking mountain of ice, some already having been transferred inside to preserve the remains of poor young Taylor Moore. George glances at the shower stall; the water is filthy now, ice mingling with porcelain flakes. He sees Truman put Taylor's wallet down, then stand abruptly and sniff the air.

"Not too long," his friend replies.

The road to Chanakkale was a vacant lot of infinite size, pockmarked by ramshackle buildings, unfinished walls and peeled plaster. The Aegean might have been a thousand miles away. Tire tracks ran parallel to the highway, punctuated by chain-link fence and rusty billboards that said *Emlak, Tekel, Pepsi.* A ubiquitous squareness, a landscape of right angles, held neither birds nor horizon. Tumble-down houses followed the highway; most were painted—blue, orange, yellow and green—yet somehow they managed no more exhuberance than unfinished cinder blocks.

A dead body had not been in the plan when they left the commissary in Izmir that morning, laden with Fruit Loops and Cheezits and Double-Stuff Oreos. Such delicacies were no longer available in Istanbul thanks to the draw down of U.S. military personnel following victory in the Cold War, which diminished the need for a commissary.

George and Truman wore short sleeves, enjoying the Indian summer. Behind them were thirty-seven turkeys and eighteen honey-glazed hams, packed in ice chests borrowed from the marines, sixty-five cans of cranberry sauce, fifty boxes of Pepperidge Farm stuffing mix, and a few odd bags of rolls that reportedly plumped in the oven. George watched the driver, Mustafa, sweat beneath his lambs'-wool jumper; it was strange, this Turkish affinity for heat, how they rode around on buses with the windows sealed and snapped their tongues at foreigners who took their babies out sockless, even if in the blazing sun. Of course, drinking cold water was forbidden, especially in August when it caused diarrhea at best, stomach cancer at worst. Instead the locals cooled themselves with glasses of hot, sugary tea.

By half-past one, they were almost to Chanakkale. The traffic was light; a few trucks belched smoke on the shoulder, a reminder of why four times as many Turks as Italians, per capita, died behind the wheel. Like over-sized Tonkas, they moved at a donkey's pace, usually without tail lights; they could be around any corner or over any hill, and usually were.

And then there were the Mercedes, passing the Turkish-made Tofashes and Doğans with arrogant speed and reckless abandon, headlong over pock-marked roads and around blind corners, racing west, always west.

People sometimes asked which side of the street they drove on in Turkey. The correct answer was both.

Truman told George his life story, and George was grateful that Mustafa's English was broken at best.

His name, Vasser, was only a generation old; it had once been *Vassiloconstandakis*, but his father had Americanized it upon arriving at Ellis Island. His first name? Dimitri, said Truman; he had been a junior diplomat in the Greek government under Metaxas, a penny-ante dictator whose government had adopted all the trappings of fascism but efficiency. When Metaxas sent Dimitri Vassiloconstandakis to Madrid, Poland was still free; but by the time his first promotion came, even Greece itself had fallen to the Nazis. My father, said Truman, had seen it all coming, and had already spirited the family fortune from Athens to Madrid, shrewdly exploiting his diplomatic privileges. In time, he had no country to return to, so began to look west. After trying and failing to obtain a visa to the U.S., he booked passage on a ship to Mexico instead, where he found refuge in the mountain town of Quernavaca. For nearly two years he lived in splendid anonymity, with a cook and two maids, one of whom, Jenebee, twenty years his junior, would eventually become Truman's mother. "Diplomats marrying their servants," said Truman. "You see, Yorgo? Some things never change!"

In due course the war came to an end, and Truman's father picked up again and headed north. His flat-bed truck was loaded with all that he could carry, and space was made up front for Jenebee. It wasn't until they reached Detroit that Dimitri put his foot to the brake; had he known that he would soon be joined by tens of thousands of other Greeks fleeing the civil war, he probably would have kept driving, at least as far as Saginaw. Or perhaps not. His rationale for stopping was succinct: "Car trouble."

"My father," said Truman, "didn't want to be Greek anymore. He wanted to be dull and middle class... *bourgeois*." So it was that he used his hidden loot to open the most American business he could think of, and called it *Burger Chef.* Beneath the sloping roof of a Protestant chapel near a strip mall in a suburb called Inkster, Dimitri married his former maid, who bore him five daughters in slow succession. By the time she finally yielded a son, Dimitri was old enough for his sperm to be suspect. He celebrated with free burgers at all three *Burger Chef* restaurants (with the purchase of a large Coke), and named the boy in honor of the president, not the author, as Truman might have preferred. Then he began to sort out his future. The revenue from thousands of burgers poured into Truman's education, which began in a private high school in Grosse Point and culminated at the Georgetown School of Foreign Service in Washington, D.C. The rest, as they say, is history. Truman passed the written and oral foreign service exams on his first try, then entered the 53rd class at the age of twenty-four. His father toasted him with champagne and feta cheese. "Don't worry about no things, my son," he said. "Just pretend to be yourself, and you are heading straight at the top." Perhaps his father's English had diminished with age. A year later he would be dead.

"Just pretend to be yourself," Truman repeated for George's benefit. "That's what my father told me. And I've never forgotten it."

Crossing the Dardanelles, Istanbul's gutter to the Aegean Sea, is enabled by two ferries that alternate departures on the hour. It is through this stretch of water that the British high command made a half-hearted thrust in the early days of World War One, losing a warship and withdrawing the rest. Had they pressed on then, they might never have had to send tens of thousands of sons, fathers and brothers—including many Australians and Kiwis—to die in Gallipoli's muddy trenches. But, then, everyone makes mistakes.

George and Truman sat on the upper deck, eating cheese toast. Mustafa was under the hood of the truck, visible from the waist down. The sky was pale and hazy, the coast to the south a faint silhouette. To the west, the figure of a soldier was carved in the mountain like the M above Missoula. Somewhere beyond was the beach where the Anzacs died in suicidal waves.

The hills had scabs, great swathes of black. A few months ago, forest fires had ravaged the area, restoring the peninsula to its condition in 1915, when naval bombardment reduced the scenery to the same charred sticks and scrub—all the more authentic for tourists.

On the port side was another site, the ruins of ancient Troy, proof that Homer's *Iliad* was more than a myth. There was a pile of rocks there, and a tacky wooden horse, four stories high, in close proximity to the tour bus parking lot.

George took a bite of toast and licked his fingers. The ferry was mid-way between Europe and Asia. Wasn't this the spot that Lord Byron had made his famous swim—when was it—sometime in the eighteen hundreds? Later, George would look up Byron in a book of poetry and find the following:

This should have been a noble creature: he
Hath all the energy which would have made
A goodly frame of glorious elements,
Had they been wisely mingled; as it is,
It is an awful chaos—light and darkness—
And mind and dust—and passions and pure thoughts,
Mix'd, and contending without end or order,
All dormant or destructive.

George remembered reading somewhere that Byron had suffered from mental illness, maybe manic depression—the *awful chaos* of which he wrote. What had he been searching for here? George finished his toast and stared thoughtfully at the water. Was he too supposed to feel something profound in this chasm, where East and West would forever stay apart? Some kind of epiphany, perhaps, as deep as the straits and as fractured as the continents, here on this frontier of rationality and spirituality and free will and predestination and a hundred different isms, in this place where thousands of years of civilization diverged and converged? The significance of this place seemed to go far beyond geography. It was all about philosophy, ideology, religion—well worth a poem if not an entire novel or at least some very serious brooding.

George spat on his fingers and wiped them on his jeans. Lord Byron had no doubt been more fastidious, but there was no running water on this boat.

When they had disembarked on the European side, they found themselves behind a pack of cars. In the miles ahead the traffic thinned, leaving them among the quiet pines, and then a dull, flat plain. The truck pitched and shuddered, and finally failed to pick up speed.

"Should there be this much smoke?" asked George. As a liberal arts graduate, he had little use for science, and knew nothing about cars. Mustafa pulled the truck over, put his head under the hood, waved dismissively and climbed back in. They made it another hundred yards before the engine died for good.

"What is it?"

Mustafa jerked his chin; he didn't know. George climbed out and lifted the hood; there wasn't much smoke now, but a burning chemical odor forced him to retreat. He looked around. The highway stretched to the horizon in both directions, running past a couple of stone shacks that could not possibly have telephones. The silence was broken only by the buzzing of insects, the bleating of sheep.

It took a full five minutes for a crowd to gather. The first Tofash to pass yielded four amateur mechanics who promptly went to work on the engine; soon there were pieces of car on the road. The patriarch from the shack across the meadow joined the group as another car stopped. Wives and daughters observed mutely from back seats as their men tinkered and talked and tinkered some more. Finally, a diagnosis: A certain part would have to be replaced. This could be done in Gelibolu.

"Let's catch a ride," said George.

"We can't leave this food," said Truman. "We need a tow."

There was an argument for the privilege of towing the truck, and the Turk with the thickest rope prevailed. He made the necessary knots, then returned to his car and gunned the engine. The bumper on his Tofash fell off and clattered on the pavement.

"H'Allah! H'Allah!" said Mustafa. "I will release the brake!"

They drove north through dusty, fallow fields, their Turkish hosts grinning with pride. George grimaced with pain as the stick shift stabbed him from below, then relaxed as it was moved to third gear. Truman was in the passenger seat, the youngest Turk in the bunch sitting on his lap. Mustafa was in the truck tethered behind them, keeping it on the road. "Just pretend to be yourself," said Truman to no one in particular. "That's what my father told me. But you know what? I've never had to pretend." He clasped his hands on the shoulders of the young Turk on his lap, who sprouted a friendly grin. George looked away. The Turks weren't ready for Truman—not with their altered boundaries of male physical affection, their middle-east hand-holding and arm-in-arm strolling while their wives brought up the rear.

"There's not much need to pretend, is there? In today's foreign service?" George had never broached the subject before, but somehow the time seemed right. With their English, they might as well have been alone in the over-crowded car.

"Some still do," said Truman, answering as if they'd been on the subject for hours. "Too many still in the closet."

"Like Daniel?" George had been itching to talk about Truman's recent house guest. Daniel had a wife and three kids; but there he had been, co-hosting one of Truman's infamous happy hours.

"Yes. I've been telling him that he needs to come out. At least to his wife."

"To his wife? She hasn't figured it out?"

"Daniel's pretty butch."

"If you say so." The car hit a pothole, forcing George to catch himself on the dashboard.

"You don't think?"

"How many straight men collect porcelain?"

"My brother does. He's straight as an arrow."

George raised his eyebrows.

Truman sighed. "Daniel is miserable. I feel bad for him."

"Try feeling bad for her," said George. He breathed in deeply, tasting sweat and cigarettes. He wondered if they were being rude, and decided to switch to Turkish. His hosts didn't want to talk about themselves; they wanted to know how much money George earned in a week. There were small gasps of astonishment. But did they realize how much it would cost him to rent a place when he returned to Washington? No, they didn't. He told them and they clicked their tongues in chorus. That better be some house, they remarked. George laughed. No, he was talking about an apartment no larger than that shack in the distance, but with lights and running water.

They left the truck in the town square, across from the obligatory statue of Atatürk. Somewhere in Istanbul, a factory churned out busts such as this in prodigious volume. Nearby was a tea house, where they sat down amid curious stares. Most of the men were playing tavla, backgammon. There were no women. The young man from Truman's lap ran off to find a real mechanic. George wondered about the wives of the men who had helped them, still sitting out in the fields where they had been left. But what was the alternative—piling into the car with a bunch of infidels?

George sipped his chi. "You know…in some ways I envy you. This is no life for families." He looked about the smoke-filled room. "It used to be a wife would follow her husband to any shit-hole on the planet. But the world has changed. Now she'll have a career; she'll know better. You're better off being gay… or at least finding some third-world spouse who won't sweat it."

"Like from Mexico."

"Yeah… well. I mean…"

"Don't worry. My Dad was a cretin. Literally!"

George nodded and observed his tea sullenly. He'd started talking for a reason; an unspoken thought, something rotten and corrosive, needed to breathe. He hoped Truman would sense it, and felt relieved when he did.

"So Margaret wanted her own career."

"She wanted more than that," said George. "She wanted her own… life." He paused. Truman had said her name like he'd known her for years. Did everyone in their incestuous little consulate community already know about his problems?

"We're not divorced," said George, eager to set the record straight. "This is a… trial period. We still talk every week. Though I suppose I mostly call to hear the baby." The *baby*, he heard himself say. Her name was Sophie, goddamit. Sophie.

"So what happened?"

He shrugged. "Maybe I just wasn't cut out to have a family. One day I was single, the next day I had a wife and we had Sophie and suddenly I realized that I'd become the person I used to never want to sit next to on a plane."

Truman's expression revealed that nothing profound, or for that matter funny, had been said. George tried again. "I suppose it was Monrovia that killed us. Margaret hated it, so of course we were both unhappy. Did I ever tell you how I got assigned? My Career Development Officer, my CDO, came to me, said our ambassador in Monrovia was gung-ho to get some real families in since the fighting had stopped—some normal people to raise morale. They didn't want the usual crowd—some cowboy whose career was on the rocks, or someone who'd just gone through a nasty divorce. Well, I put the heat on Margaret and she gave in, so off we went. But of course nine months later there was fighting again, and Margaret was evacuated without me." He laughed and went on. "So I call my CDO and tell him I want out; my wife is having a baby; send me home, and he tells me, 'Sure, no problem, just as soon as we can find someone to fill your shoes. Say, I don't suppose you know anyone whose career is on the rocks or who just went through a nasty divorce?'"

George sipped his chi and went on. "The thing was, I loved Monrovia, every second of it. Maybe I need a real crisis to keep my brain from manufacturing a phony one. You ever feel that way? But Margaret… Margaret felt lost. Who could blame her? I suppose it was just the lack of control. The lack of… *purpose*. I *believed* in what I was doing, I had my purpose, so I didn't need the control. Me, I was on cloud nine. But Margaret… Margaret was just…"

He stared away, losing his train of thought. *Believed*. Why had he used the past tense? Did he no longer *believe*?

"But I haven't lost hope," he stammered, seeking the right words, words to say it was Monrovia that was to blame, words to say it could still work out somewhere else, in different circumstances; now it seemed possible the words didn't exist. Of course, there were other words he could have used, words to describe his secret gin and tonic lunches (though to be fair, Quinine *does* ward off malaria) and the Dewars on ice that he would knock down after stepping through the door, where Margaret would be waiting in a state of near-dementia induced by fear and boredom and this thing he'd fallen short of describing before—her utter lack of purpose. No, but these words weren't useful at all. His left forearm itched; he dug his fingernails in and grimaced with pain and pleasure, then picked up his tea, wishing malaria was still a threat.

He recalled how a couple of years back, the state department had initiated random drug- testing, apparently to ferret out the closet dope fiends and coke heads. What a joke; it was the practical equivalent of knowingly searching the wrong room for a lost item simply because the light was better in there. In the foreign service, alcohol was the noble tradition.

George set his tea down without finishing it. "Eventually, Margaret's feeling of lostness, whatever you want to call it, rubbed off on me. I wasn't sure about anything anymore. Not about Margaret. Not about the future. Not even about being a father." This last statement filled him with guilt.

"Do you still love her?"

There was a commotion at the door. A policeman entered and swept the room with his eyes; it seemed a false gesture with so few there, but still it lent him an air of authority. He was middle-aged and thick around the waist, with machinery at work behind his eyes, no sheepherder's glaze. George took him for a cop of very high rank. So the welcome wagon has arrived, he thought.

A small crowd of Turks poured in from the street, all eyes on the sheriff. The cop advanced on Truman, speaking rapidly in Turkish. The word *öldü* was emphasized. Dead.

"Yes I know," said Truman. "The truck is dead." He gestured flamboyantly. "Let's bring it back to life!"

"Truman," said George. "I don't think he's talking about the truck."

It was Truman who had collected people's money for the food run, so it's he who makes the executive decision to sacrifice the meat. Using a wire hanger, he pops the plug and stands by as filthy water pours down the drain. The basin is filled with new ice, every last cube in the cooler. The hams and turkeys are still frozen, so they use those too. There is no formaldehyde here, no artificial means of preserving Taylor's body until his family can decide on its disposition. In fact, the chief of police had been reluctant to let them take the body at all, citing the need to plug it in the ground as quickly as possible. This because George had made the mistake of describing burial in America, causing the Turks to recoil in disgust. What kind of barbarians would fill a corpse with chemicals and put it on display? Were Americans so arrogant as to think they could cheat death?

Whatever the indignities to be visited upon this corpse, Turkish law required that it first endure an autopsy. George takes a closer look at the bullet hole. It's just above the left eyebrow, angled slightly inward; as the coroner pointed out, the shooter used his right hand. There's nothing to obscure the depression; all traces of blood, of detached tissue, have been washed away by ice and water, giving the wound a false, rubbery look—a glossy little tunnel into the darkness of Taylcr's head.

Much less obvious is the work so recently performed on Taylor's teeth. All have been scraped or filed in some manner, to create new angles and contours, and two fillings have been roughly removed. All this, again, according to the coroner, who escaped back to Chanakkale as soon as his work was done.

The police chief wakes for a moment, then nods off again.

"We should try calling his parents again," says Truman. By "we" he of course means George, since he's the only consular officer present.

George dials the phone using his personal calling card, hoping that no one will answer and all can be left until morning. Unfortunately, a young woman picks up; she has an Hispanic accent. Salvadoran? Footsteps on a hardwood floor grow louder; it takes Mr. Moore forever to reach the phone. George gives his set speech: Local burial is possible; cremation is not; there is a good Protestant cemetery in Istanbul where many foreigners are interred; or the remains can be shipped to the United States, but this is more expensive. Mr. Moore listens patiently, without comment. Dishes clink in the background; it's just after dinnertime in America.

"Is there anything I can do for you now?" asks George.

"No. I'll be in touch with my Congressman tomorrow. You'll hear from him shortly. Thank you for calling, Mr. McCall. Now, goodnight."

George replaces the receiver. He has handled many, many death cases in his brief career, and is no longer surprised by the reactions of friends and family. Still, he can't help but think to himself that death is a problem that not even your elected representative can be expected to solve.

* * *

The golf course called Kemer lies beyond the Belgrade Forest, in the coal mining region a one- half-hour's drive from Istanbul. Trucks heaped with coal billow clouds of exhaust as they make their way to the peasant stoves of Istanbul and back again, where other trucks, loaded with garbage and gasping like dying beasts, merge to form a herd. It's an awful drive to the links. A mile before the golf course, a mountain of trash rises five stories high, exhaling like a volcano. Seagulls swarm the ash like flies, so numerous they obscure the sun, while three-legged dogs, teats flapping, rummage for food rejected by the more discerning human scavengers. The smell of burnt toxin is jarring. It's hard to imagine any person could bear this place, yet it wasn't so long ago that several families were killed here, buried by an avalanche of garbage that caught them sleeping in their makeshift homes.

Having safely reached the links, George feels the sense of anywhere that exists on golf courses everywhere, a sameness in the artificial bumps and bunkers that is comforting to anyone who has lost his roots. It could almost be the public course in Akron, but for the din—steel pounding steel, the searing scream of torn metal, a Turkish pop station turned up too loud. The fairways are passably green, but just out-of-bounds a miniature city vomits from the dirt—vacation houses gray and square, each as perfectly ugly as the next, rising from the earth not individually but as a clamoring mass.

Ambassador Hutchins has a mean slice. With a jagged swing, outside-in, he propels his drive toward the deep rough, momentarily threatening a groundskeeper who is on his knees. The little Turk is unperturbed; he rocks gently, dipping his forehead to earth and back again, eyes closed, fingertips above his cheeks. His lips quake gently. For an instant the ambassador's Titelist, too, faces Mecca; then suddenly it veers right in a lively arc that takes it bouncing, long and low, across the fairway in the wrong direction, coming to a rest, still spinning, in a narrow gully that's been dug for no reason, then abandoned amid piles of fresh dirt. Shovels sprout like stumps.

"You can take a drop, Harry," says Phil. Is it his four handicap or his position as chief of station which gives him the right to address the ambassador by his first name? "That's ground under repair. They're putting in a sprinkler or something."

George walks separately with Priscilla, who hasn't handled a club since the second hole, when she sculled a seven-iron into the ambassador's golf bag. How she hates hosting these little Istanbul golf weekends for Hutchins; if only there was an adequate course in Ankara. "Have you spoken to the parents yet?" she asks George.

"I called them from Gelibolu. And I talked to the father again this morning."

"Moore… Cedrick Moore?"

"Yes."

"Should I know that name?"

George shrugs and Priscilla lets it go.

"I presume he wants the remains sent home?"

"Yeah. The department wired us the money yesterday. Very fast. Zimmerman's office was involved." They pause while Ambassador Hutchins swings; it's a high floater that returns to earth with a thud. Though the fairways look soft and lush from a distance, they're actually rock-hard and ill-watered, more suitable for shanks than for divots.

"The body's going home today. Our mortician sped the paperwork through. It normally takes several days. But paying the baksheesh always helps."

"Good. And the police… where was it? Gelibolu. What kind of follow-up have you had?"

"A lot." George wants to stop talking now; he has a bad lie with at least two hundred yards to the green, trees to the left, water on the right.

"And?" She has no golf etiquette. George swings badly and watches the splash.

He sighs. "And, they've gotten nowhere. Not much to go on. He was found maybe twenty yards off the highway; there was a little hole started, like they were going to bury him but got interrupted. None of the hotels or bus stations in the area remembered him, so the cops think he was killed somewhere else, then driven there and dumped. A big city drug deal gone bad, which rings true with what the professor told me, the drug dealing part…" George doesn't bother fishing for his ball. They stroll to the next tee as the ambassador putts out.

"And you just happened to be passing by."

He shrugs. "I know. It's a strange coincidence."

"I don't believe in coincidences," she says sharply. "We've not told the police about the professor's theory? Good. What have you told the family?"

"Just the facts. How he was found. That the police are investigating."

"That's fine," she says. "We don't go calling their son a drug addict, or for God's sake a PKK sympathizer, based on a few loose stories."

"I agree," says George, realizing too late that it's presumptuous to expect her to care. "But the family's going to want more. I mean, who wouldn't? And the police probably won't deliver." George knows the Turkish cops well. Their standard approach is to seize a suspect, apply "pressure," and decide if he's telling the truth. It's not so much that they're sadistic—though some of them certainly are—but rather their lack of forensic technique that makes them so dependent on testimony. Frankly, they're not half-bad at what they do. But in this case there are neither witnesses nor confessors, nowhere for the police to begin, short of shaking down all the usual suspects in western Turkey.

"Let's not borrow trouble," says Priscilla. "Let the police do their job." She thinks for a moment. "You could meet with the prosecutor."

"Tomorrow."

Ambassador Hutchins steps up to the tee, taking honors despite his triple-bogey. "Goddamn fade!" he remarks. The ball careens wildly out-of-bounds and settles near an old Turkish woman stooped in the weeds, gathering salad. She's built much like Hutchins, a formidable little man with powerful arms and an immense torso that's barely rounded with age. His jagged nose, left uncorrected from his days as a Marine Corps boxer, is a source of amusement for the embassy staff, who chuckle from a safe distance at his bull in the china shop manner and his Texas-accented Turkish. Rumor has it that he accepted this job thinking the embassy was in Istanbul. When he discovered that the government had been moved—some seventy years ago—to dusty old Ankara, he called the president personally to request a different country. Sierra Leone, he learned, was still open; also Papua New Guinea. Suddenly, Ankara had looked pretty good.

Phil tries to engage him in conversation. "Looks like Semra Hanim will join coalition talks with Fikret. That's something I'd like to see. Social Democrats and Nationalists in the same government!"

"When I see that Semra, I don't know whether to demarche her or ask her out on a date," snorts Hutchins. He opts for a mulligan, taking extra practice swings, which makes it awkward for Phil to go on. "Won this driver in a pro-am with Fuzzy Zoeller," he says proudly when he's off the tee. "Shot eighty-four that day, just watching that man swing. Haven't broken ninety since." He hunches over and rubs his legs. "Goddamn these knees," he says.

George chuckles. He doesn't share the contempt for Hutchins that most in the embassy seem to regard as an obligation. True, the ambassador to Turkey should probably be a career officer, given Turkey's strategic importance. But Hutchins has been sensible enough to rely heavily on his section chiefs, and even his detractors have had to concede that he is quick-witted and shrewd in the matters he cannot delegate. Not just any schlep can build a real estate empire from scratch. At any rate, the Turks seem happy to have him, knowing full well that a career officer would have no access to the president at all.

Hutchins hits another high one; it rests safely in the middle of the fairway, maybe two hundred yards out. "Nice shot, Mister Ambassador," says George.

"Don't blow smoke up my ass, son," says Hutchins. "I can hit it better than that."

Maybe the sting shows. Hutchins follows George to his ball. "You've got a good swing," he says. "Very smooth. Where you from?"

"Southern California. Near San Diego," says George. In fact, he's not really *from* anywhere. Chula Vista is where his father paused the longest, so it seems the best answer.

"What makes a boy from Chula Vista,"—he summons his best Texas drawl—"want to become a diplomat?"

"To see the world, I guess. And to work toward something, some kind of goal, some ideal, beyond a simple paycheck." *To do more in life than chase a buck*, he wants to add, but doesn't, suspecting that Hutchins has devoted his entire life to exactly that. And so he says instead, "My last job was as a bartender, Mister Ambassador. So I guess I joined up for the money."

They laugh together. But when George stops, Hutchins goes on. It's a millionaire's laugh now, lonely but powerful, strictly off-limits to someone making thirty-three thousand a year.

"Never forget where you came from," says Hutchins when he catches his breath. "Or you just might forget who you are. First assignment?"

"Second."

Hutchins nods. "You one of those fellows who joined for life?"

George hesitates. State Department orthodoxy requires him to say yes, but Hutchins is outside all of that. "I don't know," he answers honestly.

"I don't know," repeats Hutchins. "Now that's something I don't hear every day. Goddamn if it's not the first time I've heard it all year. Never had so many people around me act like they know every last thing, whether they do or not's a different story. You stick with that answer, son. It's working for you."

Having dispensed his wisdom, the ambassador ambles off. Phil trots to his ball and bumps it for a better lie. When he swings he finds the green.

"Phil, is it worth talking to MIT? About Taylor? Maybe they…"

"Know something? Look, like I told Priscilla…" he waits for her to catch up. "There's nothing to go on here. No corroboration."

"But what if we checked out this Euphrates Center…"

Phil spins on his heels. "Bad idea. MIT has the place under surveillance. Anyway, what's the point?"

George shakes his head; there is no point; only a lingering sense of disquiet from his conversation with—what was her name? Nazan. The way she had laughed at the whole drug angle. He lets it drop.

On the green, Phil bends low to line up his putt. George turns his thoughts to the ambassador's question. Why did he become a diplomat? It's not a career that makes much sense to anyone outside the Washington beltway. The few times he's run into people from his past he's been forced to explain, ad nauseum, exactly what he does. *You mean you're like a park ranger*? is what they invariably ask him, forcing him to clarify: For*eign* Service.

As a student, language had been his only real interest. No doubt it was a little unhealthy, his sitting alone at his favorite crummy bar booth with his happy-hour pitcher, mouthing subjunctives as the Young Business Leaders of America passed by with their suits and briefcases. How did they get there, and what in God's name did they do all day in their giant glass containers? Their lives seemed beyond his—not above, yet unreachable in a way that implied some kind of failure on his part. What they had was not what he wanted; still, he wished he could join them just for a moment, to prove that he could, to see what they saw, and then to reject it all.

So the disconnect was always there; maybe that's how he came to be here. Maybe that's why top-ranking diplomats, ambassadors even, have nowhere to go when they finally retire. After being wined and dined by ministers, feared by their staffs, surrounded by sycophants, they return to the department to pace the sanitized halls, to beg for temporary contract assignments. Newly deflated, they lose the familiar jog in their step, neglect their posture, stop starching their shirts. Yet still they hang on, hoping for a call that will never come, as if they can forever postpone their fall to irrelevance, their return to life's void, to a normalcy they've never known.

Was this what Margaret wanted? Normalcy?

He knew it was precisely not what he wanted, not if normalcy meant never seeing another Open Assignments List, the state department's semi-annual recruiting tool with jobs in every corner of the world, from Guinea Bisao to Papua New Guinea to Amsterdam. It was how foreign service officers identified their onward assignments, and in the moment of its release, every job on the list was fair game. This was the essence of the foreign service. The list spoke, and what it said was that you could do anything and everything – report on the next coup d'etat in Liberia, counsel American businesses in Ottawa, process refugees in Vietnam. It represented, quite literally, a world of possibilities.

What better for the discontented, the dissatisfied, the perpetual seekers of something more? The list offered the hope, the illusion perhaps, that the perfect job—the perfect life—was still out there. All it took was to find it. No need to huddle with the workaday masses, the rabble who could pack their lives in a box from beginning to end, and wrap it up tightly, the parameters well defined and drained of mystery, leaving little to chance, not now, not later. No need, said the List, ever to ask, *is this all there is*?

George stares absently as Hutchins three-putts. Golf courses always make him philosophical. It's a game of Zen, they say, like fly-fishing, archery.

"George," says Priscilla, bringing him back into the world. "Phil's right. Stay away from this Kurdish house. I don't want a big flap with the Turks." Her cell phone rings. Surprised, she hands it to George.

"Hello."

"George, it's Zeynep. You must come back quickly."

"Why?" He lowers his voice. "You shouldn't be calling on…"

"We are finding the mortician. To tell him he is not sending the body."

A moment later George hands the phone back, stunned. How will Priscilla react to the news? Does the ambassador need to know? How will Representative Zimmerman react if his constituents show up at the funeral home, only to find themselves collecting the remains of a stranger? When does the flight depart? All of these questions and more run through his mind after Zeynep's revelation.

"The dead boy is not Taylor Moore."

PART TWO

Take me back to Constantinople.
No, you can't go back to Constantinople.
Now it's Istanbul, not Constantinople.
Why did Constantinople get the works?
That's nobody's business but the Turks'.

—*Jimmy Kennedy*

* * *

Aya Sofya, Church of Divine Wisdom, stands quietly in the darkness, no longer under siege. The Islamist protestors have melted away, leaving it reluctantly as they found it—neither church nor mosque, but a museum for visitors of every faith.

Completed 563 years after the birth of Christ, Aya Sofya was the most splendid church in all of Christendom until the Ottomans toppled Constantinople 890 years later. 890 years. For five centuries after that, the building served as a mosque for the Islamic faithful. Since Mohammed prohibited idols and images, the portraits of Christ, the Virgin, the archangels Michael and Gabriel, and the none-too-modest emperors who'd placed themselves beside them, were plastered over or destroyed, their eyes chipped out by Turkish steel. But in 1935, after Atatürk made Aya Sofya a museum, the new government of Turkey undertook to restore the mosaics, acknowledging the building's Christian past. In the same spirit of tolerance, the Ottoman additions—notably four circular wooden plaques, immensely ugly and inscribed with the names of the early Ottoman Caliphs—were left hanging above the grand interior, a permanent blight on Aya Sofya's faded glory.

Red Halabja stands shoulder to shoulder with Zakho overlooking the nave, high atop a spiral of wide stone steps. Nervous, Zakho barks orders in Turkish and faulty English: Bedir is not to move from that door. Red, tell Bedir to wait until the Chinese have moved on (in fact they are students from Japan). Stop handling your backpack like it contains the family jewels. Give it to me. Relax.

It's not good that the Islamists were here today; they would like to see Aya Sofya stripped of its museum status and converted back into a mosque; now the police will probably blame the bomb blast on them. Istanbul's pro-West elite is always eager to finger the Islamists, the gericiler, for Turkey's problems, and just as eager to pretend the Kurds don't exist. All the more important, then, that the announcement goes smoothly. Red looks at his watch. In thirty minutes, letters describing the operation in detail will be couriered to the offices of the Sabah newspaper and the Turkish Daily News, and to police stations in Okmeydani, Fener and Umraniye, where Alevi Kurds last week were stripped naked and sprayed with cold water, as they had been the week before and the week before that, until they were persuaded to talk. Neighborhood kids will carry the notes for a few thousand lira.

"Boshaliyor," says Zakho. It's emptying.

Red puts his hand on Zakho's shoulder, and for a moment feels the warmth of his cheek. Zakho is his commander, his cell leader, but in fact there is little sense of hierarchy in the group—as it should be. Authority has withered away since their days as individuals, leaving only the group, the power of comradeship, decision-making by committee. It's an impressive achievement—a microcosm of the ideal society.

Zakho's English is on par with Red's Turkish; together they have spent hours sifting though mountains of garbage collected outside the U.S. consulate, finding such treasures as telegrams filled with unclassified but useful information on events, visitors, and other routine business. The best of it they take to Sirkeci Station once a week and stow in a locker, in case their safehouse is searched. The locker key is an unmarked duplicate, the original one destroyed.

It was while sifting through these papers that Red had come across a crumpled copy of George's cable, and with fascination read about his own reported death: "Taylor Moore… his remains were found half-buried in a field near the Istanbul-Chanakkale highway… autopsy determined that he died as a result of a head wound… police are treating it as a murder case."

A week later he would read a second cable, following up on the first, reporting the mistake. The body was not Taylor Moore's after all. The Australian embassy has identified it as belonging to one of its citizens.

How Taylor had banged his fist at that news! How long did it take for a corpse to decompose? Not long, he thought, but more than a few days if you expected the face to rot beyond recognition. In his mind's eye he saw the young Australian, the face that haunted his dreams, there in the Sultan Pub, always in the Sultan Pub, at the table where they had found him, surrounded by empty Efes bottles. That was how he would remember him—not by their walk down the cobblestoned rut, where the smell of baking bread and sewage ran together. Not in that dark place at the end of the path, where Taylor had finally crossed the threshold, where he had received his baptism by fire. There in the darkness, he'd lost sight of the young Australian's face, and had raised the gun more easily.

But in his dreams, his nightmares, the Australian's face retained its features—its square jaw and sun-baked skin and beer-bloodied eyes. Just a little rotting and it would have been a blank slate, but then the farmer had appeared out of nowhere in that muddy field and interrupted their digging. Perhaps they should have killed the farmer too, instead of scurrying away while the Australian still poked from the ground like a stump. Five hours it had taken to drive the body there—a world away from the Sultan Pub—and all for nothing. They'd picked the wrong field.

And so he had felt like crying, throwing things, tearing the room apart. Maybe it had been far-fetched after all—far-fetched to believe that he could erase his past, become truly anonymous, start his life anew, purified and committed solely to the cause. Never mind; he would not go back to being who he was—a spoiled child with no greater goal than to spend his father's money.

Now that they knew, now that his plan had failed, he wanted more than anything to go back to the consulate, to walk right in and throw it in their faces, show them that he wasn't their dupe. This he would do, of course, without telling anyone, not even Zakho.

No, he would not tell Zakho, the only one who otherwise knew all, his friend who by now had descended the steps to emerge on the great open floor below, a back pack lolling off his shoulder. The students from Japan have moved toward the exits; a few loiter at the souvenir booths, spending their yen. Two break off from the group, a young couple; arm in arm they follow Zakho to the spot that was once an altar. Red takes a breath as they stop beneath the dome and crane their necks to see the Virgin mother and child, glittering in the artificial light of well-placed bulbs. A great open space encloses them; they look small and weak.

Red watches Zakho hang his backpack on the scaffolding that rises all the way to the dome; the ceiling, which has fallen before, is in a constant state of renovation. Zakho loiters for a moment then drifts off, hands in pockets, toward the exit.

"Hadi Gidelim," says Red Halabja. Let's go.

On the Hippodrome, they squeeze past crowds of tourists, determinedly nonchalant. Seeing their guide books, Red recalls what he's read about this place, when the church was still a church and the terrified residents of Constantinople cowered inside on the 148th day of

1453 to hear mass delivered one last time. Outside the walls of the city, an army of Turks led by Mehmet the Conqueror clamored to get in. A city under siege. When at last the defenses were breached and the pillaging began, Mehmet headed straight for the cathedral and entered it on horseback, crushing underfoot the wounded seeking refuge there. Stopping at one of the large supporting columns, he pressed his palm against it, leaving an imprint in the marble, which remains to this day. At that very moment, the priest giving mass was engulfed by a powerful light from above, and with blazing trumpets spirited away to the heavens. It is said that he will descend again to finish the service on the blessed day that the Greeks reclaim their city.

Turks tell the story somewhat differently. In their version, Mehmet the Conqueror entered Aya Sofya to comfort the people who were terrified and crying in grief, and asked the priest to stand and utter these words: "I, Fatih Sultan Mehmet, tell you, your friends and all those gathered here today, that from this day forth, you do not have to be afraid anymore for your lives and freedom." And the Sultan made good on his promise, and from that day forward the Christians of Constantinople enjoyed unparalleled peace and prosperity.

These are facts.

* * *

It's nearly Christmas. The walls are tied together by red, white, and blue crepe paper, items number 143546 through 143548 in the General Services Administration supply catalog. Rudolph the red-nosed reindeer marks the exit, while Santa Claus cheerfully guards the visa refusal files. Dawn has brought in cassettes; one of them plays now, innocently refuting the separation of church and state. *God rest you merry gentlemen, let nothing you dismay, for Jesus Christ our Savior was born up on this day.*

Winston Craine has his door open, something he is prone to do more often these days. Now and then he even emerges, hovering in the doorway or passing silently among his staff, peering through the shutters that separate the visa windows from the rest of the room, scribbling in a spiral notebook that never leaves his hands. If he strays more than thirty feet from his office door, he will pause to lock it first. Rarely does he speak. No matter. His absence, like his presence, is no longer felt. They are accustomed to carrying on without him—not that this requires any true accommodation on their part, for he has always been a spectator, as omnipresent as the family dog and about as relevant.

George interviews two "black belts" from Rize, Turkey's export capital for tea and migrants, reputedly bound for a martial arts tournament in New Jersey. Though their story is novel, they can't shake the air of two Anatolians who rode into town on a couple of sheep that morning, piling on to the half million who already arrived in Istanbul this year, searching for work, burning coal for warmth, and squatting in *gecekondus*—the term, loosely translated, means "built in a night"—on the city's vast, polluted fringe. How many more Turkish gas station attendants can fit on the New Jersey turnpike? Judging by the blue sheets—the reports that INS sends whenever a visitor overstays his visa and applies for U.S. residency—there are already enough to fuel every taxi east of the Hudson.

With some difficulty, George arranges the men into position, so that the taller of the two clenches his callused fist about the shorter man's collar.

"Now," says George. "Escape."

In the pregnant moment that follows, Zeynep asks whether George has forgotten his nine o'clock appointment. "Bayan Steh-ven-sawn. She wants to renounce her citizenship again."

"Stevenson? Okay. Tell her I'll see her at nine thirty."

"It's ten o'clock now."

"Then tell her I'll be a few minutes late." He returns to the black belts, who haven't budged. Someone has turned the music up loud. *And laid within a manger upon this blessed morn, his mother Mary did nothing take in scorn.*

Dawn's voice is louder still. "Bifarmayin," she snaps at an Iranian, out of George's view. "Bifarmayin. Good day!"

"Well?" says George. The men look puzzled. Then, suddenly inspired, the shorter one pinches his eyes together and flies into action, taking a quick step backward and throwing his hands in the air as if he's stumbled into a spider web. When his hands come down, they're in the form of karate chops, and the howl that bursts from his lips prompts the other visa applicants to check for the exits. Dutifully, though he hasn't been touched, the taller of the two hobbles backward, then sinks to his knees. He seems to contemplate a forward roll, thinks the better of it, and rests on the floor instead.

George has to leave the window to avoid laughing out loud. For a moment he joins Dawn at window two. "Sir, go away," she says. "No, I'm not going to talk to you anymore. You're wasting my time. No, I said no. Go away. MARINE!"

His laughter doused, George returns to his window, refuses the black belts, and calls his next case forward—a kid who wants to attend public school in America; it's an easy refusal, but still he hesitates. He glances at Dawn. She's as stiff as a board, yet her face is pleasant enough, except for the way her lip curls as she advises her next applicant to re-apply when hell freezes over.

George remembers one thing particularly well from his training days—that a person's true colors always emerge on the visa line. How true it is. He has seen normal people turn into petty tyrants, restrained professionals become shrill and unstable, raving liberals become anti-immigration nuts. He has also seen a few flourish in the role, treating their applicants with courtesy and respect while administering the law with Solomon's wisdom. Sadly, he can't quite count himself among them—not with his compulsion for that last bit of information that always seems to be missing, that sliver of proof that never turns up, without which he can not decide. Unfortunately, he can't not decide either, for there is always someone next in a line that goes on without end.

Dawn, it seems, has no such worries; she enjoys the uncommon ability to treat every case as the best or worst she's ever seen, an almost demagogic capacity to believe her own rhetoric. Is it faith that sustains her? Just today, she passed around holiday cards to one and all, including the Turks. "Rejoice in the birth of Jesus Christ our Savior," was what they said. George reminds himself that he's a Christian too—or at least a Catholic; does that count? A pit takes shape in his stomach, a blend of disgust, envy, and self-loathing; it fails to digest, like one of those köfte sandwiches the Turks pass off as hamburgers. One or the other, friend or enemy, Dawn's life is replete with imperatives, while his is perpetually gray, as deep and dense as the Istanbul air. Good and evil, right and wrong—he understands the concepts well enough, but he no longer feels them viscerally. Is this why he envies her so?

It was Dawn who had urged him to take a closer look at Taylor's passport. "Or let Tim," she suggested. "He called to ask if you want him to come by. You know, he's an expert on documents."

Fine, thought George. Tim worked for that other Agency, doing God-knew-what. He was one of the few spooks in the consulate who declined to offer any explanation of his work, nor ever ask for help. From time to time, some shady character would stop by the consular section and request him by name, speaking one of many languages in which Tim had a working knowledge. And now it seemed he was a document expert too.

And thankfully so. Tim held the passport under the black light, while they all gathered around. Tim pointed to the smudges where the picture had been lifted to make room for another. He was impressed; the photo-substitution was an expert job; the laminate was neatly flat and the eagle, having lost some of its ink, deftly re-drawn; it took the black light to show the miniscule inconsistencies around the feathers and the tiny arrows in its talons.

"Does the quality of the job suggest PKK?" asked George when they were alone.

Tim clicked his tongue like a Turk. "No, I've seen this kind of work from the drug cartels too."

Making the call to Taylor's parents was difficult. George did it with false cheer and an overriding sense of incompetence. *Well, what do you know—it wasn't your son who died after all.* Mrs. Moore wept and thanked him for the news.

Mr. Moore called back five minutes later. He informed George that he was an embarrassment to the United States of America, and declared that he was calling his congressman.

"I'm glad your son is alive," was all George could manage, before setting down the phone. He had screwed up, falsely identified a body, put it on record with a cable to the department. He was damn lucky the corpse wasn't already on a plane.

Now the remains, whoever's they were, desperately needed a home. At George's invitation, a dozen consuls and vice consuls came to take a look, arriving at the mortician's office through the labyrinth of the balik pazar, the fish market, which offered a never-ending supply of ice. An inconspicuous back door opened to a courtyard, which was suddenly vast and wide, obscenely spacious compared to the cramped stalls of the marketplace. There, one came upon an Armenian church, grand and sturdy, and connected to it, a single stone room with a slab in the center. This was the morgue.

The British representative checked the young man's backside for a mole "the size of a bloody thumbnail," found none and left, visibly pleased not to inherit the paperwork. The Russian consul, who George assumed was KGB—or whatever it was they called themselves these days—made a cursory examination of the corpse before taking a seat where he could watch the others come and go. Even the Mexican honorary consul made an appearance, searching, he explained, for a young man last seen driving drunk out of Izmir at a very high speed.

The Russian talked and talked, doing his best to justify staying. With a rotting corpse in the room, only real consular officers would show up today, as opposed to spooks under cover. The Russian would strike many people from his list. George decided not to fight it; let the spies play their games.

"The air," said the Russian. "It tastes as my mouth is on a stovepipe." Sergei was his name, and it was the most interesting thing he'd said all day. The more George listened, the duller he found the man. Perhaps it was true what they said: When the Wall collapsed, all the talented spies quit to make money in organized crime, leaving espionage to second-rate officers still willing to work amid declining resources and prestige.

The afternoon wore on, and the corpse still failed to find a home. The mortician ceased to be his buttoned-down self, and instead sank into his wooden chair beneath a shelf of bottled chemicals. He muttered quietly. The work he'd performed on the young man, a crude embalming, carried a price tag of four hundred American dollars. It was a bargain by western standards, but a hefty sum here, and it was beginning to look like he wouldn't get paid.

George sympathized; the Armenian did great work for the consulate, but he would have to eat the loss if no one claimed the body. Tough luck, but the consulate was a steady customer, and he was one of the only Christian practitioners in town. There would be many more dead.

"Cheers," said a thin, middle-aged diplomat as the day grew late and even the Russian was gone. George was collecting his things and preparing to go. The latecomer was Australian, so he said, though not of the outback variety; this one had the refinement of an Oxford alum. He'd come all the way from Ankara to view the body, and had something important to say. "I hear you've got one of ours."

And so it was; the body was from down under. The mortician got paid and George got closure. It was late and he was tired, but relieved to hand the corpse off to someone else. It was someone else's problem now. The sting from his conversation with Taylor's father was beginning to wear off. Fuck it, he told himself, then set off for the consulate at a fast clip, avoiding the eyes of the shoeshine boys who followed him anyway, shouting beneath his senses. When he reached the Pera Palas hotel, where Agatha Christie penned her most famous work and Mata Hari once practiced her deceptions, he felt a sudden impulse to double back and did just that. Quickening his pace, he made his way up the steps of the nearby exhibition center, the highest point in the neighborhood. Over the hill, minarets spiraled and red roofs crumbled. The rat-a-tat-tat of construction filled the air. Half the city, it seemed, was perpetually rising up while the other half was falling. In the end it would all even out. Meanwhile, all the loose ends ran downstream to the Golden Horn, where six centuries ago the Turks dragged their ships through the mud to conquer Constantinople from behind. The afternoon sun was burning itself out, a crimson ember.

For a moment George almost felt good. How remarkable it was, he thought to himself, the way sulfur, ozone, and nitrogen oxide improve a sunset.

The staff meeting starts promptly at two. Priscilla kicks it off with an account of the bomb blast at Aya Sofya. A Japanese tourist died en route to the hospital; his girlfriend is expected to survive, but will probably lose an eye. The room flinches. Has anyone claimed responsibility? Yes, the PKK says they did it, but the Turks aren't convinced. Islamic protestors had been there that day, a coincidence too strong to ignore.

"The *modus operandi*," says Phil, pronouncing his Latin carefully, "suggests it was the work of the *Partia Karkaris Kurdistan*."

Priscilla shifts in her seat. "The PKK," she clarifies.

"If they say they did it," says Phil. "They did."

"I agree," says Tony, the consulate's security officer. He is responsible for safeguarding American personnel and has some of the best contacts with the police.

"Even if it is the PKK," says Truman. "The Government won't mind leaving it up in the air for a while, stir the pot a little, put the spotlight on the fundies." Truman explains the lead-up to the municipal elections, only weeks away. Islamic candidates are running strong in Istanbul. They have a shot at winning several precincts, including the consulate's—Beyoğlu.

"They want to build a mosque at Taksim Square, don't they?" asks Helen, the consul general's secretary.

"So they say in the press." He meets her eyes. "But what they've campaigned on is picking up the garbage, paving the streets, things the mainstream parties have never done. When I met their Beyoğlu candidate, all he wanted to talk about was his plans for a new parking garage. That's how you win local elections."

"If anyone believes that's what the Islamists are about," says Phil. "Parking lots. Then they're as misguided as the fundamentalists." Truman opens his mouth to respond; but Priscilla cuts in.

"Any Americans near the blast?" The question is directed at Winston, a new attendee at these meetings. He is seated stiffly behind George, his feet flat on the floor, his unopened briefcase set as always on his lap. His fingers drum the hard leather surface. When he clears his throat, his hand thrusts upward to stroke a large, balding head.

"Pardon?"

The economics officer whispers to Dawn, who hides a smile beneath her hand.

"Americans. Were there any American citizens affected by the bombing?"

"Not that I'm aware of," Winston says defensively, as if he finds the very question objectionable. He scans the faces around him, looking for help.

"Well," says Priscilla. "Why don't we go around?"

Harold from DEA reviews his plans to escort an extradition case to the United States for trial; Gwen the commercial officer discusses next week's trade show; Art the systems whiz, reports a breakdown in the consulate's mainframe.

It's George's turn. Another American citizen has been drugged and robbed, he reports. This time in Doğubeyazit, of all places. "No it's not our consular district; but the kid has a return ticket to Istanbul, so this is where

Ankara has advised him to go. Never mind he's transiting Ankara to get here."

The group laughs. Most in the room have served a consular tour or two, and know the easiest way to get rid of a problem is to make him someone else's.

"What? No. He's okay. Just disoriented. And a little hypothermic. Someone slipped him a mickey and he woke up in a snowbank. He's a writer or something. The cops found the guys who did it, but unfortunately they couldn't retrieve any of the money they stole. I'll probably need to deal with him this weekend. Fortunately, he has my home number now." More laughter, this time it's sympathetic.

George wants to change the subject to the dead Australian, to show he's pulling the pieces of his fumbled death case together, but he is distracted by Zeynep peering through the half-open door. She motions; her expression is plaintive, then desperate when he hesitates.

"What is it?" She is half-jogging away by the time he reaches her. Stares follow him out.

"Taylor," she whispers. "He's here. In the waiting area!"

"Taylor?"

But when they get to the consular section, the waiting room is occupied only by a couple of old expats chatting with Umit through the bulletproof glass.

"Umit Bey, where'd he go?"

"Chikmish," shrugs Umit. *He must have left; but I did not witness it personally.* Leave it to the Turks to have a verb tense for hearsay.

"Taylor Moore?" George is skeptical. "How do you know it was him?"

Zeynep retrieves the photo that his parents had sent, for posting at bus stops and hostels. "This boy was here. And he's been here before. More times than one. Tim was meeting with him."

George takes the photo and grabs his coat.

"And he left something," Zeynep calls as he heads to the door. "With Tim's name."

"Whatever it is, don't open it! Give it to the marine."

"I opened already!" She shows him a cucumber, ripe and about six inches long. George ponders the vegetable for only a moment, then heads for the exit.

Outside, he has a choice to make. George picks left, and starts jogging. A dirty drizzle falls. He passes a group of derelicts, drinking raki beneath an unlikely cluster of trees, and tackles the steps of the trade center two at a time. The gray-slabbed building blends with the sky above.

There, Zeynep's words catch up with him: Taylor's been to the consulate before? And he met with Tim?

A shoeshine boy blocks his path; George nudges him out of the way. "Git," he says, but the boy hangs close. He releases a twenty-thousand lira note from his pocket; it flutters in the breeze. The boy chases it down.

There!

Half a block away, Taylor Moore is strolling up Mesrutiyet, in the direction of the British consulate. Though his back is turned, George knows at once he's not Turkish, something different in his gait and too much color in his clothes. George slows to a walk, and realizes he's breathing hard. The taste of Turkish winter fills his mouth.

He has no plan, considers confronting him, but decides against it. They enter the balik pazar with barely a dozen meters between them. Why the hell has Tim been seeing him? And why did Taylor send him a cucumber—the old Turkish *fuck you*?

George looks back to find the twenty thousand note was a mistake. A gang of shoeshine boys follow him into the market place, chattering loudly. He digs in his pockets; only a few hundred- thousand notes left, worth about three bucks each. He can't afford to let those go, not at his salary. "Git," he breathes, trying to look mean. It's a tough sell. The boys close in.

The torso of a young sheep, skinned and bloody, hangs before a butcher's stall. George takes cover behind it, as Taylor slows to a stop. "Buyrun," says the butcher, shielding George from the urchins. Can I help you? Around them, the shoppers are thick as the flies, with tomatoes, peppers, eggplant and onions, piled high in every direction. Crates of spice cramp the alley, square unfinished wood and multi-colored sands of infinite depths, like litter boxes, everything open to the air. For Western senses, it's too much, beyond one's capacity to absorb, an explosion of sight, sound, and smell. A Turkish pop song wails from a scratchy boom box, like chunks of metal sawed apart. "Hadi git!" screams the butcher. A shoeshine box bounces off the window of his stall, rocking the hairy carcass of a goat, spraying the feta cheese that's stuffed inside. The butcher flies past and delivers a slap to the guilty youth. There are more slaps, and the shoeshine boys scatter with shouts and taunts. Laughter all around, and a single angry butcher. George buries his head deeper into the sheep's torso, so close he can smell its death. In Istanbul, the city once called Constantinople and before that Byzantium, a nest of spies since the time of Christ, it should be possible to follow someone with more dignity.

Taylor regards the noise behind him, then walks on. At the mortician's, he turns left and heads downhill toward Kurtulush, the Armenian slum. George lags well behind, uncertain if he's been seen, feeling conspicuous among the unwashed children, wiser than their years, scurrying beneath carpets and laundry draped across the cobble-stoned streets.

It seems silly now to skulk in corners; the temptation to confront Taylor grows. He resolves to do it, but what will he say? George picks up his pace, then falls back against the wall. A car has stopped, and an open door takes Taylor in. "Wait!" Too late. George breaks into a run, then slows as he nears the corner where the car has turned. He slips, and his suit meets the slippery cobblestone; he scrambles to his feet, soaked, and watches the vehicle move away, slowly, struggling past parked cars with inches to spare on either side. Up ahead the alley ends. The car will have to turn right. Or left. If he runs after it, they'll see him in the rear-view mirror, sprinting like an idiot. Think! No, don't think. Act!

George turns left, gambling that the car will do the same. He prepares to turn right at the next street, but finds it's a dead-end. He runs on, past a group of pre-pubescent kids who miss him with their pebbles. Farther downhill, the alley opens wide where four streets converge. There's a market there on Sundays, and today... a taxi! The driver sits on the trunk, smoking with a heavy-eyed friend. They look up to find George descending the slope, feet no longer grasping the cobblestone, unable to stop. This time he really falls, feet flying above his head and hands across the cobblestone, gathering rocks and garbage. Back on his feet, he gives the men a warning stare. The driver moves quickly to open the door. George leaves a streak of black mud as he slides in.

"Gidelim!" he shouts. Let's go.

They drive forward, turn right, then do a little circle and advance again. Taylor's car is nowhere in sight. George thumps his hand on the seat; pain climbs his arm. I've been lied to! If Tim has been meeting with Taylor, then of course Phil knows more than he let on. What are they hiding? The traffic thickens, forcing the taxi to slow. They have traveled about ten blocks, and are closing on a major street. George has lost all sense of direction. "Nereye?" asks the driver, turning around. "Where to?"

"Goddamn it," says George. Slumping back in his seat, he instructs the cabbie to return to the consulate, tracing his fingers along the hem of his jacket. He finds a tear, then another. He inspects his aching right hand; the scrapes are turning red; the wet soot glitters. What do his suit pants look like? Maybe he can file for reimbursement; the process only takes about a year... When George looks up, Taylor Moore is sitting in the car next to his, closest to the window. Taylor! For an awkward moment their eyes meet; Taylor looks interested, almost friendly, and for a moment they are merely two lonely expats in a sea of Turks. George smiles nonchalantly and looks away. Mere feet separate them, as the cars compete in heavy traffic for a single lane. George is relieved when Taylor's wins, forcing the taxi to fall into place behind it.

"Araba'yi takip et!" George tells the driver. The phrase, in Turkish, fails to resonate—at any rate, they have no choice but to follow that car, locked as they are into bumper-to-bumper traffic. It's an absurdly slow chase. Keeping up is easy; not accidentally passing them is a challenge. George studies the back of Taylor's head, and the heads of three others, none of whom look American. He sinks into his seat. Goddamn Phil. He stood there and listened to me talk about Taylor, and pretended he'd never heard of him… Who is this kid? Who the hell am I following?

The road clears, and George instructs the driver to drop back and switch lanes. "Okey dokes," says the driver. Then, in Turkish, "You are CIA, right? I am a good driver. You will see. I won't let them get away. They are Russians? KGB?"

George nods, trying to be agreeable. They weave through frenzied traffic across the Galata Bridge, into the old city, falling back until the car is almost out of sight. This guy knows how to follow, thinks George—probably a standard skill for Turkish cabbies. The Bosphorous stretches north, the horizon lost in the gray. The sun is an unhealthy red, giving the fishermen a radioactive glow; their poles dangle minnows only inches long—not bait, as one might assume, but the actual catch, soon to be dumped, bones and all, into pots of boiling grease, somewhere up in the gecekondu hills.

They enter Fatih, where Islam is strong, then turn off the main thoroughfare into a smaller street where the cabbie stops.

"What are we doing?"

"No exit," says the driver in Turkish. He points to the street where Taylor's car has turned. The houses are new and barely crumbling, box-like and plain but for doors and windows painted green. A bearded man with a turban strolls by, two steps ahead of a woman in a black chador. Only her eyes show through. The driver clicks his tongue in contempt and declares he will stay in the cab.

George asks him to wait.

"Okey dokes."

George reaches the corner in time to see Taylor disappear through the door of an apartment building, as featureless as its neighbors. He takes a mental snapshot of the place. More ghosts in black sheets materialize, then cross the street to avoid him; a teenager with baggy pants and clumpy hair on his chin makes no attempt to hide his curiosity. George turns away; if he stays, it will take just seconds for a crowd to form.

They drive back to the consulate, the cabbie taking advantage of the frequent stops to draw a simple map in reverse. At the top of the page he scratches the address. George slumps back in his seat, overcome with exhaustion. The chase is over, but what has he found? He can't get Phil's lies out of his mind, so lets it go blank, indulges in emotion instead—the sting of being duped, the rush of success in tracking his quarry, the sense of inadequacy, of being in over his head. George digs in his pockets for fare and finds little left over for a tip. "Problem yok" says the cabbie. "Today I help you catch Russians. Tomorrow you help us catch Greeks."

"Did you find him?" asks Zeynep when George walks in. She is sticking a note on Craine's door, adding to the three already there; as always, the sound of an old typewriter can be heard inside. When George shakes his head, no, she gives him a dubious look.

George takes a seat and loses himself in his inbox; it's easier than thinking about his damaged suit – or about Taylor Moore.

At the top of his pile is a fresh *Welfare and Whereabouts* cable with Taylor's name on it. Its tone is shrill, which can mean just one thing—Zimmerman has raised hell with the department over George's little foul-up with the body.

There is also an envelope in his box, a letter from Nazan; he smiles despite himself. Zeynep watches him read it. "You will tell your wife about your girlfriend here?"

"Just as soon as I get one," says George. "For God's sake, Zeynep, this is just a visa case." He tosses her note in the garbage; it contains a few kind words about their lunch—plus a phone number. Later, after Zeynep has left for the day, he'll go to retrieve it, only to find the wastebasket has been emptied. Damn it, Zeynep.

A visa case. Yes, that's right. That's all she is. Vram, her Armenian friend, was back in line only yesterday, making his case to Dawn, who turned him down in a flash. Nazan must have dropped the note off afterward.

Is it only the visa—Vram's visa—that she wants? His thoughts turn to Margaret; he hasn't spoken to her all week. How old does that make his daughter? Is she nine months now? He begins to do the math, then loses track of the months. Why doesn't Margaret call?

A decision would help. A decision about something, anything. Angry with himself, George rises from his desk and strides out into the rain, half-jogging across the parking lot until he reaches the Palazzo. The unlit foyer fits his mood. Upstairs, he finds Tim loitering in the political section, chatting with Helen. He is lean and erect, with a fastidiousness that seems a different era's. George has seen Tim once or twice at the Pera Palas, elegantly dressed and taking tea with lunch.

This is not as George planned it. "Do you know what a cucumber means?" is the first thing that comes to mind, and so he says it. Helen looks expectantly at Tim, waiting for his answer.

There is no response.

"Have you ever gotten one before?" George persists.

Tim crosses his arms. "What do you need, George?"

"I can think of one or two ways to use a cucumber," volunteers Helen. "I mean, besides putting it in a salad." Her intervention gives Tim the chance he needs to walk away, not slowing down until he reaches his office. George is on his heels.

"Close the door," says Tim. As always the radio in his office is turned up loud, complicating the work of eavesdroppers. On Tim's desk, plain as day, is the offending vegetable.

George complies.

"So, what do you need?"

George points at the cucumber. "Tim, I know this guy's been in to see you, my welfare and whereabouts case, the one I messed up. I've got the department breathing down my neck. But c'mon, am I telling you anything you don't already know?"

Tim sighs. It's an exceedingly long exhalation. "Look, George, I know you're only doing your job, and I'm not trying to screw you. But I can't help—it's strictly need to know."

"Okay, so I don't need to know. But let me ask you this. Am I in danger if I meet with him?"

"What are you talking about?" Tim had been fidgeting with a pen, turning it over and over in his hands. Now the pen is still.

"Just what I asked."

"Are you telling me you know where he is?"

George says nothing.

"George..." He places the pen on his desk, meticulously lining it up with the rest of his papers. "Let's go see Phil."

They meet in the room where their words will not be heard. George has been here only once, for his orientation briefing. Of course, not all his questions were answered that day. He glances about the room, taking in the pea-green paint, shoddy furnishings from the disco era. Must be hard to stay fashionable when the tables and chairs have to be handled with the care of weapons-grade plutonium, lest a bug work its way into the room.

George feels no particular urge to be helpful, only to stay out of trouble; he sits in silence as Phil talks. It's the kind of chatter that reveals nothing. Finally, the question:

"Where is he, George?"

"Fatih."

"Where in Fatih?"

"What are you planning?"

Phil tips his chair back. He exchanges a knowing look with Tim. Testily, he answers. "We plan to bring him in George."

"How? The police?"

Phil waves his hand as if to say, whatever.

"For what? Drugs? Or is he really…"

"PKK? My turn to ask a question, George…"

"Why didn't you tell me before? I've been in the dark…"

Phil sighs and shakes his head. For a long time they are silent. George is grateful to see the door open, and Priscilla walk in. "Can I join you gentlemen?"

When George looks to her, she barely smiles. He runs his fingernails across his arm, hard enough to leave red marks. Making amends for his fiasco with the body has driven him here; now he's in over his head.

"What's up?"

"Just hoping for a little inter-agency cooperation, Priscilla."

"Yes, Phil. I'm aware how much you value coordination."

Phil's face is flushed.

"I've seen Taylor," says George.

Phil winces at his mention. "Tim, why don't you and George grab a cappuccino?" George glances at Priscilla, who nods. Without a word, they close the door behind them and head for the makeshift kitchen.

The pressure builds, but Tim doesn't wait long enough. He frees the valve several seconds too early; the trickle of steam warms the milk but produces no froth. "Cheers," he says, eyeing the cappuccino-turned-latté. They click cups. Tim shakes his head and smiles. "Let the chiefs sort it out, eh?"

George nods uneasily. Someone has draped the walls with tinsel, and on one of the doors there's a *Twelve Days of Christmas* collage. The seven maids a milking have a faintly sexual appeal, which George finds troubling. He resolves to call Margaret when he gets home. There is no point talking to Tim. He indulges in a slurp. A Christmas tape is playing again. *Don we now our gay apparel, Fa la la la la la la la la.* George tries to imagine Christmas this year in the Moore household. Happy? Worried? At least their son, once dead, has been reborn.

Fa la la la la, la la la la.

* * *

Stop. Listen up. Do you remember the unfortunate American citizen who George mentioned in the staff meeting, before Zeynep interrupted with news of Taylor, and started the chase? The American citizen who was drugged and robbed in Doğubeyazit? Who was pulled from a snowbank with a touch of hypothermia and put on a plane to Istanbul and given the consulate's number? Well, that American citizen was me.

I arrived in Istanbul a little worse for wear from my Doğubeyazit adventure, but still hungry to find Winston Markey and get my hands on the file. As for Winston Markey's underling, George McCall, a later reading of Markey's memos, a vigorous cross-analysis, would demonstrate that at the very moment of my arrival in Istanbul, George was indulging himself before the mirror in his large Bebek apartment, where not everything worked but still looked like it did.

In my mind's eye I imagine him thus: Lifting his work shirt, which is sadly spit-free, George pinches a wad from his belly and grimaces in disgust. A side view confirms that he is circumnavigated by a layer of fat. Everything in life, in his life at least, tends toward the middle. With a sigh he lets his shirt fall back into place, reaches for the ceiling and clasps his hands together, stretches right, left, then right again. Then he stops, doubting that he has accomplished much. He moves to the kitchen and builds a sandwich. With Margaret gone, fruits and vegetables have no place in his life.

George expects me to call, yet doesn't think twice about tying up the line. He dials Margaret's number in Virginia. No answer. When he replaces the receiver, only then does he realize how desperate he was to get through. He tries the number again, on the off- chance that he mis-dialed. The phone rings and rings; even the answering machine ignores him.

He surveys the apartment, a place where he spends too much of his time. There are too many hazards for a nine-month old: A glass-top table, a teetering lamp, ashtrays and tile coasters with sharp edges. What kind of father is he, to live in such a place? Then again, what kind of father is he to live an ocean away from his child? Was his absence even felt anymore? He sits down heavily and feels the floor throb. His neighbor, Orhan, is sharing *Bolero* with the neighbors. Meanwhile, the call to prayer is sounding in the distance, a discordant wail without rhythm. Orhan employs technology to solve the problem. He turns up the volume.

"What the hell am I doing?" He wonders. There is no one around to respond, but this doesn't stop George from asking another question. "What must Priscilla think?" His hands search for something to do, to hold. They feel empty without a drink.

Tim had been right; the chiefs would sort it out, though not in George's favor. When Priscilla had emerged from the room, George could see it in her face. "Where is he?" she had asked. To his credit, Phil had looked away, more bored than smug.

George had described the neighborhood, right down to the colors of the cars in the street, and the exact location of the flat. Since he had no address, he had offered to take them to the spot. Phil had hesitated, then agreed. They would go together the following day, he'd said, once he'd had time to round up the the Turkish police. He would call in the morning. Until then, not a word was to leave this room. It had been obvious from Priscilla's expression that the discussion was over.

"Jesus Christ," Priscilla had said when they were alone. "I thought you had more sense than this. Do you know what could happen to your clearance? This is a career stopper! Do you understand? I'm not going to have you curtail over some cloak and dagger nonsense. Now, please, hear me when I tell you to stay out of it!"George knows he's lucky there's no alcohol in the apartment tonight. The place seems clinically bare. He considers his options: There's the Sherlock Holmes bar in Etiler where the women stake out western men. How easy it must be to take one home! He's heard they'll do almost anything short of actual penetration, kinky things that western women won't, so long as they retain their virginity, technically speaking. *I can relate to that,* thinks George. *After all, I'm only technically married.*

He feels deflated. Taylor had been an adventure—that was the simple truth. The cloak and dagger nonsense was exactly that, but for a while it had woken him up from what seemed in retrospect a long and sterile slumber.

He decides to call Truman, who is slow to pick up the phone.

"Good God," says Truman. "Go out and have some fun! Me? Oh, I'm sorry. Timur's here. We're watching videos. Well, sure, stop by. But I should warn you, Liza Minelli is the only star I have on tape who keeps her clothes on."

They agree to meet tomorrow instead. George picks up the Turkish newspaper and reads that Shariah law is inevitable if the Islamists win the mayorship, that the Greek Orthodox Patriarch is scheming to create a mini-Vatican in Fener, that the leaders of the mainstream parties have accused each other of corruption, that twelve more PKK terrorists have been captured dead on Mount Ararat.

Always they're captured dead, thinks George. But which comes first, the captured or the dead? He thinks of Taylor Moore, scott-free for at least a few hours more. But what then? Would Phil have him arrested? As a consular officer, George is supposed to help his countrymen out of trouble, not into it. Captured dead. The words linger long after he puts down the paper.

He has to talk to someone. If I had called just then, that someone might have been me. But my mind was elsewhere. To be exact, my mind was accompanying the rest of me in a cheap hotel not a hundred yards from the consulate, trying different arguments to convince the bartender to let me run a tab. And so I wasn't available to talk George out of his next move, which was to search the pockets of his suit for a crumpled napkin from a fish restaurant in Emirgan where he had eaten eggplant several weeks ago.

He used it to call Nazan.

* * *

George McCall has to hear it from Mr. Moore: His son, Taylor, has been arrested. The call comes at ten in the morning, still the middle of the night in Great Falls, Virginia. George fumbles the phone trying to reach it from his beside. He had too much to drink the night before, thanks to Nazan, and is remembering what a hangover feels like.

"No. He didn't leave a goddamn phone number," says Mr. Moore. "I thought you might know your way to the jail by now."

George covers the mouthpiece as he clears his throat. The room is gray and ill- defined, like a photocopy short of toner. A pair of pants, presumably his own, lies draped over the corner chair. The window is fuzzy with streaks of rain. George feels the impulse to check the sheets, his clothes, the carpet, to make sure he hasn't been sick. "Of course, Mr. Moore. We'll find him. Did he say anything else?"

"I didn't speak to him. He was on the phone with his mother. Said it's all political, a set-up. They wouldn't let him talk long. Then they got interrupted. The line went dead. God knows what they did to him."

The police probably just hung up the phone, thinks George—when it dawned on them that Taylor was calling the United States. The gall to dial international from a police station!

There is a long pause from Taylor's father, then, "Mr. McCall. My son has his… issues. But he's a good kid. I have significant resources at my disposal and I am prepared to get on a plane right now if you think it would…"

"That shouldn't be necessary Mr. Moore."

"Then I hope you'll act quickly, and keep me fully informed."

"Yes…" George recalls what Nazan said about Taylor and his father, her hints that they were estranged. "Mr. Moore, you should be aware that we need a Privacy Act waiver from your son before we can discuss his case. Taylor will have to give us permission before we can go into…"

"Now listen, Mr. McCall. I've already been on the phone to a dozen people in the state department. Everybody puts me on hold, then tells me to talk to someone else. Goddamit, I'm sick of the run-around and I've had my fill of bureaucratic claptrap. This is my son we're talking about. Just find him and call me back when you've done that!"

"Mr. Moore, I'm sorry. I know it's frustrating but this isn't a matter of bureaucracy. This is legislation that was passed to protect..."

"Don't tell me about red tape, Mr. McCall. I pay seven figures a year hiring people to cut through it. I'm sure my congressman will be interested to hear..."

"I'm sure he will, Mr. Moore. And I hope he'll explain to you that it was congress that passed this law, not the state department..."

They are silent for a while. George feels his hands shaking; is it the alcohol, or is it his nerves? He pulls the sheets over his bare chest and props himself against the pillow. It's not easy to play the part of diplomat, official representative of the United States of America, in just his socks and boxers.

"As soon as I get off the phone, Mr. Moore, I'll start calling police stations. I'll get back to you as soon as I've learned anything. Okay? You can call me at this number anytime."

But George doesn't call right away. He takes a long shower instead; in the mist his head clears. He didn't sleep with her; he didn't even kiss her. His hand drops down and his heart races with pleasure and guilt. The need for reassurance is strong. He says it aloud, "I didn't do anything." Relief comes quickly.

He recalls shots of lemon vodka at Rejans, an empty bottle as they rose to leave. The waiters had helped him with his coat but not hers, as is the custom in Turkey, and she'd nearly fallen over trying to wrest it from her chair. Walking up Istiklal, he'd found himself in a shoving match with a pack of teenagers who stunk of glue. He remembers it now! The boys, children really, had held their ground, shouting curses. Nazan had tugged at him, trying to pull him away. "Siktir ol!" Fuck off, they'd shouted. And he'd slurred back at them, "Yari kafalar. Annana koydum!" Penis heads, I stuck it in your mother.

Nazan had been impressed with his Turkish.

George towels off on his way to the kitchen. He drinks water straight from the pitcher and leaves a pale film where his lips touched the rim. Margaret always hated that. I'd better call, he thinks. In his living room corner, the answering machine blinks, illuminating the adjacent window. Four times. Could he really have slept through four calls? Or did Mr. Moore call back that many times while he was in the shower? Perhaps Phil had called as well? George sets the pitcher on the air filter; it hasn't been cleaned since July. It whirs and grates, struggling to digest the coal dust, sending tremors across the water.

Click.

Beep.

Beep.

Click.

No message. Could it have been Nazan? George feels slightly ill; he wonders if she'll call back, both hoping and fearing that she will.

Beep. "George? Hey it's Gwen from Commercial. I'm on duty this week. Listen, I'm sorry about this, but you'll be hearing soon from an Amcit, a Mr. Moore, who's got a problem with his son. I couldn't find you last night, so I told the switchboard to put him through to your place. So you might be hearing…" George hits fast-forward. "Hey, Gwen again. Listen, I got a message from some whacko American, says he needs to get a hold of you. His name's Bill Bigelow. I think he's the guy you mentioned in the staff meeting—the one who was drugged and robbed out east? Anyway, if you get this message give me a call will you? And if you don't… well then you're lucky. This duty officer thing's a pain."

George drinks again from the pitcher. As a consular officer, he is more or less always on duty.

Beep. "Um, hello. My name is Bill Bigelow. I'm the writer who called a couple of days ago from Doggy-bey-zit. Um. This is George McCall? Look, I don't wish to bother anyone but I find myself in need of some money. You see, I ran into some bad characters of Kurdish persuasion a few days ago… well, I think you know my predicament. I have some money back in the states… what remains of a modest inheritance… I simply need to find out how to access it. Oh yes, there's also the small matter of my passport. If you'd like to call me here… I seem to be staying at the Yoo-jelt Hostel. The number is… one, five, one, three, six, one, five, seven, two, nine, seven… My goodness, that's certainly a lot of numbers. Well. I hope to hear from you soon. Goodbye." Beep. Beep. Click. The cassette rewinds.

George puts down the receiver and stares out the window. The rain has eased, but gray matter cloaks the nearby apartments, reducing the bodyguards next door to mere silhouettes. He reaches for the phone, dials, then hangs up without finishing. Let Gwen deal with Bill Bigelow, he decides. He starts to dial the consul general's number, changes his mind, and calls Craine first.

Felicitas, Winston's wife, answers on the first ring. "He not here," she says. "He gone since yester. Day. Leave boys here to me. If you see him, you tell him come home. Right away." George doesn't bother leaving a message. He has done his duty by reaching out to his supervisor; now he's entitled to call the consul general.

"Priscilla? I'm sorry to disturb you at home, but there's been a development in the Taylor Moore case."

"Mmm?"

He tells her about the call from Cedrick Moore. "I'm going to start searching for him right now, although I have a feeling he's not in any normal sort of..."

"That won't be necessary, George."

"Won't be necessary?"

"Phil called me last night. He's already been out to see him. They're holding him in Mecidiyeköy in some... special department."

"Why wasn't I..." He stops, unsure if he wants an answer.

"He's been visited, George. I understand you have a consular responsibility to do that. But it's been done. Let's all take a deep breath 'til Monday. Phil can brief you then. I'll personally see to it that he does."

But George is barely listening. The words, *out of the loop*, race through his mind. Is it possible he slept too late and missed the action? But no, Phil had never tried to contact him, even after promising they'd go get Taylor together. It was clear now; Phil never intended to wait. It was a lie, and not the kind of lie he hears on the visa line; this one stings.

"Priscilla, I'm sorry, I'm not trying to be a pain. But a visit by a... another agency doesn't satisfy our obligations. I mean... did Phil give him a list of lawyers? Did he have him sign a privacy act waiver? Did he try to contact his parents?"

"George..."

"Priscilla, we're on shaky ground. You're on shaky ground." He knows his tone is all wrong, but there's no stopping now. "Priscilla, I'm giving you my best advice as a consular officer. You can reject it but you're going to leave yourself... open. We've got an American citizen in custody on serious charges. An Amcit! His family is asking about his safety. They know we know he's been arrested. And! And we have Zimmerman checking up on our work. These aren't the usual form letters he's signing, he's actually interested! I think we should play this straight, Priscilla. I know this puts us in a tight spot with... But we don't have a choice. Our butts need covering too."

George makes himself stop; he has made his point, and feels vaguely euphoric. His hands, which shook a moment ago, have steadied.

At first, Priscilla says nothing. In the silence George listens to the gentle drumming of the rain against the window. Whatever the outcome, he feels a burden has been lifted. He has said his piece. Somewhere outside, a muezzin wails. He hears himself breathe and takes another sip of water. It dawns on him that he doesn't know where to begin looking for Taylor. Normally he would go to Zeynep and ask her to check around; but if he discloses anything about this case to an uncleared Turk, he will leave himself exposed.

Mecidiyeköy is not a neighborhood that George knows well; arrests normally take him to the Foreigners' Police in Sultanahmet, or to Sağmalcilar prison where *Midnight Express* took place. The story is well known: a young American drug-runner, tired of being tortured, acts crazy to get himself transferred to a mental ward where he assumes security will be porous. But the plan backfires when he is confined to section thirteen with the violently insane.

In fact, Hayes did manage an escape from Turkey, not by killing a guard but by awaiting a transfer to a minimum-security island prison where there were no walls, only water. A year or two before he was to be released anyway, he crawled on his belly to the beach, untied a fishing boat, and rowed off into the night.

A petty crook was free. The Turks got their comeuppance. From that day on, Turkey would forever be associated with sadism and torture. The audience cheered for this strange happy ending.

There is anxiety in Priscilla's voice when she finally responds. "Okay, George, go find this American and do your job. I'll back you up."

He hangs up the phone. He thinks to himself, Priscilla is alright.

The sun peeks through the December gloom, dragging the temperature to its highest point in weeks—a balmy 15 degrees celsius. The patrons of the Bebek Hotel make the most of it, pouring from the bar's smoky innards to the deck on the Bosphorous, where the surliest waiters in town unstack soot-darkened chairs and, with a strike of their cloths, pronounce them fit for habitation. The drinkers are giddy with delight, almost perplexed; they drink faster than they should, and order things they've seen on the menu a hundred times but never tried—florescent drinks with curly straws and colorful fruit and tiny umbrellas. It's a sight to see; normally the customers here will nurse a single beer for hours.

A Russian tanker plows downstream at double speed; in its wake will come the supertankers, mammoth crafts hauling crude from the newly developed oil fields in the Caspian Sea. When a ship is that long, special care must be had to guide it down the channel. The slightest miscalculation and the ship will run aground—like the cargo vessel that collided with a seafood restaurant a few years back, around six- thirty in the evening. Luckily the Turks eat late. But what about next time? From one end of the Bosphorous to the other, tinderbox houses start at water's edge and ascend uphill, fire's favorite direction. One day it will be a supertanker that runs aground, and the flames will burn long into the Istanbul night.

George finds Harold in a corner near the water, alone with his heels on an empty chair, staring at the waves. He is looking for Russian submarines; they are obliged by treaty to surface through the Straits, but few pass this way any longer, not since the Black Sea Fleet ran out of money and began to rust. Anyway, it's hardly necessary to look out there for Russians; three Natashas sit at the nearest table, chain-smoking Turkish cigarettes, while their Turkish pimp shouts into a mobile phone.

George takes a seat and orders an Efes. "That stuff'll kill you," says Harold, sipping a Bacardi and Coke. "Turkish beer eats me up inside. Even worse than the wine. Once I've had one of those, my girlfriend won't even be in the same room with me."

George takes a cautious sip; he's embarrassed to admit that he's never had the local brew. In fact, not since Monrovia has he had a beer of any kind. The aftertaste makes him wince.

He waits for Harold to finish his critique of Turkish beer, wine, and booze, and tries to keep his impatience in check. Working for DEA, the Drug Enforcement Agency, Harold earns twenty-five percent on top of a salary that is already larger than George's. How could this be, without even a college degree? George swallows his resentment with a bolder swig of beer. In fact, they have made a good team. Some months back, George had helped by issuing a visa to a known drug trafficker so that Harold could accompany him back to the States and bring down the U.S. distributor. George had also managed to surreptitiously copy key documents as part of the visa interview, without blowing Harold's cover. The operation had been a success, and reflected well in Harold's file. Now, it's time for his colleague to return the favor.

George explains the situation, omitting fewer details than he should, punctuating every sentence with a swig of beer. Harold's been to every jail in town at one time or another, even more than George, often working side by side with the spooks. But George knows his attitude toward the Agency is ambivalent; it's they who generally come to him for help, not the other way around.

"Mecidiyeköy, huh? Yeah I know the place. MI6, British intelligence, took me there once. Our own guys wouldn't." He greedily attacks his glass, swishes the ice cubes around, and looks for the waiter. He is nowhere in sight. "These guys are worthless. They've got to be the worst waiters in town."

"Can I get in there?"

Harold shrugs. "You're asking me? At least you speak Turkish. I wouldn't try it without an interpreter to steer me through." He is momentarily distracted by the Turkish pimp, who is out of his seat and pacing like he owns the place. Harold sighs and turns back to George. "But you just wave your diplomatic passport and they let you in. Right?"

Sure, maybe, thinks George, but this is no ordinary jail. He asks Harold to scribble down the address, then leans back and empties his glass; there's something dead in the taste, something in the water that's not quite rocky mountain fresh. A mild diarrhea threatens then recedes, replaced by the alcohol that softens the edge of the early afternoon.

George feels warmed by a faint nostalgia, though of what he's not sure.

"Want another?" asks Harold. The waiter strikes a pose that says there's a million places he'd rather be. "You are the sorriest son of a bitch I've ever seen," Harold tells him as he points to his empty glass. "Iki tane." Two more. The waiter sulks away and Harold turns to George. "Don't worry, he doesn't speak English."

George studies the address and thinks about leaving, but now there's a beer on the way. At the next table, the Natashas and their pimp have gotten louder, inviting stares from the other drinkers, mostly young unmarrieds with cell phones on the table.

"That maganda's going to ruin my day," says Harold. Now the pimp is on his feet and his arm is around the the smallest whore, steering her to the edge of the deck where off-season construction has left a gaping hole in the rail. Laughing heartily, he pretends to toss her into the oily drink. She struggles helplessly, alternating between nervous giggles and genuine protest, lowering her eyes at the crowd, too unworthy to expect their help. Some of the customers mutter ayip, shame, but no one moves a muscle. The pimp has a round face and Turkmen eyes; his shoes are Italian leather. He is worse than maganda, nouveau riche; he is pis, garbage, and he is enjoying his game.

At last the whore is set free. With a slap on her behind she scurries back to the table looking humiliated but relieved.

George reassembles his thoughts. He wants to ask about the cops in Mecidiyeköy, whether Harold remembers any by name, whether he should mention Harold as an ice-breaker. But he is still distracted. Coming to the woman's rescue was a fleeting idea, quickly dismissed and never quite real.

It's not my country, thinks George. I'm only a spectator. His mild drunkenness makes him philosophical. *Life is theatre,* he reflects, *better observed than lived.* And how much easier to observe overseas, where anonymity is the natural state.

But if that pimp stumbles over here, then what? With all those Turks watching?

When George turns to Harold, he is surprised to find an empty chair. The pimp is still at water's edge, lighting a cigarette and watching a yacht go by. Perhaps because a large portion of the rail is missing and because the pimp has drunk a good deal of raki, it is almost too easy for Harold to tip him off the deck and into the water, where he lands with a flop then falls beneath the surface. And it may be because he is so heavy, or so drunk, or because he is covered head to toe with the oily slime of passing ships that the pimp has so much trouble lifting himself back onto the deck of the Bebek Hotel, a dozen yards downstream. By the time he gets to his feet, gushing goo from the Straits and brandishing a knife from his breast pocket, Harold has had ample time to sit down and finish his drink, draw a handgun from his tote bag, and ask George how to say "Sit down" in Turkish.

"Formal or informal?"

"I think *informal* is better."

"Otur," says George.

"Oh-tour," repeats Harold, leveling his weapon at the pimp's groin. The pimp does exactly that, leaving George and Harold to resume their conversation. But now George hears nothing but the creak of the pimp's chair, the heavy breaths that come less fitfully now, the silence that will turn to rapid footsteps when the pimp finally launches his attack. He consoles himself with something he read once: All intelligent men are physical cowards. Wasn't it Graham Greene who wrote that? Would it be any less true if it were Danielle Steele?

When the pimp gets up and walks away, George wonders if he'll return with friends carrying guns larger than Harold's.

"I think we should move on."

"No. I'm going to hang for a while," says Harold. Without another word, he reclines in his seat and eyes the Natashas who chat like nothing has happened, which could be true since hookers have seen just about everything in their lives so, for them, perhaps nothing has.

As it turned out, Harold's information was enough to track down Taylor, who seemed no worse for wear when the guards led him into the tiny cement-block waiting room. George had argued his way into the building, past the sullen guard who reluctantly left his post to escort him up a wide flight of stairs that smelled of ammonia. Rounding a corner into an office where a radio blared, George had found himself face to face with Tim, who couldn't quite hide his surprise. After whispered debate they struck a deal: George could meet with Taylor, but Tim would stay in the room.

Two hours later George was back at the consulate, able to advise Taylor's father that his son was in good health, and had competent legal counsel—a lawyer from the Diyarbakir Bar Association, famous for representing Kurdish activists and himself under indictment for *insulting the military*. For the moment, at least, Taylor's father seemed satisfied.

It had been an extraordinary conversation, George's meeting with Taylor, and one well worth recounting here, if only there were time. But in George's absence the American citizen complaints have piled up: *I've been bitten by a dog. No one will cash this check. Where is my tour group? My husband died. My passport's been stolen. My train ticket's been stolen. My wallet's been stolen. I said my husband died. They stopped me at the airport. Can't you make an exception?*

George leaves *American Citizens' Services* and surveys the visa waiting room through the bulletproof glass. It's a wriggling, writhing mass of rich and poor, ignorant and educated, strong and weak, globbed together in a way that seems unnatural, if not unholy. George guesses he could adjudicate half the cases on looks alone, without ever seeing a document, possibly without ever asking a question. Fashion, dialect, dirt beneath the nails, skin complexion, posture—though it can't be acknowledged, these are what distinguish good cases from the bad. The documents are just icing on the cake.

George calls forward an immigrant visa applicant whose marriage he suspects is a fraud. The Turk lives in Tekirdağ, a coastal blemish on the main route to Greece; his brother owns a grocery store in Brooklyn. His new American citizen wife, who has filed the application on his behalf, is pale and malnourished, as if she has relied too heavily on happy hour snacks. Out of sync with her costume jewelry is a diamond on her finger, large but cloudy, which she fusses with self-consciously. They met in the covered bazaar, she explains, on the first day of her vacation. Five days ago they were married; now she intends to take him home.

That he doesn't speak a word of English and she not a word of Turkish is not reason enough to deny an American citizen the right to bring her spouse to America. George needs more. "Have you consummated your marriage?"

he asks. As a visa officer, he has the right—no, the duty—to ask the most personal of questions.

"Have I what?"

"Have you... Have you been intimate? Have you had sexual relations?"

"Sex? Oh. Well, yeah. Of course. We're married aren't we?"

"Where did this take place?"

"The sex?"

"Yes."

She pauses. "At his house."

"And where is his house?"

"In... what's the name of that city? Tecker-dog."

"And you stayed the night?"

"Well, yeah. That was sort of our honeymoon, I guess you could call it."

"Could you raise your right hand please? Do you swear that all the information you have given and are about to give is true to the best of your knowledge?"

She hesitates only slightly. "Uh huh."

"Thank you. How many nights have you spent in his bedroom?"

"Well." She counts her fingers. "Since we were married, about five nights I guess."

"Could you please describe his bedroom to me?"

Her eyes widen a little. "It's like a normal bedroom," she says.

"Could you please draw a little diagram," he says, sliding pen and paper beneath the bulletproof glass.

"I can't draw very good."

"Nothing fancy. Just show me where the bed is in relation to the door. Okay. Now, are there any windows? Good. Any furniture in the room? No? Okay. Are there curtains? What color are they? Which side of the bed did you sleep on? Just circle the side where you slept, please. Where does your husband keep his clock?"

When she is done, he takes her drawing and lays it flat on his side of the glass. "Thank you. Now can I show you the picture your husband drew?"

She is shouting now, but George tunes her out. There are boxes to fill and lines to initial before the rejection will stick. And he is distracted by Dawn's shrill voice at the adjacent window.

Dawns whirls in her stool, so that the applicant no longer hears. "You know the Turkish word for Iranian... acem... is the same as the word for liar? Now I know why."

"Actually, it means excessive exaggeration," says George.

"Whatever," she says. "Say, any word on your household effects?"

George forces a smile. "Yeah, they're in Haifa. The company went bankrupt as the ship was passing through the Red Sea. The question now is whether the cargo will end up in an Israeli court. If it does, I'm screwed; we won't see it for years."

"That stinks."

"It's fucked," he corrects her, but notes her sincere tone.

"You're in a nasty mood."

"Sorry." He tries to return to his work.

"You know, you shouldn't think I'm homophobic or anything," she says.

He is taken aback by the non- sequitur. "Okay."

She glances around. There is no one within twenty feet except for the visa applicants, and they're inconsequential. "My oldest brother is gay, and very much in the closet," she says gravely. Then, "You're one of the few people I've ever told."

The implication that he's in elite company only makes her revelation odder. "Dawn, is there something on your mind?"

"I shouldn't have said what I said to Truman. He's not, like, a bad guy."

"You were mad."

"Yes, I was. Still…"

"Forget about it; I'm sure he has." It's a lie, but it feels right to say it.

"I have no desire to pry into your personal life."

"*My* personal life?" He is taken aback. He had thought they were talking about Truman.

"What you do outside the office is your own business is how I feel."

"Dawn, what are you talking about?"

This time she considers the visa applicants and yanks down the shade. "What I'm talking about is Phil interrogating me about *your* love life. Like, what could I possibly know about your love life? The only time I ever see you is on the visa line." There is a touch of despair in her voice that George ignores.

"What do you mean, interrogate? About me? What did he want to know?"

"He wanted to know if you dated, if your marriage was still… stable, whether…" She pauses. "Look, he wanted to know if you're gay." There, she said it.

"*Gay*?" He says the word like he might say "syphilis," full of fear and loathing. "My God, Dawn, I'm not *gay*."

"I didn't think you were, and that's what I told him."

"Shit, I mean, I'm married for God's sake." But this argument fails to convince even him; after all, wasn't Truman's friend, Daniel, married too? And didn't he have three kids to George's one? That is, three times the evidence?

"I told him, I told him," says Dawn. "But he said lots of FSO's keep a wife at home. They use the separate maintenance allowance for their alimony."

"Jesus, so, I mean, what, what else did he ask you?"

"That was it. He said you claimed you weren't gay on your security clearance. So if you were lying it would be a problem."

He stares in disbelief. *Problem*—now that's an understatement. "They've looked at my clearance?" His chest feels hollow and for a moment he's afraid to breathe. The sense of invasion is total.

Dawn goes on, more animated now, oblivious to his anguish. Or is she enjoying it? "I think it was the food run with Truman that did it. Let's face it; it didn't look good spending the weekend with someone so open and notorious." *Open and notorious*; these were the words that Truman used to describe himself, but tongue in cheek. Truman didn't have to fear for his clearance; he'd been out of the closet from day one. Only those with something to hide could be labeled security risks, since it was they most prone to blackmail. This was why the Pentagon's "don't ask don't tell" policy made so little sense.

"Does Phil know we had a corpse in our hotel room? Did he think that was romantic?"

"You and Truman stayed in the same room?"

"Dawn, I'm not..." He puts his hands to his head and turns away.

"I hope you'll keep this between us."

"Between us? How can I, Dawn? I've got to defend myself."

George slides from his stool and begins to pace. What kind of onward assignment would he get if his security clearance was yanked? A dead-ender for sure, certainly nothing overseas. What had Priscilla called it? A *career stopper*.

George does the rest of his twenty-seven interviews in a funk. Three of the cases are borderline; he refuses them all. It's time for lunch. He eats a döner kebab standing up, then walks a long way up Istiklal, right up to Taksim before reversing course. By the time he returns he has made up his mind. Sexual blackmail—wasn't that spycraft 101? Never mind that it's normally for recruiting foreign spies, not bringing down colleagues. Either way, it's effective.

He enters the Palazzo Corpi and walks straight to Phil's office. The chief of station looks up from his desk, his lips tightening into a smile at the sight of

George's stricken face. The threat hangs between them, as obvious as it is unspoken. George indulges a moment of silent contempt, then says evenly, "Let me know if I can help in any way on the Taylor Moore case. Otherwise, I'll stay out of it. Getting involved was a mistake. I'm done."

When Phil nods sagely, George understands that the matter is closed.

* * *

Mustafa Kemal Atatürk, Father of the Turks, was a brilliant commander in the First World War, but it was events to come that would ensure his place in history. Though they stood firm at Gallipoli, the Ottomans could not forever postpone defeat to the Allies. In due course, the Empire's forces were on the run and Istanbul found itself under British "protection." The end of the war was not a good time to be a Turk. The Sultan was a British stooge and his citizens resigned to whatever fate the Allies had in store for them, namely an empire dismantled and doled out to the Greeks, Italians, and Armenians in little bits. In the rush for spoils, even the Kurds were promised some sort of state of their own.

Allied designs were reflected in the peace treaty signed at Sevres, a city known for its fragile china. But not all—for the British had already made secret agreements with the Russians, the Italians, the French, the Jews, the Arabs, and the Greeks, most of which conflicted with Sevres, and with each other. The Greeks, for example, had received private assurances of spoils on the coast of Asia Minor. When Sevres failed to deliver, the Greeks took matters in their own hands and landed twenty thousand troops in Smyrna, the present-day city of Izmir. From there they drove east, aspiring at long last to realize their megali idea of a greater Greece encompassing all the lands where Hellenic influence had been paramount through the ages.

But as the Greeks headed east, so did Mustafa Kemal, the hero of Gallipoli. Four days after the Greeks landed at Smyrna, Kemal landed at Samsun on the Black Sea coast and began to organize small pockets of resistance into a single army. His recruiting efforts were aided by the Greek attack, which awakened the Turks from their slumber. To fall under British domination was one thing, but to be conquered by the lowly Greeks, Ottoman subjects for so many centuries, was a humiliation too great even for the dispirited Turks to bear.

Kemal's new army clashed with the Greeks at Sakarya, well on the way to Ankara. The fighting was pitched and bloody, but soon it was clear that the Greeks had overreached. Having marched thousands of miles to the front, their supply lines were stretched beyond the breaking point. Greek troops, taken prisoner, begged their captors for bread. At the end of twenty-two days, the whole of the Greek army fell back, retreating in an orderly fashion at first, then collapsing into a chaotic, headlong rush to the sea.

The first stage of Turkey's War of Independence was over; now only the British remained to be beat, and afterward the monumental task of building a nation from the wreckage of an empire. Seventy-five years later, Mustafa Kemal Atatürk's achievements would inspire Hollywood to capture his life on the big screen—until pressure from the Greek-American community forced the project to be abandoned.

Maybe that's why Atatürk looked so angry now, hanging from the wall in the müdür's office at the Mecidiyeköy jail, where George and Tim sat together in silence, sipping tea, waiting patiently for the prisoner to appear. George studied the face in the frame. Here, the father of the Turks was clean- shaven and fez-less, respectably aged but still charged with the manic energy of youth. Hard to believe that only a few years later, Atatürk would have to take refuge on his ship, the Savarona, where in the cool Bosphorous breeze he would scratch his legs until they bled. To the very end his doctor refused to admit that the father of modern Turkey was dying from cirrhosis of the liver, such a human ailment, though it would have been obvious to any first-year medical student.

When the inevitable came, at precisely 9:05 a.m. on November 10, 1938, the clocks in Dolmabahce Palace came to a stop, never to start again. And so it has been on the same day every year since, that a shot rings out at the precise moment of Atatürk's death, shutting down the country for one full minute. In those sixty seconds, when no Turk may chatter, pound a hammer, play the radio, or holler "yes please" loud enough for the next Turk to hear, Turkey continues her long crawl westward, the secular revolution living on. It's the only moment of peace and quiet that Istanbul ever gets.

"My name is Red Halabja, Unit Commander, Military Wing of the Partia Karkaris Kurdistan," said Taylor Moore, in such a way it was clear which words were capitalized.

"You're a screwed up kid who should be jacking off at home, not blowing up innocent people in a foreign country," Tim replied.

The two of them glowered at each other, but it was anger tinged with boredom; clearly they had been down this road before. George tried in vain to make eye contact with the pale young man, who looked short where he was sitting and as narrow as a fence post. There was a welt above his right eye, and freckles below; otherwise he had the weathered look of an older man.

"Would you prefer we did this with Americans only?" George asked. Then, smiling pleasantly at the Turk who sat with them in the room: "Zahmet olmazsa." If it's no trouble.

The Turk wore a well-pressed cotton shirt and an Ottoman-patterned tie that looked suspiciously expensive. MIT evidently paid better than the police. The Turk's expression was cold, but there was machinery at work behind his dark eyes. "You may speak to me English. And if you wish I may go." But still, he made no move to leave.

Between Tim and George and Taylor and the Turk, there was little space left in the room. Oddly, they sat facing each other in a small semi-circle, as if in therapy.

Tim tipped his chair back, bringing the front legs off the floor. It creaked loudly. There was no radio blaring, no television, nothing, not even the ritual offer of chi. "That's all he's going to tell you, George. Right, Red? Just your name, rank, and serial number."

Taylor stared insolently. He was only twenty-four years old, but if he was nervous he didn't show it; if anything he appeared to be gloating. Only his hands suggested otherwise. His fingers danced on his lap and clenched into fists; his palms pressed his thighs, drawing taut the handcuffs that fastened him to the armrests on both sides. He tipped his head at George. "Which of you is supposed to be the good cop? I can't tell you apart. You're both such *esekler*."

"Watch yourself Taylor," said Tim, rising ever so slightly from his seat. Though his Turkish was remedial at best, he knew a good number of slurs, including the word for *bastard.*

Taylor smiled warily. A vague knowing passed between them; how familiar with one another they seemed. Had Taylor been that many times to the consulate?

"Sikim ashağida kasimpasha," said Taylor, flattening the A's in his Boston way.

The MIT man smiled.

"What?" said Tim. Here was an insult he didn't know.

"Kasimpasha is under my dick," said George, by way of translation. It's... You know. Beneath him. Like Kasimpasha, the neighborhood down in the valley..."

Still looking straight ahead, Taylor congratulated George on his Turkish; but his tone was no warmer than before.

Tim fidgeted in his chair. "You want a ride back to the office?"

George ignored him. Again he asked the MIT man to leave, quoting from the Vienna consular convention, faking the parts he didn't know. At last, the Turk stood up, clicked his tongue and left.

George touched his finger to his eye. "Have you been hit?"

"Breaking news," said Taylor. "You're in Turkey."

George sighed. Taylor might be a terrorist, but he was also an impish kid. George recalled his own state of mind at twenty-four; it wasn't hard, being only five years ago. He said evenly, "We'll complain, make sure it doesn't happen again."

Taylor only smirked.

"Taylor," said George. "You're in a lot of trouble." When this failed to eliminate the smirk, George decided his tone was too earnest. Still he plowed on, explaining his role as a consular officer. Guilt or innocence made no difference, he said. He was here to ensure that Taylor received fair treatment. On the table was a list of lawyers and a backgrounder on how the Turkish legal system worked, plus some issues of *Time* and *People*. "Sorry. They're pretty old. I had some newer magazines but we've had a lot of drug busts lately."

Taylor regarded the backgrounder with disdain. "You think any of this applies here?" He looked at Tim. "How long will I be here?"

George gritted his teeth; this was his job, not Tim's. Unfortunately, however much he wanted to tell Taylor what to expect next, what court he would go to and when, in fact he had no idea what happened in the state security courts. He knew vaguely that the rules were different, allowing for things like incommunicado detention and sealed indictments. Sticking to familiar ground, he produced a Privacy Act waiver. For the moment it was the only purpose he had.

"I'd like you to fill this out, Taylor," said George. He dropped the papers on his lap. "It allows me to discuss your case with your parents. They're desperate for information as you can imagine."

The handcuffs just allowed Taylor to bump the papers until they scattered on the floor. Tim picked them up, stood menacingly behind Taylor for a moment, then returned to his chair. Taylor bristled. In that brief moment, George glimpsed a physicality in Tim he'd never noticed; under the bow tie, the breast pocket handkerchief, there was hard bone and muscle, good for something besides desk work.

"Jesus, Tim," said George. "You've seen too many damn movies."

Now it was Tim who bristled. "Nice stunt with the cucumber, Taylor. How does it feel knowing you're the reason your friends are dead?"

For the first time, Taylor's facade seemed to crack. His eyes glistened as he looked thoughtfully from George to Tim and back again. "I've spoken to my father. He knows what he needs to know. No more no less."

"Taylor…"

"Don't call me that!" A flash of rage, then he was calm again. "Call me Red Halabja or nothing. Do you understand? Taylor Moore is dead. I killed him. Oh don't look shocked. Of course I killed him. Not that Australian fuck; it was me I killed."

Tim tries to interrupt, but Taylor won't stop.

"What's one more missing fascist in the great scheme of things? You should have let the Turks bury my body right then and there."

George's head spun from the strain of understanding. So the mix-up with the body was no fluke: Taylor had killed the young Australian, and he had done it to steal his identity. But why? So that he could go completely underground? To completely shed his former self? George might have entertained the thought further, but now Taylor was speaking loudly and pedantically on the history of the Kurdish struggle from Saladin the anti-Crusader to the Republic of Mahabad to the meaning of Newruz. Genocide, state terrorism, villages emptied out across the whole of Kurdistan, millions forced into shantytowns on the fringes of Diyarbikir, village guard programs that turned neighbor against neighbor and forced Kurds to kill their own. Electric shocks and squeezing of testicles and truncheons rammed up women's vaginas.

Taylor's voice had lost its agitation, had become a cool breeze. For a moment, George let himself see the world through Taylor's eyes, surrendered himself as he often did to foreign tongues, as if this diatribe were an accent he could make his own. What a marvel it was to lose himself this way, and how frightening, to empathize so completely, as if nothing bound him to any particular manner of speech, to any point of view. But just as suddenly he returned, the vision having failed to soothe; the words were rote, spoken by a madman with a switch gone off in his head.

But, no, this wasn't madness he was hearing. Taylor wasn't crazy, not psychotic, for his ravings had an internal logic, sure enough. No, he was simply unencumbered by the arbitrary distinctions of fantasy and reality, of fact and fiction. How nice it must be, and what an advantage.

Abruptly, Taylor turned to Tim. "Let's get on with it. When will I be sentenced? Do you think I'm afraid to die?"

"Die?" George laughed anxiously. "No one's even found you guilty of anything yet." Anyway, he thought to himself, there must be a reason he hadn't already been *captured dead.* Was it because he was American, or had Phil protected him?

In truth, he'd merely been lucky. George had been with Nazan, lifting his fifth lemon vodka at Atatürk's one-time hangout, Rejans, when the police made their move on the safehouse that George had described. Under cover of darkness, they had crept through the alleys to surround the building unnoticed. On both sides, neighbors were startled to find their doors forced open by mean in black ski masks, men who instructed them to wait in other rooms. When 8/12 Devrim Sokaği, Revolution Street, was finally breached, Zakho was fiddling with the television antennae, trying to improve the reception on a film about bobsledders. Long before he felt the bullets enter his stomach, Zakho was blinded by shards of glass from the TV where only a moment ago John Candy had been speaking in a Black Sea accent, but which now exploded without warning. Only one of the terrorists made it to a weapon before he was asked to surrender, then shot anyway. Taylor was fortunate to be suffering from diarrhea for the third straight day, and was in the best possible position to release his bowels with fright. More to the point, the young officer who entered the toilet was too proud, too embarrassed maybe, to shoot him as he squatted with pants around his ankles; instead he half-dragged, half-kicked Taylor into the living room where his red-speckled body filled the dozen armed men with wonder.

"I'm PKK," said Taylor, pronouncing it the Turkish way, like a crow, *pay-kah-kah.* "I deny nothing except the accusation that I am a terrorist. Our fight is a just one. To help the Kurds win their…" And so on.

George asked, "Did you plant the Aya Sofya bomb?"

Tim stood up and began to pace, running his fingers through his hair.

"*We* planted it. What difference does it make if I was there personally? In the movement, the individual doesn't exist."

"But why? Why kill a bunch of innocent tourists?"

"No innocents were killed," said Taylor. "Non-combatants died and that's regrettable. But that's war. If only they'd listened to our warnings and not come to Turkey to spend their money! Where does that money go, except for weapons that are used to commit genocide against the Kurdish people?" A long pause. "American weapons of course."

"The bus is leaving." Tim said. He was standing by the door, arms crossed.

Taylor stared at the door in silence. George wondered if there was anything else to say. His training as a consular officer had included an empty office decorated like a jail cell, phony spider webs and hash marks on the wall, and a colleague posing as a prisoner. Fun and games. Now what?

"There's a congressman who's interested in you. If you don't want me to tell your folks, fine. But I'd like to get the Hill off my back. We can amend the Privacy Act waiver to reflect..."

"Telling Zimmerman's no different than telling my father," said Taylor.

"How did you know it was Zimmerman?"

"Who else?" For the first time Taylor deigned to look George in the eyes. "Do you know who my father is, mister *vice consul*?"

"I don't know anything about your father."

Taylor looked at him skeptically. "You've heard of Quintet Industries?"

"Well, sure." Quintet.com was among the fastest-growing start-ups around. George had a couple of their CD-ROM games; they also made business applications. But these were just asides; most of Quintet's software was defense related—target acquisition, friend or foe, war games scenarios. Almost overnight Quintet had grabbed a huge market share in the third world, mainly the Middle East, piggy-backing on sales of F-16s and attack helicopters.

"You don't know that my father's the CEO?" He laughed, but also eyed George carefully. "And Zimmerman... Zimmerman's his cheerleader. For a fee, of course. Excuse me. Soft money."

"Well, isn't that ironic," said Tim. "The son undoing his father's work. Nice little Oedipal complex you have there." He said it with a swagger, but to George it seemed to mask a growing desperation.

Taylor noticed it too. "I told you, his son is dead. I killed him myself." He smiled and kept his eyes on George, who nodded and rose.

"That's interesting, but I don't know what to do with it. Here." He tossed a business card on the table. "Call me if you change your mind about signing the waiver. I'll be in touch."

But Tim seemed to speak for both of them when he said, "Goodbye, Taylor."

They were almost to the door when Taylor said, "Give me that." George sat as Taylor filled out the waiver, carefully stipulating that only his mother should know the circumstances of his arrest. No one else—not his father, not the press, not the U.S. House of Representatives—was to be informed of his plight.

"Tell her I asked about her, okay? And that I said there's no reason for her to worry. You saw me and I'm fine..."

"That's sweet," said Tim.

The rage returned. "Amine koyayim. Ebeni sikeyim!"

"What?"

"He says he'll have sex with you and your grandmother," said George. "I'm not sure in which order."

"Charming," said Tim. "Why don't we call the Turk back in."

"Casusuydum! Beni öldürecekler!" Taylor virtually spat out the words. But a sidelong glance at George, almost a wink, belied his anger.

"What's that?" Tim demanded.

George hesitated. "You don't want to know."

But of course he would have liked to know, for Taylor's outburst explained a lot. Why, for instance, he had been coming to the consulate for all these months.

It all makes sense, is what George thought to himself as he stared out the passenger side window, plying Tim with stupid questions to feign his ignorance. Tim was tightlipped, which suited George fine, and soon they lapsed into silence, barely speaking even after a close call with a pedestrian who lingered in the street a moment too long. The Turks were like that. Fearless, they were always plummeting through traffic with split-seconds to spare, their arms stiff as they marched in fast- motion. One foot was always in danger of being left behind, reaching the curb only inches ahead of the grinding wheel. But sometimes the timing was wrong and an ankle or a heel didn't quite make it. In Istanbul, life and limbs were cheap; like the cast of a Fellini film, half the city seemed to walk with a limp.

Casusuydum. I was his spy. *Beni öldürecekler.* They're going to kill me. George replayed the words in his head. The words were meant for him, not for Tim.

I was his spy. A dirty agent, that's what he was. An asset who had turned against his handlers, who had maimed and killed while on the Agency's payroll. Similar cases in Guatemala and elsewhere had been murder on the CIA's image. And this time it was an American. Weren't there rules against recruiting one's own citizens? George wondered how far they would go to cover it up. *They're going to kill me.* That's what Taylor had said.

George stared out at the night. So now he knew, he knew just about everything, it seemed, but what could he do with it? The answer to that question would come soon enough with Phil's veiled threat, with his insinuation of sexual deviance, a blackmailable offense, in Priscilla's words a career-stopper. And so he would never have to decide; the matter would be closed. The CIA had played its spook games with Taylor and lost. So what? George would not jeopardize his career to bring it to light.

Hard, wet pellets slapped the windshield, caking the glass with something like snow. At six o'clock it was utterly dark. In a few weeks there would be even more cars, for then it would be Ramazan, and everyone would be racing home for the ritual iftar, the daily feast which broke the fast, all of them short-tempered from lack of food. But then the weather would be better. Hard to believe they had sat on the Bosphorous that very morning; in the evening's callous gloom the Bebek Bar was a distant memory, no longer real. The slushy embankment was spattered with mud. Tim tightened his grip on the wheel as traffic slowed to a crawl, then stopped altogether. In such weather, no one in this country knew how to drive.

* * *

Days and weeks just sort of passed by. Christmas came and went; some of the Turks put pines in their windows and pictures of a jolly fat man in red, and called him Father Christmas. Baba Noel. The decorations, they explained, weren't for any religious holiday; they were for the Yeni Yil, the New Year.

On the first day of the Yeni Yil, Islamic fundamentalists assassinated the cardboard Baba Noel adorning the lobby of the Marmara Hotel. Also caught in the blast were a pine tree and a couple of tourists sitting nearby.

George sent Margaret an Angora wool sweater from a window display on Istiklal, noticing too late that it might not fit, but dispatching it anyway. For his daughter he assembled a box of imported baby toys, which had cost a small fortune at the Akmerkez, Istanbul's gala shopping mall. Packing such a large box had brought on a kind of euphoria, but when it was gone, entrusted to the U.S. military postal system, to corporals and staff sergeants and non-com clerks, he again felt empty, as if he'd tossed a piece of himself into the void.

The sky was dark and as heavy as lead; every day it rained more than the day before. Sometimes it snowed, heavy wet flakes that turned the mosques white, then morphed to mud in the afternoon. The city's doormats failed to keep pace with demand; grease and gunk flowed in from the streets, and remained in the shape of footprints.

George tried to forget about Taylor. Every couple of days the Turks would move him to a different jail, and every couple of days Zeynep would track him down, only to hear that George wasn't interested. It was a lie, of course; in the middle of a visa interview, he would stop to ponder Taylor's words and reflect on his dilemma. No, he told himself, he would not even tell Priscilla. What match was she for the Agency?

And then there was Truman, who probably had a right to know considering his part in Phil's little make-believe scandal. But Truman was too far out of the closet, too much the activist, too likely to go off half-cocked and make things worse for George. Hell, he was practically shouting his sexual orientation from the rooftops. Truman just didn't have enough to lose.

Congressional letters on Taylor arrived one after the other and, every few weeks, a phone call from Zimmerman's staff. Had Taylor been formally charged yet?

Due to the Privacy Act, I cannot discuss details of his case.

Why isn't Taylor allowed to call home?

We are not aware of any such restrictions. With respect to further details, I must refer you to the Privacy Act, which prohibits the release of information on Mr. Moore's case without his expressed consent.

What is the consulate doing to get him released?

The American Consulate General is working closely with Turkish authorities to ensure that all American citizens who are detained or arrested receive fair treatment under Turkish law...

Etcetera.

Worse were the calls from Taylor's father, who took it none too well that only Mrs. Moore was authorized to receive information about their son. Finally, one day, the announcement came; Cedrick Moore was coming to Turkey. And so George awaited his arrival.

In the meantime, there was other work to do. The day after Christmas, an elderly American plunged through the porthole of a tour boat and broke his hip. A group of Hare Krishnas from Oregon were arrested for handing out tracts at Istanbul University, and spent three nights in jail. In the middle of the night an American was found directing traffic in the nude at Taksim Square.

Insane people are like that—intelligent and fond of travel, obsessed with God, the mafia, and the CIA, and always removing their clothes at the worst possible times.

George couldn't get Taylor out of his mind. "Casusuydum." *I was his spy.* "Beni öldürecekler." *They're going to kill me.* Even as the visa applicants sobbed at his window the words stayed with him.

Was the Agency really capable of that?

Now that I was in Istanbul, I saw George every couple of days, though it was really Winston that I was looking for. But while George was always in, Winston was always sick or on vacation, in a meeting or talking on the phone, or out traveling around. Or so they said. Every time George lied to cover for his boss, he squinted and scratched his arm. What had they done with him, I wondered. Had Winston been disappeared for knowing too much, like so many others before him, who had dared to challenge *It*? And what of the file, the hundreds of pages stamped CONFIDENTIAL bunched up with rubber bands? My fingers ached to turn those pages; my eyes watered to read them.

But I never let on to George, only kept my eye on the consul's office and carried on my vigil.

Of course, spending time with George served a useful purpose too, for he was the one who doled out my modest allowance for the price of a few forms. It wasn't much—only twenty or thirty bucks each time I came in—the idea being to keep my head above water just long enough for my own funds to arrive. But in fact the income allowed me to manage quite well. Most importantly, having cash in hand did wonders for my credit rating, and thus I regained the power to deficit spend like the Reaganite I never was.

And so it was that every three or four days I would exit the consulate with a spring in my step, buy a pastry and a mini-bottle of Glenlivet and retreat to my hotel room to sleep away the afternoon, awakening from time to time for munchies and scotch. Then it was back to bed until the sounds of the night returned—car horns tooting and beds creaking and Russian maidens squealing and red neon blazing through the window like some weird toxic episode. At some featureless hour I would get out of bed and work again for hours on end.

It was this routine that sustained me through Chapter Three.

George saw less and less of Truman, which bothered him more and more. There were few people in the consulate he could talk to, most being older and strange in their own ways. Dawn was the closest in age, except for some of the younger spooks who formed a cliquey, secretive bunch. George couldn't blame them; their entire lives were elaborate constructs, tight capsules to be revealed only on a *need to know* basis. It must have been exhausting, all the inventing they had to do, an occupational hazard; how much easier to be with each other, where they still could deceive but at least be understood.

They wouldn't really kill Taylor would they?

Truman's frequent absences had a lot to do with Timur Iskender, heir to the largest fortune in Turkey. Timur took Truman to his family's island in the Sea of Marmara, where the ground was scattered with enough antiquities to fill a museum. There, under stars that sparkled in the smog-free sky, Timur and Truman found they had much in common; for example, they both enjoyed going down-market on occasion. The following night they did just that, riding in taxis until they found a driver who was young and passably handsome, and who repeated over and over that he was not a homosexual while doing things that argued otherwise.

That was the remarkable thing about Turkey, Truman explained. It was almost ridiculously easy for a homosexual to get laid. The issue wasn't gay versus straight—it was submission versus domination. Truman was willing to elaborate, but George felt he'd heard enough.

Anyway, there was bigger news afoot. Mayoral elections were held across Turkey, and the Islamists won big, tossing out the mainstream candidates whose parties had grown cozy with graft. For the Islamists, years of distributing bread in the villages and paying for funerals had paid off in spades. The following day, shell-shocked and crest-fallen, the consulate's Turkish employees staggered into work warning of headscarves and Shariah law, while outside the Islamists set about picking up the garbage and paving the streets. There were, after all, still national elections to be won.

Inshallah, perhaps they'd even tackle the pollution. Beneath the city, natural gas lines were already in place, the perfect alternative to dirty coal, but no one was willing to flick the switch, lest an explosion swallow the city.

And so it was that Istanbul's air remained the color and consistency of meconium. Even inside the Akmerkez, the air was like soup. Teenagers loitered in the food court, buying the occasional box of cigarettes. There were hamburger stands and pizza joints, corrupted by köfte and Turkish spice, but there was also Wendy's, gloriously air-conditioned, with globalized Frosties. Movie-goers cheered Arnold Schwartzenegger and Jamie Lee Curtis as they took on the Arabs, right after the preview, a bank advertisement, showed an incongruously blue-eyed Turk in a row-boat, trout fishing with his dog. The problem was this: Never, ever in the country's history—not even once—had a Turk gone trout fishing with his dog.

Outside, in the real world, Apo – Kurdish freedom fighter, bloodthirsty terrorist—remained on the lam. There were reports that he'd landed in Athens, and the Greeks had panicked and sent him elsewhere. As usual, the news was conveyed in clipped remarks and hushed tones. Surely someone knew where he was, thought George. In this day and age, was it really possible to fly a plane round and round Europe without being seen?

Zimmerman's staff showed remarkably little interest in current events when they called to confirm their arrival in Ankara on such and such day, and in Istanbul soon after. The Chairman, they explained, wanted to meet with Taylor, a proposal that sent Phil flying into Priscilla's office to protest. But there was nothing he could do. Without Taylor, Zimmerman lacked an airtight justification to visit Turkey's most fascinating city. Clearly, he'd learned his lesson the year before, when Al Kamen of the Washington Post had snickered at his eighteen-day junket to Indonesia, Australia, and Tahiti. *That dirtbag Kamen*, Zimmerman reportedly fumed. *He always exaggerates. The talks with the*

Indonesians were damn useful, and let me tell you Jakarta's no Las Vegas.

It wasn't going to happen again. Taylor was one of his constituents, by God, rotting in a Turkish prison for a crime he probably didn't commit. I'll be damned, Zimmerman told the press, if I'll sit still while one of our own goes through that kind of hell. Anybody here see *Midnight Express*?

Later, Zimmerman's office would do a press release clarifying the Chairman's position on U.S.-Turkish relations. *We fully support Turkey's legitimate defense needs, and urge the administration's strong support for all pending arms transfers.*

Zimmerman's visit was now less than two weeks away. Truman was named control officer, while Dawn was given responsibility for the control room, the hotel's nerve center that would provide support to the delegation, as needed, or more likely as not needed, twenty-four hours a day. George was assigned to do baggage—the shittiest of jobs; it felt like a demotion.

As it turned out, the Honorable Art Zimmerman would never see a Turkish prison, because his constituent would get there first. At the baggage claim, surrounded by gasterbeiter on a Friday afternoon, Cedrick Moore was met by Phil and three glum Turks who whisked him through customs and across the city without so much as a bathroom break. The problem of his son's detention was solved by the spooks before the weekend was over. No courts, no interrogations, just splendid U.S.-Turkish cooperation and an awkward hug from father to son before the group made its way back to the airport in a consulate vehicle, flanked by unmarked Turkish cars. Had Taylor been wearing handcuffs, they would have come off to avoid upsetting the airlines, who otherwise saw him as just another seedy backpacker, exhausted and unshaven and heading home with Dad. Taylor presented his boarding pass with a dazed look and was gone. Istanbul, Athens, JFK. The flight left on time.

The Turks were pleased to see him go.

Phil stood on the runway and studied the sky, until it was empty of Taylor and his father, long after the roars of the engine were gone. What kept him standing there was anxiety, or something closer to propriety; a gnawing concern that he had let something come undone, like a parent with kids home watching videos who suddenly remembers with horror the one in the back, the one his wife begged him to destroy. Yes indeed, that's what he should have done.

George was on the phone with Truman. "Well, yeah, of course. Control ought to be the political officer. It's your job. I don't know why she promised it to me in the first place..."

"Baggage is important," said Truman, with a surprising lack of irony. "It takes a lot of organization."

"Yeah, but... Baggage!"

"God help you if anything goes wrong. It is important." He laughed. "You know what I'm doing now? The ambassador has decided the delegation should attend a black tie event that's happening on the Savarona. One of the most exclusive events of the season, and I'm supposed to come up with two-dozen free tickets. Hell, you know the congressmen won't pay. Let me tell you, if I succeed, at least one of those tickets is going to be mine. Black tie! Can you believe it? They're planning to take the boat out onto the water—not just leave it parked at the dock like they usually do."

Built in 1931, the Savarona was Turkey's most famous yacht. It was the size of a cruise ship, yet designed to sail with only thirty-four passengers in seventeen sumptuous suites. The rest of the ship was a discotheque, a conference room, and a Turkish bath built with sixty tons of hand-finished marble. Originally owned by the granddaughter of the engineer who built the Brooklyn Bridge, it was very nearly purchased by Hitler, but he withdrew his bid when he learned that Atatürk wanted the ship—perhaps hoping that Turkey might still join the war on Germany's side. In any event, the Father of the Turks enjoyed it for only a few months before moving his deathbed to Dolmabace Palace. Decades later, the yacht was leased to a private company and henceforth rented out for tidy sums—currently thirty-five thousand dollars a day.

"Priscilla knows I'm the only one in this consulate who has the contacts to come up with these tickets," said Truman. George nodded, imagining a room full of gays with telephones ringing, gathering intel on events around town.

When the phone rang again, it was a young-sounding intern in Zimmerman's office. She began to read. "The best Byzantine mosaics to be seen this side of Ravenna, and in fact some of the best mosaics in the world, are in the Kariye Museum, once a mosque, but originally built as the Church of the Holy Savior in Chora, out near the city walls. The church, like Sancta Sophia, dates from the time of Justinian..."

"Where are you getting that?"

"Frommer's. But it's a few years old. It may be out of date."

"As long as it was published after 1321," said George.

"So we could do that on Saturday, right after the Bazaar."

"Yes, but wasn't the refugee camp on Saturday morning?"

"No, that's been canceled. Do you know that's three hours out of town?"

"Um, yes, I do." The camp was near the border with Bulgaria; George had been there to see the Bosnians, to chronicle their tales of murder, rape, and torture. Never had he been so depressed. Now the Bosnians were gone, replaced by Kosovars with the same sad stories. The Grand Bazaar was undeniably more upbeat.

"Can you give me, like, an update on this Taylor Moore person?"

"He's gone," said George, too distracted to see Nazan enter the waiting room. A thin young man with an unhealthy pallor followed her halfway in, then with a nod withdrew to the visa queue. Nazan tugged at her black skirt, bringing it back to knee-length, then adjusted her wool sweater, which was tight enough to draw an outline of her small but upright breasts. She was attractive without being pretty and had a scent, a residue, that both attracted and repelled—a blend of shame, pleasure, and disgust.

George watched her take a seat next to one of his American citizen charity cases.

George was on the telephone as I took a seat in the waiting room to wait for my cash. My eyes scanned beyond the bulletproof glass, but as usual only Zeynep met my eyes, giving me one of her motherly winks before resuming her work. She was so studious, so officious. I made a note in my pad to that effect, then described the rest of the room: paint peeling on the walls; four ugly government-issued waiting room chairs; a map of Anatolia pulled from someone's subscription to *National Geographic*, the eastern half colored red; a plain table strewn with information on taxes and customs and how to take your dog to America.

I read my two pages of notes, then, disgusted, tore them up. Somewhere in the background I heard the buzzing of flies—louder, I noticed, with each passing day.

When my head cleared, I saw that a young woman had placed herself in the seat next to mine. She wore a short black skirt and a tight wool sweater that worked rather well as a topographical map.

I had been a long time on the road. I watched as the young woman combed her fingers through her hair. I imagined they were mine.

After a while she tired of my stare. "Hello," she said. Her tone was not what I would call friendly.

"Looks like we're waiting for the same person."

"Oh," she nodded. "Well. You were here first so..."

"A Turk who believes in lines! Now I've seen it all." Did I say that aloud?

I flushed as she said something in return, the words drowned out by the blood rushing to my ears. No matter, the accent alone was worth savoring. How I loved that high-falluting British way of talking and quickly told her so. By way of reply she forced a smile, an act that seemed to require all the strength she had to shift the requisite muscles into place. No, no, don't get up!

"Perhaps we could have dinner?" I said. No, too soon! Too soon!

Now she smiled with less effort. "Who are you?"

George answered for me. "Mister Bigelow," he said from behind the bulletproof glass. "I could be about twenty minutes. Do you want to have a chi and come back in a little while?"

"Thank you, George. If it's all the same to you, I'll wait." I watched him cringe.

Nazan carried her smile, unbroken, to the window; perhaps it would have been difficult to reconstruct it from scratch. "I haven't heard from you," she said.

"Nor I from you." *Nor I from you?* George's left eye ticked, and I saw that he regretted the pretentious turn-of-phrase as much as the implication that he'd missed her. This had started badly. He didn't want to play games; or did he?

"You're the consul, you're very, *very* busy. I'm sorry, I shouldn't have..."

"No, please, don't apologize."

"But when we had dinner a fortnight ago, chok hosh! And what you told me..."

Having run with the bulls in Pamplona and crossed streets in Cairo, I knew well what panic looked like. Eyes wide, George tensed to hear what would come next, like a man who has stupidly run a knife through his finger, and in that split second of clarity anticipates the pain to come.

"I..." He glanced my way, and I winked supportively.

"Well. It's not *really* important," she said.

There was a long pause, which Zeynep stepped in to fill. "Excuse me, miss." Her tone was cold. "George, there are too many notarials to be signing. And have you forgotten you are having a three o'clock appointment..."

"I haven't forgotten," said George.

"And I don't want to kill a dead horse, but after two hours you should call your wife. Remember you asked me..."

I saw his look of shock, but I was paying more attention to Nazan, who swallowed the revelation as gracefully as the circumstances allowed. Did she know? Judging from her reaction, I believe that she did. For her expression didn't change. Only her eyes blinked a little faster than they had before, then slowly lost their focus.

"Thank you, that's fine," he snapped. But Zeynep was already gone, mission accomplished.

When Nazan finally spoke, her tone was upbeat. "Well. I should go to my friend. He is here again for the visa, and is probably wondering why I've gone missing. And if he is unsuccessful *again*, and he is always unsuccessful, canim, dear, then he is going to want my shoulder to cry on..." Here she stopped, her gaze resting a moment too long on the bulletproof glass between them, the glass that prevented touch unless she gambled and slid her fingers through the slot where the passports went. George had seen visa applicants wrestle with this decision a hundred times. When the fingers came through they were at your mercy: You could grab them and twist them or stab them with a pen or crush them with one of the heavy staplers if you wanted to. Or in this case, you could simply not touch them.

She never gave him that chance. With a casual hoscha kal, she left.

* * *

The story is told of a journalist who comes upon a small village in Bosnia-Herzegovina and finds it utterly destroyed; smoke rises from the ashes of the rubble and fresh graves litter the square. "What happened here?" he asks an old Serb, strolling amid the ruins.

"In 1384 the Turks came," he replies. "Our men fought heroically but they were outnumbered ten to one. In the end, they slaughtered even the women and children."

""No, I mean…"

"In1878 it was the Austrians. They said they were here to liberate us from the Turks. But then their army stayed and took what they wished."

"No, I mean…"

"In1940 it was the Germans' turn. They came in tanks and reduced our village to stones. Then they stole our food and left us to starve through the long, cold winter."

"No, no," he interrupts. "I mean, what happened here yesterday?"

Listen up. Early this century, something happened to the Armenians—exactly what, I don't know. Maybe a million and a half were shot, hacked, raped, or bludgeoned to death. Or maybe just a half million perished, from occasional massacres or from long walks in the cold. A half million? A million and a half? I suspect it only matters if you weren't one of them.

But there in Beyoğlu, in my little hotel room a hundred meters from the consulate, the numbers meant a lot. Sprawled on my bed in a neon halo, I wrote as if I'd seen my own mother violated before my eyes, dismembered, and fed to the Kurds in bloody chunks. Page after page, I argued that the Turkish propaganda machine had blinded the world to the truth. In time, I would know better: What propaganda machine? When God handed out public relations genes, the Turks must have been off eating köfte. For what is their image abroad if not dead Armenians, tortured Kurds, or how the Greeks hate them so. What is their archetype if not *Midnight Express*?

The only Turk to appear on M*A*S*H was a thug who barked unintelligibly and menaced Hawkeye with a meat cleaver. Was that a fair portrayal?

First Lieutenant Frank "Blister" Bigelow, my father, who saw that war first-hand, had his own story about the Turks, which went something like this: The UN forces had formed a cordon to prevent the enemy from slipping south at night to sabotage their supply lines. The Chinese wanted to do just that, so sent a group of soldiers through the Turkish sector, anticipating that these third-world soldiers would be the weakest link. Unfortunately for the Chinese, they did not account for Turkish pride. The infiltrators were captured and, with the exception of a single soldier who was tied up and made to watch, sliced into small pieces. The survivor was then allowed to report back to base. Not surprisingly, the Chinese chose a different route the next time.

To this day, I can't help but smile when I tell this story, nor could my father before me. And this makes me wonder: Who are the bloodthirsty ones—them or us?

In the alley beneath my window, the shop owners talked up a storm and played tavla and hosed down their storefronts for the umpteenth time, sending mud next door only to have the favor returned with the next blast of water. I moved my table away from the window and there resumed my work. In long fits of held breath, I wrote of Turkish sadism and Armenian suffering and the injustices of the world as if I'd lanced a boil that needed draining. But the effect wasn't cleansing; the anger, the horror, the indignation washed over me and with every page I felt dirtier, more depressed, more filled with shame and self-loathing as I re-read the pages and tucked them beneath my mattress with the hope that tough editing would someday set them right, knowing well that it might not.

But of course there was no question of stopping, not when the words in my mind kept raining down like tetris blocks, descending from an inverted hell. I had no choice but to catch and make sense of them, to fit them snugly together and ward off the chaos.

I guess you could say I was feeling depressed.

To lift my spirits I took the bundle of words, which I called Chapter Three, to the posh Marmara Hotel. In the air conditioned business center I faxed them to the *New York Times*, the *L.A. Times*, the *Detroit Free Press*, the *Chicago Sun-Times*, *The Atlantic*, *USA Today*, the *Cleveland Plain Dealer*, the *Milwaukee Journal*, *Newsweek*, *Time*, the *Economist*, the *Chicago Tribune*, the *Milwaukee Journal-Sentinel*, the *San Francisco Chronicle*, the *Village Voice*, the *Boston Herald*, *Newsday*, *Entertainment Weekly*, the

Boston Globe, *Mirabela*, and the *Philadelphia Inquirer*. Then I went back to my room to catch and arrange more falling words.

In the days that followed, my naps grew shorter until they vanished altogether and it was not so easy to distinguish sleep from wakefulness, dream from reality, and the completed pages before me looked the same either way. More than once I woke to find that my narrative had veered off course, that my pen hadn't kept up with my thoughts, and so I took to plotting future projects, things I would write about next, and then after that. These included the miracle of flight, the miracle of the Virgin Mary statue in New Jersey that shed real tears, the number of Turkish gas stations in Trenton, the general economic fortunes of immigrants in general, General McArthur, McCarthyism, Paul McCartney, Pope John Paul, and Pious the Twelfth. The list went on and on.

In the hours that I felt good I still felt very, very good. I was one with everyone and everything around me, selling kebab off the spit, or moaning in Russian, my legs spread wide, or begging in rags at Taksim Square, high on glue. On those days I would walk around for hours on end with that wonderful feeling, entering and leaving the lives of the people I saw, like a ghost, none of them the wiser, just like I had in Budapest during that brilliant summer so long ago.

Pitter patter
Flitter flatter
Wop de who de who
I am magic
Life is tragic
Who the hell are you?

And then, without warning, the tide would reverse, and I would lie in bed and count to sixty and watch the shutter flip on the digital clock, then start over, never missing a second, so that I accounted for every minute, every hour of this long, tedious life. And as I stared at the clock, I would pray for a shutter to fall across my consciousness, to separate this day from the next, for my life had been reduced to a single day of infinite scope, sometimes light and sometimes dark, but always the same day nonetheless. And in such circumstances, what was the point of washing my hair, or brushing my teeth, or changing my clothes? The thought of doing anything, when I would only have to do it again later, exhausted me.

This was my state of mind when I heard a knock on my door and opened it to find Nazan and Vram standing there. A real woman, and a real Armenian—it seemed too good to be true. As I stood there slack-jawed, Nazan took a look at my room and said, "Let's go somewhere for tea, shall we."

I suggested a bar nearby, where the waiter brought us chi in coffee cups. When we had sipped for a while, I let Vram show me his passport. The last page had an "APPLICATION RECEIVED" stamp, and there were three dates to match the number of times he'd tried and failed to get a visa. I smiled. The most recent was today's. At that moment, I knew we would become fast friends.

"How did you find me here?" I asked.

"Why, you're at the consulate nearly every day," said Nazan. "I hope it doesn't trouble you that we followed you home." She smiled meekly, as if by way of apology. Then she went outside and hailed a cab.

We sat in the back seat, our scents mingling; for the first time in weeks I regretted not bathing. Vram still hadn't said a word. "Do you want to know where we're going?" she asked.

I forced a nod, but in truth I didn't care. It was enough to be surrounded by flesh and blood, in a more or less comfortable space. I watched the wiper blades go left, right, left, right. This was no rain; it was a downpour, a deluge, a terrible torrent that held the driver in its grip, hunched forward in his seat. When I was seventeen and stoned, my friends would make me pull over if I failed to keep my back against the cushion. But these were different times. I inched my legs apart and felt the warmth on both sides and listened to the frictionless swish of the wiper blades. A burst of light brought the faces of my friends into sharp relief, then all was dark again.

Nazan paid the taxi driver when he dropped us in a place called Shishli. Soon a small and airless elevator strained beneath our weight. Three floors up the noise was gone. Now we could hear the water on the stove before it boiled. When we were seated, the water was poured into cups by Vram's sisters who then retreated to the kitchen. I looked around and saw shelves littered with crucifixes, an extraordinary number, reaching their zenith on a homemade shrine by the color TV. There were brass candlesticks and incense burners, mirrors and figurines. At the center was an icon of the Virgin Mary, and at the fringes little doilies and other crap. There were framed photographs too; one of these caught my eye—a ruined church on a dramatic landscape that looked like the end of the world.

"That's Ani," said Nazan. "The lost kingdom of the Armenians. There is gold there, buried by the families who fled. It would be chok hosh if you could bring an American metal finding machine. We could take you there. The Turkish machines are only good at finding silver."

"Who's the photographer?"

"Vram's Uncle Hikmet. He is very professional."

This was confirmed by a small, crooked man whose grand entry to the room brought Nazan to her feet. It was Vram's father. He eyed me suspiciously, then motioned us back to our seats where we resumed sipping chi. "Yes," said Nazan, interpreting for the old man as seamlessly as if she were his aide de camp. "My younger brother, Hikmet, is the artist of the family. He is our photographer, our painter, our writer, our little capitalist. He has many talents."

"A Renaissance man," I offered, forgetting that the Turks had missed out on this rather key chapter of human history.

The old man barely looked up. Instead, he studied his hands as he spoke, as if their very existence amazed him. He talked about Hikmet some more, then turned to other members of the family. It was a monologue that foresaw no end. Nazan maintained her interpretation, as if this had been her role all along, her raison d'etre. I let the words wash over me, a balm for my muddled brain. In time our chi cups turned empty, prompting Vram to check his watch. The females of the house stirred from the shadows and switched us to coffee, as black and oily as the Bosphorous.

I ran my tongue across my teeth to wipe away the grit, and tried to remember why I was here. I could think of no good reason. Still, it was easier to stay than to leave.

Vram's father went on, and what he had to say was this: Vram's mother had died some years ago, God rest her soul, leaving him to raise two girls on his own. And what good was a father to girls? Hikmet was no help at all, off in America with no family of his own, a *bachelor*, said Nazan, unwittingly employing the twenty-first century word for *gay*. And the boys were no easier, with the exception of Vram, who had stayed close to home as he was supposed to, keeping up the family business.

Now Vram spoke up for the first time, in broken English. "He says I am similar as him. We only think business. Not crazy dreams and adventures. I and him are the responsible peoples. Couches and practical."

"Cautious," Nazan corrected him.

It was quite the opposite with Vram's older brother. "Rabo," said Nazan, continuing her interpretation, "was his mother's son, may God watch after her. Wild and impulsive, but so full of life. He was always in trouble. Once, late at night, when he was only fourteen, he went into the mosque and replaced the call to prayer with his own music cassette... No, no, the call to prayer is not a real muezzin anymore. It is just a recording... And in the morning, that is what was heard by the gericiler, the backward ones—rock music instead of the call to prayer." At this the old man laughed sharply, then seemed to catch himself. "But of course that caused a disturbance. We were all worried when the Imam brought a crowd and then someone was cut with a knife." The old man brought his fist to his stomach and clenched it with a tremor. "And so of course the polis came, and were very cross, and went to all the houses in the neighborhood, but especially the Hristyan ones..."

"*Do you remember? Do you remember how frightened we were*?" He glared at Vram, who smiled weakly. "*And you said we should all hide in the church*?"

Nazan lowered her voice as she continued her interpretation. "The only one who was not frightened was Rabo. When the polis came to our house, Rabo went to the door and opened it himself and spoke to the polis for all of us... Only fourteen! And he said..." Vram's father slowed to recall the exact words. "The person you are looking for is a defender of Atatürk fighting against Shariah, Islamic law. Tell the Imam to lock himself in his mosque if he wants to be safe."

With a look bordering on reverie, the old man sighed. He was smiling, but there was dew in his eyes. I chose the moment to give up my coffee cup, while Vram wandered off to relieve himself.

"Imagine," said the old man, with Nazan's assistance. "My son, Rabo, the defender of Atatürk." He sighed again. "And they believed him!"

"How did he wind up in prison?" I asked, rudely jumping ahead in the story—past Rabo's childhood pranks, his vandalizing of government buildings, the anarchist tracts that were found in his room. Even past his decision to forego the family business and join the Armenian terrorist group, Asala, where he was assigned to make bombs from coke cans and fertilizer.

The old man recounted these facts now. Rabo's destiny, it seemed, was to plant a bomb beneath a silver-gray Mercedes belonging to the Turkish consul in Frankfurt. But the car pulled forward when it should have pulled back, and the only ones who got hurt were Rabo and his comrades when the police caught up with them. In the safehouse they found handguns and enough fertilizer to re-plant Frankfurt's zoologischel garten. Rabo was sentenced to a minimum of six years in prison, two years more than his co-conspirators, for refusing to disclose the identity of his contact at the next highest level. This was where he remained today.

So Vram's brother, Rabo, was a terrorist? Now this was interesting, but when I asked for more, Vram's father turned away. Nazan, in good interpreter's fashion, did the same. I felt a flash of annoyance and put my hands to me head. My thoughts were noisy.

Vram came back to the room, carrying a pile of paper in both hands. When he handed them to me, I recognized an affidavit of support from Uncle Hikmet. Despite his protests, I crumpled it up. "A dead giveaway," I said.

"False documents and lies. Why not simply tell the truth?" said Nazan, so adept in her role that I nearly forgot it was the old man talking. Vram reminded me by rebuking his father in Armenian, Turkish or, for all I knew, Gaelic. "*Do you think Rabo told the truth when he applied for his German visa*?" is what he might have said—or perhaps not. It's what *I* would have said.

Poor Vram, stuck without a visa in a country where he could be rich, perhaps, but never respected. A country where the biggest taxpayer was said to be an Armenian madam who owned the brothels in giraffe alley, so called because passersby had to strain their necks above the window sills to check out the merchandise. A country where the officials who collected her taxes had to be Muslims, not by law but by practice, which was all that mattered.

Nazan sat next to Vram, so close their knees almost touched. She caressed his arms like a worried mother.

Were these thoughts worth adding to the chapter I'd sent off last week? I supposed they were, but then I was off again on other thoughts, too many thoughts to be contained on this page, or on any number of pages. How frustrating to know that before I could write my thoughts down I would be on to the next thought, and the next one after that, so that none would add up in the end. I consoled myself with the thought that this was the mark of true, unfettered creativity, but then that thought too was gone before I could seal it in that cranial vault where three unfinished novels were already stored, and where a miniature rock opera played ceaselessly at full volume.

"May I use your telephone?"

After recruiting Nazan to share with me the receiver, I dialed the Marmara Hotel. "The hotel clerk says there has been nothing for you since you rang yesterday," Nazan interpreted. "But he must advise you again regarding your docket."

"Aha!" So my credit was out at the Marmara. I turned to Vram's father. "Do you have scotch?" Then I sat heavily in a seat of my choosing. I felt my face tick, and hid it by surveying the room yet again. The crucifixes sparkled like prizes from a cereal box; if I slipped one into my pocket it might fetch a nice price. Vram's sister brought a glass of milk-white raki; I drained it with a swallow and sent her off for more. Oh, why did they stare at me so? Fuck it! With drink in hand I glared back at Nazan, forcing her to look away. Choking down my second raki, I mentally undressed her, stood her up, and bent her over the armrest. That's where she remained for a long while, until Vram took my hints and invited me for dinner. I accepted, then we settled down to work.

Vram located his form OF-156, and I helped him fill in the blanks. *No, scratch that out. You have no uncle Hikmet in California. And you're going to need a new passport, since yours is full of refusal stamps.*

"I will tell you about our family," said Nazan, renewing her interpretation for the old man. Vram's father sidled up beside me, sharing a space too small for one. He placed a withered hand on my arm. "When my father was half your age he lived in Harput. His father owned three hundred sheep, which he paid the Kurds to graze. My grandmother was the only literate person in the village; she spoke French, and owned a hundred books. Her husband, my grandfather, could not read, but was still a great man, a leader, rich from trading with the Russians. He ate his meals with the mukhtar, the village head, who would come to his home once each week, knock three times, and let himself in, saying, 'It's only me.'"

"Come," said the old man, rising from his seat. Nazan made to follow, but the old man waved her off, beckoning me instead. I drained my raki and walked with him in silence. Behind us I could hear Vram mutter.

Rabo's room seemed not to have been touched in many years. There was dust on the bedspread, and a young man's clothes in the closet. There were more of Uncle Hikmet's photos on the wall, and a map of Turkey that started the old man talking. "Ermenya," he crowed, drawing his finger over a portion of the map crayoned in red. He opened a drawer and began pulling out books, tossing them one by one on the bed. When he had finished emptying the drawer he cursed and, with a flourish, knocked the books to the floor. With mounting vigor, he dove into the closet, discarding more books. I got into the spirit too, ripping open a drawer and studying its contents—mostly socks and underwear. I left them there and joined the old man in the closet, combing the top shelf which was out of his reach, finding more dusty books, old shoes, a nifty hat, parts of a transistor radio and an old wooden box laced with mother-of-pearl; the lock was easy to pick. The old man froze when I took out the gun. It was a tiny thing, a Turkish Saturday Night Special, or so I figured, never having seen one up close. When Nazan and Vram appeared at the door; the old man shouted them away, then turned to me and grabbed at the box. I clamped it shut and put it back on the shelf. This I insisted on doing, though he probably could have done it himself—for in the moment that his back was turned I had lightened the load considerably.

Would anyone notice the lump of steel in my pants?

At last the old man found what he was looking for—a weathered old textbook adorned with black and white photos. Wasn't that Woodrow Wilson, the spectacled one among the old-fashioned gents with top hats and handlebar mustaches? I smiled pleasantly, causing the old man to redden; angrily, he slammed the book shut and showed his brown teeth; his breath smelled of aniseed. When he called Nazan's name, she returned at a fast clip.

"President Wilson promised the Armenian people that they would have their own nation," she explained, evidently familiar with the old man's shtick.

The old man went on. "One day my father returned from school to find my grandmother crying. The mukhtar had been to the house, the same man who had taken dinner in our home for ten years. But on this night, instead of knocking three times and announcing 'It's only me,' he let himself in quietly. My grandmother, who had known this night would come, threw herself at the mukhtar, scratching at his eyes until the jandarma saved him. The men took her and passed through her honor. Then they took my grandfather away. The barbarians! Later, there would be more killings, many more; the Turkish soldiers threw babies in the air and caught them on spears. They swung them by the legs and crushed their heads together. I am alive today only because my father ran away and escaped to the city."

At that he was quiet. My mood blackened as the raki turned to poison in my veins.

Back in the living room, Vram smiled wryly. "You like the stories? Oh, as a child the night terrors I have." He sought help from Nazan. "Has he been telling you about his grandfather in Harput? The one who sold guns to the Russians and was thus sent to prison, leaving his family alone? The shame of his confinement was so great that she left Harput, and came to the city, to Istanbul. There was no rape. She had a child outside of marriage—my father's father. So, you see, the seeds of destruction were planted by our own dishonor. When my father's father was released from prison, he never went home. Instead he went to Trabzon and drank until his liver was gone. He died in the street like a dog. Yes, he was killed by the Turks—by those who distilled his raki."

The old man stared at the floor as Nazan completed her interpretation. For a moment it seemed he would fly into a rage, but he only sat down heavily and started picking the skin on his hands. He looked tired, but his eyes burned. Vram looked away; he shuffled his feet and stuck his hands in his pockets.

I stared out the window, forgot for a moment what the point was, indeed if there was any point at all.

With a flash of lightning the window became a mirror and I glimpsed myself before I disappeared.

Through Nazan, the old man spoke again. "In a very narrow sense my son is right," he said. "But I know this is true: If we had stayed in Anatolia we would have been massacred with the rest, because we are Armenian and the Turks are butchers. Yes, yes, my son is correct… literally. But politically…" he shook his head. "He is a liar."

PART THREE

Good and bad, I defined these words
quite clear, no doubt, somehow.
Ah, but I was so much older then.
I'm younger than that now.

—*Bob Dylan*

* * *

Red Halabja is back.

He cuts through an alley one half mile from Sağmacilar Prison, too close for comfort in his view. He stops and eyes a street sign, the first he's seen for nearly ten minutes, and breathes a sigh of relief; a wrong turn could spell disaster. It is not yet five-thirty in the morning, a stupid time for him to be wandering these streets. He searches his jacket for warmth, finds none; steam pours from his lungs. His right hand is cold from the plastic bag he carries; he switches hands, shoves the cold one into his pocket and walks on. A ragged dog steps from a doorway, stretches lazily and watches him come; Red hesitates, then passes him by.

Why meet at this time? A few hours later the neighborhood would be teeming with life. Without the crowd he is absurdly conspicuous, all alone in the street, pale and freckled and glittering in the first light of dawn. At least his hair is no longer red, not since he colored it with the dye he stole from the barber shop back in Komotini; his scalp itches unpleasantly. Zakho would never have made an arrangement like this. No, don't think that way. Zakho is gone; he can't be replaced. Is that what he's trying to do?

He considers the possibility of a set-up. But that's no way to think either; life in the movement requires trust—trust that's absolute. His instructions are all he has; ignore them and he might as well turn around and head back to Greece. He imagines crossing the Evros again. Never. The icy water had squeezed his chest like a vice, had left him gasping and shivering on the eastern bank, unable to move. When at last he'd regained control and slipped into dry clothes, a freak thunderstorm had come from nowhere, soaking him to the bone again. How the lightning made the shadows dance! The landscape mocked him; every tree was a Turkish soldier, every mound of dirt a Turkish mine.

Lost and alone on the border. It was the first time he could remember feeling real fear. Killing the drunk Australian, even getting arrested and contemplating torture, had been easy by comparison, maybe because, on the Greek-Turkish frontier, between east and west, he had found himself truly alone.

Yes, truly alone—alone and doubting himself, questioning things.

Twelve-forty-three Ülkücülük drive. They'd told him to commit the address to memory, don't write it down, but of course he'd been too anxious. Turkish words were tricky. He glances at the note, then, like a character in a cheap spy thriller, sticks it in his mouth and chews. The house rises before him, a three-story wooden structure with a flower-less balcony; the place looks on the verge of collapse. Upstairs a light shines dimly. Red knocks on the door.

"Efendim?"

"Allah Kavushtursun," says Red Halabja, taking care to pronounce the words correctly. May God reunite you.

"Efendim?"

This is not the expected reply. He wonders if he's at the wrong house, but remains at the door for what seems an eternity, uncertain whether to knock again. He feels a nervous ache in his bladder, and regrets not having stopped to relieve himself. Suddenly the door opens. He starts to speak, but they are not interested in hearing, only in searching; he is manhandled, up and down, in the darkness. Then he is brought, blind and stumbling, up a long flight of steps where at last he squints from the light.

"Hosh geldiniz, efendim," says a dark, baby-faced man, so short he is almost a dwarf. You came pleasantly.

"Hosh bulduk," says Red. I found the coming pleasant.

"Please," says the man. "For you to sit."

A chair bumps against him from behind, absolving him of choice. He sits heavily, then makes to lean forward but instead finds himself flailing in reverse, all motion dictated by the searing pain in his neck, which disassembles the room. His tongue lashes out and his whole body retches; fingers, his, but with lives all their own, draw blood as they search for routes beneath the metal wire that staples him to the backrest. He feels his eyes bulge; there is no air to be found, not anywhere. Amid the frenzy a moment of clarity, a single thought; so this is how I die.

The wire falls loose. "Who your cell leader was?"

"I cannot say," he croaks. He has had nearly a minute to consider his answer, the length of time it has taken for air to re-enter his lungs.

"But you not."

"No, not me. Someone else."

"But you made contact."

Red nods. The question is not unexpected, but somehow his prepared answers are gone, exorcised by the wire dangling at his chest. In any guerrilla cell there is only one cadre authorized to contact the next highest level. Zakho broke that rule by sharing a cell phone number with Red, many months ago.

"I understand. It was a lapse of security, a foolish thing." He struggles to recount the events that led him here: the raid on the safehouse, the death of his friends, his interrogation by MIT and the CIA, expulsion from Turkey, escape from his father, and his journey to rejoin the movement.

Gone was any notion of trying to explain his long association with Tim, his recruitment as an agent, the attendant payoffs in cash. Of course he had nothing to be ashamed of; his career as a CIA informant was by order of the PKK—an instruction handed down from above. In all respects, the operation was a success; he had given Tim a wealth of information—all of it false. "Noise" was what they called it. In return, he'd gotten a glimpse of the Agency's techniques. By the time Tim had grown wise to his game, Red had cut off all contact.

But how to explain this now? Of course it couldn't be done, not without someone to back him up. And so he only says, "I told my captors nothing. I did not put the movement in danger."

"Every person says some things when he is under torture."

"But I was not tortured." He all but spits out the words, such is the shame. "Because I'm an American. They thought they could make me go away quietly." He gasps for air and pulls himself up. "But they could not. They underestimated me."

"We have many time to discuss what was you said to CIA. Many, many time to talk. But now let me tell you the true. I do not want your being here. What does a foreigner, a yabanci, understand about our struggle? Only enough to put us in danger." He glances at the young men standing at the window; their eyes don't leave the street. His face comes closer. "But our commanders think you have something is important." He throws his chin back and clicks his tongue loudly. "And I am unlucky only one to be knowing English. So you are my problem. These are my orders. I will obey. And also you will." With a wave of his hand the wire is gone.

Red slumps in his seat and breathes deeply.

"Show me in your bag."

Red empties it on the table; there are diagrams of apartments where diplomats live, schedules of visitors and events, invitations to various receptions, even a slew of U.S. government documents—the sum of their cache at Sirkeci Station, which he'd retrieved at considerable risk the day before. With the key lost in the raid, he'd had to pry the locker open with a screwdriver in broad daylight. He had expected the CIA to be there waiting for him, but had risked it anyway. It was worth it; without the documents, what use was he to the movement?

The Kurd with the metal wire hovers dumbly at the table; his hands are grotesquely large and matted with hair; the tool makes an awful sound on the floor, like nails on a blackboard. The eyes of the little man widen as he reads; Red feels his confidence return.

"Look here," he says. "See how the road narrows? He walks by each morning at five after eight. The only problem is how to manage the escape." He takes his hand from his throat, which is moist with blood. "Or, here. This diplomat's apartment backs into a hillside where there is only a cemetery; this is out of the vision of the guards, who are around the front and do nothing but play tavla. Or, if you prefer, there's this one. When she visits her friend she parks her car in the alley; nobody would see us plant a bomb..."

The little man nods. "Yes, yes, if we want to kill just one, but better to kill many... Galip!" The gorilla comes running, then is dispatched to the kitchen and returns with a tray of bread and olives. "I was knowing Zakho from Boğazici—Tabii, I was there. Zakho was good fighter."

Red is relieved that he can call him by name. "Zakho was my friend."

The little man doesn't bother to look up. "Salaklik. You are fool." But he says it with no more malice than if he were commenting on the weather.

Red looks away. For now, it's enough that the little man likes the papers spread on the table. But what a man! With his stunted torso, his oversized head, he resembles a troll, an ugly elf. Is this what second-cousin marriages produce? But no, that might doom half of Turkey to this horrid fate.

What a contrast with Zakho, so taut and lean and light on his feet, his face plucked from a Gucci ad. Red scolds himself; how superficial can he be?

"This is all very excellent," the Mongoloid nods. "Chok güzel."

Emboldened, Red takes a piece of dry bread and chews it slowly. He regards the room with more than a little self-interest—my new home. There are mattresses on the floor, with paper-thin blankets and no sheets.

The only furniture is a card table and some folding chairs, the only light a single bare bulb that swings gently in the draft. Air seems to flow from all directions; the floor is bare wood; paint peels from the walls. There is a coal-burning stove in the corner that gives off equal shares of heat and dust; Red feels no urge to remove his coat.

"Taurus and Zagros; do you know what happened to them?" he asks. After the raid in Fatih, Red had seen the police drag Zakho's lifeless body away, but the fate of his other comrades had been less clear.

"Captured dead."

Red nods without emotion. There really had been no need to ask. Perhaps it was for the best. If captured alive, they surely would have died under torture. They were not American like him. Again, he feels the shame.

"I am Gazi," says the little man, scooting his chair so close that their knees almost touch. "I am sorry for your neck. Before I not..." He jerks his chin with disgust. "But now, you know, everything is change." He grabs a chunk of bread and presses it into his hand. "It is pain?"

"Yes."

"Good to eat. We will make action soon, of our choice. I was sorry you are with us, but now..." He gestures at the papers. "My mind is change. Before they arrest Apo, we waited all of time for orders. Now there is no command. Not any orders now. Only we are in command. We decide to make action, or not to make action. We choose. Better like this, değil mi? Always I hated the waiting for orders. It is hardest thing."

Red lets the confusion show on his face. What about Apo? He has the sense he's entered a conversation in mid-stream.

"Before they say kill only soldiers, only agents of state. Now no more rules. This is good. We can make a war on tourists too. We decide. Did you see in Nederland today? We captured the Greek ambassador. We will not shoot him, of course. Today is to protest for Apo, but tomorrow the struggle..." He stares with hunger at the table.

Forgetting his fear, Red crosses the room and pulls a newspaper from atop a stack in the corner. There, on the front page, and on the second, third and fourth, are pictures of Apo looking haggard, shell-shocked, possibly drugged. He is harnessed to a seat amid black-hooded men; tape covers his mouth. On the next page is a close-up; tape pinches his skin; he is in pain. Now he is standing before the Turkish flag, a police line-up; for the first time in history, there is fear in his eyes.

Red, still reading, drifts to the window. The morning sun, weak though it is, still hurts his eyes.

"How did you not..." Gazi looks puzzled. "Ah, but you have been running..." He gets up and starts pacing. Angrily, he recounts Apo's flight to Athens, how the Greeks refused him asylum and forced him to Kenya instead. There, the Greek ambassador gave him sanctuary, but soon lost his nerve and allowed Apo to fall into the hands of the CIA. Now Apo is on Imrali, a Turkish Island prison built for one. He is unable to give orders, even through his lawyers. What will happen to him there? The genocidal government will torture him, of course. And then he will be killed.

"The CIA?"

"Turkey can not do such things by himself. Of course it was..." he pauses before saying the words. "Your government."

Red struggles with the newspaper articles. It is slow going; the Turks care little for commas, and their sentences stretch entire paragraphs. No matter, the pictures tell the story. Apo, leader of the armed struggle, is in Turkish custody; it is a disaster for the movement. Red's fear turns to depression. He has no one to talk to. If Zakho were here they would talk long into the night; Zakho would get teary-eyed, as he did when the body of the Australian was discovered; only he had understood Red's disappointment. He was like that, as hardened as any guerrilla, yet soft and sensitive, like a brother. No, more like a sister.

Could it be that he was really gone? There had been no last words, just a gurgling cry from lips too bloody to work. In death, he'd released his bowels like everyone does; never mind Hollywood's dignified endings. Red plays the image in his head, Zakho sprawled wet on the floor, Zakho, who was never ashamed to play the saz loudly and terribly, who bounced soccer balls off cars in the faculty parking lot, who made love to a prostitute while Red watched from the bed, back before the movement governed their lives. Red gazes at the rows of apartment blocks, so cramped and colorless; there is no room here, nowhere to stretch out. This place is foreign, he thinks to himself, a foreign place. He feels an urge to go home.

Gazi sees Red's melancholy but misreads his mind; he stops pacing and returns to the table. "I am sorry to tell you about Apo..." He trails off, gestures at the notes and diagrams, forces a smile. "Gechmish olsun. May it pass. You are a part with us now."

Somehow Red doubts it. Exhausted, he collapses on a dirty mattress and sinks his face in his hands. In the dazed confusion of the weeks following Zakho's death, he has not even had the time to mourn his friend; now seems like the right time.

* * *

FROM: American Embassy Athens.
TO: The State Department and American Consulate General Istanbul. February 27.
SENSITIVE BUT UNCLASSIFIED.
SUBJECT: Disappearance of Amcit Taylor Moore.

On February 26, Amcit Cedrick Moore advised consular officer that his son, Amcit Taylor Moore, had disappeared from Athens International Airport. Mr. Moore and son had arrived from Istanbul on Olympic Airways Flight 412 earlier that same morning. They had been scheduled to board an onward flight to Paris en route JFK the same day.

The following account was provided to us by Mr. Cedrick Moore: Taylor had until recently been a student at Bosphorous University in Istanbul. After encountering unspecified legal problems, Taylor terminated his studies and departed Turkey accompanied by his father. Taylor left Turkey voluntarily, but after arriving in Athens, Taylor became agitated and indicated he wished to return to Istanbul. When Mr. Cedrick Moore disagreed, the two scuffled. Taylor stole his father's carry-on baggage, which included his father's passport and roughly USD 2,000 in cash and travelers checks. Mr. Cedrick Moore received minor injuries but did not require hospitalization. We are currently assisting him in applying for a new passport.

ConGen believes Taylor Moore has returned to Istanbul, or is currently en route there. At Mr. Moore's request, we have not alerted the Greek police. We believe ConGen Istanbul may be familiar with this case, and are forwarding this information for appropriate action. We have been contacted by the office of Representative Zimmerman with a request for information. As we anticipate further congressional inquiries, we would

APPRECIATE ANY INFORMATION CONGEN ISTANBUL CAN PROVIDE. ALTERNATIVELY, WE CAN FORWARD SUCH INQUIRES TO ISTANBUL, IF REQUESTED. THANK YOU FOR YOUR ASSISTANCE. —MICHAELS

George reads the cable with a grim smile. So Taylor gave them the slip. It serves them right, he thinks. God, if I could see Phil's face…

Or is he being petty? Phil has been a new man since Apo's capture: Pleasant, friendly, almost human. But he's not the only one; lately every spook in the building has walked with an extra spring in his step. Whatever role the Agency played, or didn't play, in catching Apo—and of course George knows nothing more than what he's read in the papers—there's no doubt the PKK has been dealt a historic blow. And whatever one's sympathy for the Kurds, it's good to see this cold-blooded killer finally behind bars.

George runs the cable through the photocopier and leaves it with Phil's secretary on the way out. The air looks toxic. He revs the engine. It has been an eventful day. Aside from the cable from Athens, there was a cable from Tel Aviv bringing rare good news on his household effects—the Israelis have released the cargo ship and now it's en route to Istanbul.

It might already be here, thinks George. Allowing for customs clearances and the necessary red tape, he could have his stereo, his television set, his sheets and towels, his bike, his books, his alarm clock and computer within the month!

There is another piece of correspondence in his briefcase, which he chose not to read at the office. The envelope bulges; it's a thick letter. When he gets to his apartment, he sets it on the table and turns on the air filters; the room rattles and hums. He opens the curtains to see the Bosphorous; a cruise ship makes its way north, a festival of lights; the evening is strangely clear. He procrastinates further, decides to read the letter over dinner. There is nothing in the refrigerator but mustard and ketchup and skinny plastic tubes of sweetened ice. He chooses lemon-lime and decides to order pizza, one of the advantages of living in Bebek. Holding the ice in his teeth he stands over the toilet and relieves himself, neglects to wash his hands, then returns to the kitchen and takes a bottle of raki from the cupboard. He is troubled to find it half-empty, just two days old. He squeezes the flavored ice into a government-owned glass, and adds the alcohol. It turns yellow-green and milky. He sips. Not bad.

What will Margaret say when he tells her about their stuff? His darkest fear is that she'll be ecstatic, but that nothing will change. He sighs, picks up the phone, and calls Truman instead.

"I have great news too," says his friend. "Timur got me twenty invitations to the Savarona event. Twenty. That covers all the congressmen and more."

"That is good news," George replies, though he couldn't care less.

"And, listen… Timur fixed it so that they can spend the night on his island. The Savarona's going to take them there! We'll check them out of the hotel before they go, so they'll have their baggage. And you know what that means."

"A logistical nightmare?"

"A baggage control officer! The ship can't sail without one."

George mulls this over. Would he need a tux if he's only handling luggage? That sort of thing wasn't reimbursable. At least he could enjoy the booze. "What are you doing tonight?" he asks.

"Timur's here. I'm going to thank him with dinner." Then, cupping the telephone, *No, no, this will be my treat. Uh uh.* A pause. "You want to come?"

"No, that's okay. I'm just going to… Get some work done." It's a lame thing to say, but Truman doesn't press the issue.

George holds the phone long after Truman has hung up, then slips a CD into the boom box borrowed from the Marine Gunny, a poor substitute for his own stereo lost at sea. The music seeps out, the most melancholy selection he could find.

Dear Georgie,

The letter is in an elegant cursive. Margaret has wonderful handwriting.

I'm sorry it's been so long since I've written. I don't blame you if you're furious with me. It's just so hard sometimes, writing down what any other married couple should be able to say face to face. Sorry, I'm bitching already.

Sophie's doing great. She's in the 90th percentile for height and weight. Must be my family's genes (sorry again). She's been cruising for a few weeks and can even stand by herself for a few seconds, which is pretty advanced according to the book. She even drinks from a normal cup. Best of all, she still knows you, since I show her your picture every day. It's the one of you with the ambassador and that faction leader. You have the double-chin thing going, but otherwise you look good. Maybe you should send a few more, or is the camera in our sea shipment too? I don't remember.

Do you know where my suits are? I could use them now; I started a part-time job last week, editing for a non-profit refugee organization. Very appropriate, don't you think? Don't worry, it doesn't interfere at all with Sophie since mostly I work at home on the internet. It's the perfect arrangement; I work a couple of hours when she naps, and then a couple more at night after she goes to sleep...

George skims the news from her family. Margaret's sister is having a wedding shower or some such thing that she plans to attend. The brothers are fighting; her father's health is no good. George slows down when he gets to the next page. The separate maintenance thing, the allowance she gets for living apart from him, is getting more complicated. The Department wants an OF-155, or maybe an OF-455; for sure it ends with a five. How long can she draw the allowance? The stupid people at the office couldn't give her a straight answer. George scratches his arm; he is not bothered by the bureaucracy, only by her efforts to sustain their separation.

I like my job, but Washington doesn't feel like home anymore. It's too expensive and it's such a transitory place, full of unhappy people who came here to be somebody and mostly struck out.

George feels his pulse quicken. He fingers his raki and reads on, a little faster now.

...although I have made a few friends who have kids. We have a mother's group, which is good. Next month, I'll have them all over for Sophie's birthday. Yes, that's how exciting my life is—I'm planning my child's birthday party a full month in advance!

Yes, yes, fine. He reads on.

Georgie, what are we going to do?

For this most important of questions, she has switched from black ink to blue, an indication that the letter was put aside and later resumed. How long? Hours? Days? The next sentence is indecipherable, scratched out with excessive vigor; not a single letter survives. What did she write there? An insult? A profanity? *A call for divorce?* More likely, knowing Margaret, it had been an outburst of sentimentality that she'd regretted. It was her cynicism, her edge, that he had always loved. George gives up trying to decipher the sentence, takes another drink, and feels his throat swell.

> *Georgie, I think it's time for me to leave Washington. You're not coming home (home, where is home?) for a long time, so why should I stay? My plan is to stay through April, when the lease runs out, then move in with my parents for a while. With my mother watching Sophie, I'll have plenty of time to find a job and jump-start my life. I've already sent out a couple of resumes, to publishing firms in Madison. Before you get mad, think about it. There's nothing for me here. I don't know why I've stayed as long as I have. I suppose I honestly thought you would curtail and come back, that you would try to make this work. To make us work. More than anything, I wanted Sophie to have a dad...*

Wanted. Her use of the past tense is jarring. He tilts his glass and finds it empty, but he doesn't get up.

> *I'm sorry that we fought the night before you left for Turkey. We should have aired things out. I don't think you ever understood how I felt, why I couldn't return to Monrovia and why I couldn't go with you to Istanbul. It wasn't the third-world hardship. It was because I was never my own person—I was always an appendage of you, a "dependent spouse." Do you know how repulsive that term is? It's not easy to be strong when you have no identity of your own. No identity and no purpose.*
>
> *Did I tell you I've been taking Sophie to church? A Catholic one. I tried the Unitarian Church first, but it wasn't what I was looking for. A bunch of ex-hippies and a gay minister, and everyone feeling "spiritual." I know what you're thinking—I'm trying to find myself. Maybe I am, I don't know. I knew who I was before we went overseas. Now I'm less sure. I thought I would sleep again when I got back to the U.S., but I haven't. It's either this or Valium.*
>
> *A book I'm reading says people get anxiety for one reason only—because they feel out of control. How do you feel in control*

when you're bouncing around the world, not knowing where you'll be from one month to the next? How do you keep from losing yourself? I don't know how you do it, Georgie. I can't.

More black ink. George blinks. Good God, he thinks. Self-help books.

I know you don't like decisions, but this is one you have to make. I'm not staying beyond April. Call it a deadline if you want, but one of us needs to force the issue. How long am I supposed to wait? Until after Turkey? Why should I believe you'll be back after that? That you won't get yourself assigned to some other crazy place? I have to move on. Maybe what you're secretly wishing is that I will.

Call me soon. Love, Maggie.

George repeats the words to himself. *Love, Maggie*. For a long moment nothing else in the letter matters. Since when did she call herself *Maggie*? He remembers experimenting when they first started dating, in those anxious days before *babe* and *sweetie* seemed right. *Maggie* had never worked; she had told him she preferred Margaret, so Margaret she'd remained.

Maggie. What did she mean by *that*?

* * *

It was not at all easy to get to Shishli. From the doorstep of my hotel, I would walk up Istiklal to Taksim Square, past the McDonald's and the luxury hotels, then veer left to avoid the descending stairs to the futbol stadyomu, and pick up a bus heading west, never the same bus twice, until the traffic slowed to a stand-still and I knew I was close enough to resume my journey on foot. With a little help from my fellow pedestrians, I would finally arrive at my destination two hours after I began.

Vram had taken to buying me the English-language *Turkish Daily News*, which I read with the soles of my feet on the floor out of respect for Vram's father. Today's headlines were about Apo, as they were the day before and the day before that—Apo calling on the rebels to lay down their arms, Apo apologizing to the families of the thousands killed, Apo promising to end the war if only he were spared. Apo this and Apo that. The stories repulsed me; I couldn't get them out of my head. Had he no shame? No honor? Pleading for his life was bad enough. But to admit the cause had been for nothing? After so many thousands killed?

After so many miles traveled?

I dropped the newspaper and put my face in my hands. My thoughts fell in a torrent, as prickly as sleet. Processed one by one, they were manageable, but in such volume they rattled the senses; they overwhelmed. Ah, this world, where things are precisely not what they seem, where people shake their heads to show they're sincere, where soaking too long in water will dry you out. I thought of Winston, how he'd enticed me here, then slipped away. With the file he'd promised everything! I felt the anger of the betrayed. Isn't it the fellow traveler we hate the most? Because when he disappoints, our own horizons shrink?

For George I felt nothing—not anger, not hatred, only a faint pity at best, nothing I could sink my teeth into. He was just a bureaucrat, passionless, irrelevant as they come. Only when he conjured the image of a medicated life did he make any sense. Of course! It was not the first time that they had tried to silence me. Did they really believe I'd consent to go back in my box? That

I'd sit and let the lid slam shut? Where would I be—what would I be—without my writing? A seller of golf equipment? A waiter? One doesn't shed one's ideas, one's purpose, one's essence—one's very self—quite so easily.

People used to tell me I was trying too hard to save the world, and I agreed. Now I know I was only trying to bridge the chasm in my life, the chasm in all of our lives, that separates what we are from what we think we are. What is life, but a tiresome expedition to connect these dots, to square the circle, to close the loop?

Right then and there I swore to myself, I would never go back. My sane, moderate, medicated self was as dead to me as if it were plugged in the ground.

Vram's Uncle Hikmet, Los Angeles jewelry store mogul and writer of affidavits, was, it has been noted, also a photographer of very modest talent. In fact, he was good enough to cover society for the *Turkish Daily News*—the same *Turkish Daily News* that Vram brought home each day for me to read—snapping photos of celebrities and politicians at gala events, while his brother-in-law minded the business in Los Angeles. "He doesn't need to work," Vram told me through Nazan. "He owns four jewelry shops in the covered bazaar, and a chain in California. But he prefers to drink for free."

That's where I came in. With my empty socks and my unanswered faxes, I declared I would take a paying job for Hikmet. He put me to work on the bylines beneath his photos for two hundred thousand lira an hour, which was either two or twenty dollars, depending where one put the decimal point. Whatever the case, I was suddenly less reliant on the consulate's money, which isn't to say I stopped accepting it since my ties there were as useful as the cash.

I was happy in my new job and pleased to help Hikmet. His writing was awful, but nothing that a little editing couldn't fix. "Pictured above are Minister for the Economy Rafik Erdoğan and Czech Consul General Jan Kavan at the grand opening of the International Hospital's new intensive care unit," he wrote. Dull! Dull! And so I changed it to, "Minister for the Economy Rafik Erdoğan discusses with Czech envoy Jan Kavan the implications of EU expansion, a potential tonic for their respective nations, whose shared destinies include languishing on the frontiers of Europe for most of the twentieth century." In fact, what they were discussing were the little hot dog things, which looked grossly undercooked, but one could hardly write that.

Occasionally, Hikmet took me to events, like the reception at the Swiss Hotel where the U.S. vice consul failed to recognize me in my smart dinner jacket, a loan from Hikmet who was tall for a Turk. After doing a double-take, he strolled in my direction.

"Mr. Bigelow? I'm George McCall. From the consulate."

"Yes, yes, I know who you are."

Still he handed me a business card, as if pre-programmed to do so. "I'm a little surprised to see you here."

I made to tuck the card in my jacket pocket but then remembered that already there was a large chunk of steel. "I must say I'm surprised to see you too. A wonderful exhibition, don't you think?" It was all I could do to be civil. My head ached from the early afternoon; the card shivered in my fingers.

George glanced at the wall, where two nudes collided with savage force. There was violence in the rapid brush strokes, and an Elvis-on-felt cheapness to the silhouette of Atatürk superimposed on the scene. It was secular shock art with a message—to be for something, one had to be against something else. The painter had made a career of thumbing his nose at Islam, much the same way that many a western artist had won fame and fortune dunking Jesus in urine.

"Not exactly my style," replied George.

"The contrasts derive from Singer Sargent, don't you think? Though clearly the composition is a play on Le dejeuner sur l'herbe." It was one of several stock comments in my repertoire; perhaps it was even true.

"I wouldn't know," said George. He was smiling, but when he scratched his arm I knew I had him.

Across the room, Hikmet was positioning the guest of honor and prominent guests for a photo shoot. The ice in my Chivas fell against my teeth. "Would you excuse me, Mr…? I must get back to work."

"McCall," said George. "But please call me George." He fell in step with me. "So you've gotten a job since I last saw you."

"No. I already had a job. A writer always has a job." We moved toward the bar. "The difference now is that I have an assignment." I ordered another Chivas. The waiter offered to replace George's half-full glass; he hesitated, then nodded.

"How does this affect your plans to leave Istanbul?"

"Oh, I won't be leaving Istanbul; certainly not before I finish what I came here to do." I tracked the movement of my glass, from the moment the bartender selected it until it sat before me, filled. Satisfied that it had not been tampered with, I drank. The glass almost shattered when I put it down. "Aha!" I said.

"What?"

"Hmm?"

George looked away, then back at me. "Mr. Bigelow, I thought we'd agreed…"

"Is Mr. Craine here tonight? Or is this event beneath his rank?"

George ignored the slight, sipped his fresh drink carefully. The artist, who seemed profoundly unhappy, began to speak at the microphone; spoons clinked on glasses and the crowd slowly hushed.

"The loan you've taken from the consulate is for repatriation," whispered George. "If you've decided not to return to the United States, you're going to have to repay it."

"Oh, I plan to," I counted my fingers. "As soon as I receive my advance."

"Oh? Have you sold something?"

I wanted to scream out, but somehow held it in. "Are you familiar with the writing business?"

"Are you alright?"

I pulled my hands away from my ears and forced my voice lower. "Do you really think lack of money will stop me? You people are all the same."

He only stared.

I took another drink. At the microphone a plump Turk was butchering the English language. No one seemed to mind. All around us, waiters ran about, preying on half-full glasses.

"Bill, I'm only trying to help you. When the consulate gave you money it was to tide you over until your own funds came. Two weeks ago, you said it would take only a few days."

"Unfortunately, most of my assets are tied up in cash," I replied. In fact, I had just received a cashier's check from the Bank of America, in the amount of two hundred and fifty six dollars and thirty-seven cents. I couldn't bring myself to cash it. Even after losing eighteen thousand dollars from my sock in Doğubeyazit, I refused to believe that my aunt's inheritance had dwindled to this paltry amount. Who could have taken the rest? Was it my jealous brothers and sisters? Or the FDIC? George's face was blank. The accompanying letter had said, "We regret your decision to close your account and look forward to providing financial services to you in the future." Oh, they were good. I wondered if keeping a record of my transactions would have helped. I swallowed hard. No, don't be naive.

"There are other ways of getting you home, Bill. Maybe someone in your family…."

"Tell me, Mister… Mister…" Again I was at a loss for a name. "Why is it the government is always so interested in sending me to this place it calls *home*?"

George shuffled self-consciously, as if there were a hundred places he'd rather be. An old woman to his left seemed annoyed. "Bill," he whispered. "The consulate just got your bill for the Akdeniz Hotel—sixty eight dollars, mostly liquor. Add that to what you've borrowed from us, and your debts come to nearly two hundred. Of course, those are just the ones we know about."

I had forgotten the Akdeniz. It seemed a lifetime ago, though it was only a week. I was at a different hotel now, running a different tab. I motioned to the bartender. George did the same.

"Chivas," we said in one voice. Matching drinks appeared on the bar and we eyed each other carefully, like partners in crime. He sipped and put his hand on his hip, then removed it when I matched the gesture.

"Piss off," I muttered, or rather something deep within me muttered. A moment later I had apologized on its behalf. My head was so cluttered I missed most of what George said next. My face stung; only then did I realize I had slapped myself.

"…means you can't renew your passport until the loan is paid back."

"What do you mean?" I felt dizzy; why was the room fading? A half dozen drinks could not possibly explain it. With horror I realized I had not watched the bartender pour the last round. I felt the tickling on my ear and slapped again.

"When I annotated your passport, I explained that the loan. It had to be paid before you. Could renew it. Are you okay?"

"But I need my passport," I said coolly. "I'm going to Israel next, then to Iran. Just as soon as I get the file." I was talking too much, but what did it matter? George must have known everything already. God, didn't he see the flies. I pressed my fingers on my nose, then swept them over my eyes.

"Are you alright?"

"I know my first amendment rights; these aren't the rules." My hand felt for the lump of steel, but it was too big for the pocket and refused to dislodge. I felt the fabric start to tear.

"Why don't we…" George motioned toward the exit. Why was everyone staring? "Okay, okay!" he said. "I'm listening, I'm…"

I hadn't realized I was talking—with such intensity, in fact, that I had to stop and gasp for air. I inhaled and felt the flies pour in, causing me to choke. Slowly, deliberately, or so I thought, I picked them one by one from my tongue and went on.

"Please, slow down."

My mouth was vomiting names. "Balzac, Faulkner, Fitzgerald, Christian Anderson, Henry James, Hemingway, Dickens, Emerson, Melville, Zola…" I counted them off on my fingers. Famous writers. Where was I going with this?

"Woolf, Wollstonecraft, O'Neil, Dinesen, John Bunyan, Malcolm Lowry, Ibsen Greene, Graham Mary—"

My arm jerked. Pressure that had been there a moment ago was gone. A Turk was yelling at me, but I plowed on, recycling fingers, losing count, trying to hear what my mouth was saying.

George responded in a dozen contradictory ways; the result was no motion whatsoever.

"Shelley James Barrie Arthur Benson Maxim Gorky Tennessee Williams William Inge Twain Nikolai Gogl Joseph Conrad Lewis Grassic Gibbon Robert Louis Stevenson Leo Tolstoy John Parkman Francis Rushkin…"

Now the commas were gone. I drove on, ignoring the swarm of flies that came at me from all directions. Stupid, suicidal, they secured themselves to my lips, my ears, my nostrils; they drowned themselves in my moisture, begging to die. Damn Australian flies, Goddamn, damn, Goddamn things, immigrants from some third-world country, somehow got past customs on infested fruit, aboard rattan, multiplying, always multiplying. I resolved to ignore them, to let them be, no longer bothered to spit them out. I yelled right past them, chewed right through them, opened my eyes wide and let them stick. A shriek exploded through the buzzing, like Turkish pop music, metal sawing metal, bringing me back to the world. I swallowed lumpy spit. George's fingers were awash in my tears. I slid aside and left them dangling. More cries. The man at the microphone stopped. Beneath me an old woman flailed and pounded at my legs, her skirt hiked obscenely, broken glass in her hand. I was shoved backwards, spun around, and stumbled toward the exit. A Turkish beer blocked my way; I sent it flying.

"Aha!"

On the street outside the wailing was an echo, then only honks and engines droning, the reassuring sounds of traffic. I turned and jogged downhill, outpacing the cars. The air was cool and clear. I sucked it in, turned left at the water, felt my way through the gathering crowd. No escape! I slowed to a walk, out of breath. My eyes watered, but the view was clear now. The swarm was gone. The faces were familiar—the bartender who had spiked my drink, much older now, flogging sandwiches of sheep entrails; I raised my fist and he retreated behind his stand. And there, the old lady I'd stepped on, younger but still fashionably dressed; at my approach she quickened her pace.

I went with the current. The water was vast and empty before me, and beyond that the dim lights of Asia. How hard would it be to swim across? God knew what lurked beneath the waves. I teetered at water's edge, turned inland, searched out darkness, then rested on a merry-go-round too rusty to rotate. When I stood my pant leg was torn and my leg bled. The pain alerted me to danger. "Who's there?" I called. My hand drifted to my pocket like a gunslinger. This time the weapon came loose, the fabric tearing on its way out. "I won't go back," I said, trying to keep the gun from wobbling. A group of students approached, nursing cans of Efes, then hurried on. With my free hand I fumbled through my pants pocket for pen and paper, something, anything, to write on, but all I found were wadded napkins and greasy toothpicks from the hors d'oeuvres. They fell to the dirt as I swallowed a sob. "I won't go back. I won't."

I eased my grip on the weapon and allowed my fingers to absorb its texture. The chill was absolute.

I took it away from my head.

What was the best angle? In the movies it was often the mouth, but that seemed so unsanitary to me. Gratuitous violence was not my cup of tea. Nor did I want to peril anyone else. It seemed important somehow to be responsible—to shoot in such a way that body and gun fell together in the water, nice and symmetric, safely away from the flimsy swings, the rusty shards of the merry-go-round, the slide with the gaping hole at bottom. This playground had too many hazards already.

I watched the Bosphorous flow by, creating two continents where there should have been one, pretending to head south while doubling back in the depths below, returning north to the Black Sea. I screamed at the water. Its duplicity ensured its filth, demonstrated that all progress was illusion. I stared at it long and hard, and as the drizzle fell and the flies returned, I tried and tried and tried to make up my mind.

* * *

Eight p.m. has barely come and gone when the phone rings, catching George asleep. Something he ate the night before, maybe at the reception, had disturbed his stomach, and for every tenth visa applicant he'd had to make a trip to the bathroom. At three o'clock he'd beaten the rush hour traffic home to get sick in his own toilet. Was it the börek? Try as he might to forget, he could still taste the cheese.

He hears a woman's voice. Nazan's.

He sits upright and swings his feet to the floor. His head clears. "Yes, I remember the restaurant. The one in Emirgan. I'll be there in half an hour."

He wipes the sleep from his eyes. What would Phil say? That she's off-limits? Is he breaking the rules by meeting with her? No, George tells himself, this is not about Taylor. For days he's been waiting for Nazan's call, though hardly expecting it. Their last meeting at the consulate had not gone well; damn it, Zeynep. It frustrates him that he lacks the strength to put an end to this charade, as if he is waiting for her to do it first, at once hoping and fearing that she will.

And there's another reason to go. Margaret is supposed to call tonight. He hasn't yet digested her letter. God, how he wants to miss that call.

He descends to the shore road and comes to a stop in traffic. The road is crammed with young men who, if not actually drunk, bear a close resemblance. One soccer team has lost and another has won; supporters of the latter parade bumper-to-bumper, shouting and waving flags from the windows. Fireworks pop in the distance.

He finds Nazan occupying the same table where they first met and talked. It seems such a long time ago. Of course she could have sat anywhere. Aside from the waiter, the restaurant is bare. "I'm sorry I didn't wait for you," she says, pouring him raki from a half-empty bottle. She tops off her own glass.

"Traffic," he says. "Sorry."

"Yes, Galatasaray's supporters are devoted."

George still hears sounds of celebration, but muted now, a long way away. He sips his raki and notices the same waiter from their visit before. Nor has the music changed; Frank Sinatra still croons from a worn-out cassette. At least it's not the Gypsy Kings, whose music plays everywhere—bars, restaurants, supermarkets. In Turkey, things tend to repeat; the government collapses, the lira loses value, Greece behaves badly, the PKK is defeated; the same half-dozen spices find their way into every meal, even at so-called Chinese restaurants.

"Have you tried the patlican?" asks Nazan, glancing at the menu.

"Yes, I've had the eggplant once or twice," he says touching his stomach. Déjà vu, he thinks—déjà vu all over again. "I'm not hungry."

Nazan bites her lip. They are silent for a while, and George feels a guilty pleasure for wrecking the mood. He gives in and makes small talk, but Nazan is already rummaging through her purse. Without comment, she sets a photograph on the table.

"That's…" George sits upright. It's a candid shot, Tim sitting at a table littered with used plates and coffee cups, obviously a café. Though facing the camera, his eyes are elsewhere; to be exact, they are focused on a young man in the shadows, whose face is a dark silhouette, backlit at the edges; only his red hair stands out. Where light meets dark, George sees a blotch of pale, freckled skin.

"Taylor."

"These are better," says Nazan, setting two more photos on the table. In one of the pictures, Tim and Taylor are laughing, jovially sharing a joke.

"Where did you get these?" His mind races. Now he's certain that he is breaking Phil's rules.

Nazan pulls a camera from her purse and smiles. She settles back, arms folded.

George takes another drink of raki, feels it rush to his head. Has he ever had such strong raki? He glances at the waiters. They stand at the entrance, or in his case the exit. Their faces are stern; is it the lack of business that they're upset about? Why is the place so fucking empty? Shouldn't there be other customers on a nice night like this? George feels a lump in his throat. *It's fine*, he tells himself. *Take it easy.*

"What are you thinking," says Nazan.

"What I'm thinking," says George, collecting himself, "is that you haven't been honest with me."

"Maybe you're not asking the right questions, canim." She smiles coyly.

"Why are you showing me these?"

"To make a point. That I can be useful."

"Useful? How?" His eyes sweep the room; he half expects Taylor to walk out of the kitchen donning a floppy chef's hat.

Nazan cocks her head. "You already knew, didn't you?" She fingers one of the photographs. "I wanted to see your reaction. You act surprised, but I know that you are not."

"Surprised about what?"

She laughs crudely, but still seems sober—more sober than he's used to. "That Taylor was working for the CIA. That you paid him for information, five hundred dollars a week. Are you really a vice consul as you say?"

"And who—what—are you?" He glanced at the bottle. Was this all just an elaborate game of spot the spook?

"Five hundred bloody dollars a week! For what? He told you lies. Don't you know that?" Her voice cracks, surprising him. Her sudden despair seems genuine. "When he said the PKK would plant a bomb at the Pera Palas, you were ready. But instead they bomb the Aya Sofya. Is this kind of information worth five hundred dollars! Oh you're mad. With intelligence like that, I can understand why your government was caught unaware by the collapse of the Soviet— Where are you going?"

"To my car. And I'll keep these." The photographs are in his pocket as he heads for the door, wondering how far he'll get. The waiters object as he nears them, exchange looks of mild panic. *The toilet is there, efendim; the food is coming. Ne istersen? What do you want?* A moment later George is outside, alone. He scans the shadows as he crosses the parking lot; headlights crowd the noisy road alit with stop-and-go tail lights. Through leafless branches he sees an oil tanker, plowing downstream. The air is unseasonably warm; otherwise the night is like any other. Or is it? He circles his car, stooping every few steps. He unlocks the door and climbs in—a stupid move if his instincts are correct. But they are not; the engine starts quietly. Yes, he tells himself, he is paranoid. He shuts it off and sits awhile. Nazan is arguing over the bill when he returns.

"I thought you were gone," she says. Her hand shakes as she pours out the rest of the bottle. Her anxiety relaxes him. "The government doesn't pay my rent, canim."

George sighs and takes the bill.

"That was cruel of you to leave. Why are you so cross?"

"Why did you show me these?"

"I… I want to help you. Now that they've arrested Yavuz Bey, there is nothing left for me to do at the University."

"Doctor Yilmaz? The professor? He's been arrested?"

She eyes him skeptically. George is reminded of Margaret's expression in the old days, the way she would look at him whenever he'd tell her he had had just one drink.

"Bollocks."

"It's late," he says. "I should be going." George scoots back his chair.

"The anti-terror police. They came for him last month." She checks his reaction.

George laughs wearily. "That harmless old…"

"He was not harmless," she says sharply. Then, calmer, "He knows much more than you think. And they will know it all soon enough. When he is tortured…" She trails off, too tired to finish, or even to take a drink. She stares a long time at the reflection in her glass. Her eyes are limp.

"Because he's a Marxist?"

She falls back in her chair. "Because he's PKK." *You idiot,* she seems to say. "How else would Taylor have joined? Do you think they have a public sign-up? As if it's a… a cricket team?"

"So Yilmaz got him in." He pauses. "But then why would Yilmaz ever have agreed to meet with me?"

She pauses while the waiters clear the table. George grips his glass tightly; there's still raki at the bottom. Nazan orders another half-bottle without seeking his counsel. "To play with you. To throw you off the scent."

George considers this possibility. True, with his accusations that Taylor was dealing drugs, Yilmaz had muddied the waters a little. And the professor had asked plenty of questions himself. He feels dimwitted, having this explained; a cocky grin is his compensation. "Something tells me it was no coincidence that we met."

"No coincidence at all."

The bottle comes. George's initial buzz has faded, absorbed by eggplant puree. He allows her to pour him another glass. In time, she will pour him another, and another. But it is too late to get pleasantly buzzed; the moment has passed. Now it's a heavy drunk, turgid and sour. Nazan pauses to hear *New York, New York* from beginning to end, then talks without stopping until it plays again. George contemplates donating some of his old cassettes to the restaurant; he has grown to like the place but is tired of Sinatra.

Nazan tells him everything. She concludes her story with the observation that they have a great deal in common. "For example," she says, "you are a spy…"

"I am not a spy."

"Hmm," is her reply. But it's enough. It is all clear to him now. The only question left is how he will explain it to Phil.

"She works for MIT," says George. Turkish intelligence. There's no way *not* to tell them. Any contact with a foreign intelligence organization, friendly or otherwise, is a reportable event. "But she's not a professional spy. She's an informant, an asset. Like Taylor," he says, looking Phil in the eye.

Priscilla has come from a planning meeting for Zimmerman and the other members of congress—due to arrive the next morning. Now she rises from her seat and drifts to the window, remains there with back turned and dark hands gently clasped, the pinks of her palms showing through her fingers. Maybe it's her way of letting Phil take the floor, or maybe she is longing for happier times. There is nothing to see in the garden, only wetness and filth and drizzle falling on a dug-up yard. The wall some fifty feet away, the same wall that blocked the Dev Sol rocket some years back, is fuzzy in the pall. Fifty feet! Come spring, Priscilla will eat lunch at the iron table on the edge of the garden, surrounded by blossoms. Wasn't it a white table once? The surface is pockmarked by rain.

"Has she pitched you?" asked Phil.

"Has she what?"

"Pitched you. Has she tried to turn you? To recruit you?"

"I told you, she's not a spook. She's an asset," he says, deliberately employing one of *their* words. He wonders if he sounds naive. "That's what she told me anyway. She said *they* recruited *her* when she was at Istanbul University. They sent her to learn English in the U.K., then back here to work on… terrorism." Priscilla returns from the window and sits, tossing one leg over the other. George goes on. "She's attached herself to an Armenian family. One of the boys is a member of Asala, just got sent to prison in Germany. She didn't say so, but I think she made the case against him."

George leans back in his chair, wondering when to release his bombshell. He could play Phil like a trout, make him squirm as long as he wants to. But that takes ice water in the veins; George only has raki.

"What else?" says Phil. The chief of station looks nonplussed. His eyes are half-closed, either deep in thought or half-asleep.

"Well…" George tosses the photo on the table; it is not one of the better pictures, but more than adequate for the purpose. He feels himself stiffen like a boxer awaiting a punch, ahead on points and needing only to survive the round.

He has rehearsed the answers over and over, but is unprepared for this: Phil turns a little pale, then smiles a self-deprecating smile and hands the photo to Priscilla. The sleepy look is gone. He rises and takes Priscilla's spot at the window.

"She has more…?"

"I think so," says George. What he doesn't say is that so does he—in his breast pocket. If asked to show it he will, but only if asked.

"One of our mistakes," says Phil, still wearing the same sad smile. He shakes his head. "What's that game my son plays? The one where you have to keep hammering all the little guys that pop up—every time you hit one, another pops up somewhere else…" His voice trails off, but his hand still thumps away with the imaginary hammer. For a fleeting moment, George almost feels sorry for him. *No, don't. This is the asshole who contrived a gay sex scandal to wreck your career.*

Priscilla shakes her head as she studies the photo. "So this is the famous Taylor? For God's sake Phil, if you can't cover your tracks better than this…" She trails off, too exasperated to finish. It takes her a moment to recover. "First things first. How do we extricate George from this little mess? From *your* little mess?"

George is grateful, and a little surprised, that her first words concern his well-being.

"*Our* mess! Now wait a second," says Phil. "Who is this girl to you, George? What's your relationship?"

The question is expected; still, piecing the words together is tough. "I know her, sort of. Met her on the visa line—she was interpreting for someone…" *A bad visa case,* he could add, but doesn't. He breathes deeply. "We've gone out a couple of times, but there's never been anything…" He considers *untoward,* but the word seems ridiculous. He says nothing.

The look on Priscilla's face suggests his explanation didn't play as well out loud as it had in his head. At least now he is building his credentials as a heterosexual. Why not let Phil believe he had an affair with her, if for no other reason than to prove he's not gay? Ah, but what a tangled web.

"Priscilla, there's nothing I would like better than for George to extricate *himself* from… *this* little mess. But he needs to come clean."

"What do you want to know?" asks George, sitting up in his seat. "She told me Taylor was on the Agency's payroll for years, but that all he did was supply false—" Phil's reaction makes him stop. This isn't where he wants to go.

"I don't buy it that this… this girl… is a simple asset," says Phil. He turns the photo in his hands with the suggestion of pent-up violence. "Either she's—

" He regards George and stops.

"You think she might be, what? PKK," says Priscilla. "Or Dev Sol?" Maybe it's a factional dispute? Maybe—"

"Could be," says Phil. "What did you two talk about George? Did she ever ask you how much you make? How many debts you have? She ask you how happy you are in your job?"

"We might have talked about—"

"Your finances? Try to remember, George. I think there's every possibility that you've been targeted for recruitment. Simple asset my—" He glances at Priscilla. "Think hard, George. Maybe they think you have some skeletons in your closet?"

"Goddamit, you know I don't."

They glare at each other in silence, then Phil slowly nods and disappears from the room. Priscilla seems to prefer silence in his absence, drifting back to the window while George thumbs a coffee table book, comprehending nothing.

Phil returns with a sheet of paper in hand—a questionnaire. He gives it to George. "Fill this out. Do it here. It doesn't leave this floor."

George looks at Priscilla, who nods. He studies the sheet. Do vice consuls stumble on bungled CIA operations so often that they've created a standard form? He reads it through, then stops, recalling yesterday's nausea. Does he need a lawyer? Yes, he's been told, if ever he finds himself the target of investigation by the State Department 's inspector general. Isn't this worse?

He knows it's a mistake to fill it out. He knows he will do it anyway. To George's relief, Priscilla and Phil leave him alone to consider his answers.

Is pissing off the CIA the worst career move a diplomat can make? Possibly, though starting a war or insulting the ambassador's wife also rank high. But, of course, nothing compares to losing a congressman's luggage. Make it the suitcase of the chair of the congressional committee that controls the State Department's budget and you really have a problem.

Normal people, when they travel, don't give much thought to luggage. They might spend some time deciding what goes in their bags, whether to check them or carry them on, but once they're airborne their thoughts turn to other things, the in-flight movie, for example, or their choice of meals. On arrival, they'll grab their bags, haul them to a taxi, and trust the hotel porter to get them to their room. Leave the bags to the professionals; it makes sense. But it's not how congressional delegations operate.

George looks at his watch. It's five past seven and he's late getting onto the tarmac to meet the delegation's aircraft. He kills the engine, steps from the car and shows his ID to the uniformed Turk. Ryan is nowhere in sight; Colonel Ryan, the congressional delegation's military liaison, the man in charge of logistics, not just baggage but *the whole ball of wax*, as the Colonel himself seemed fond of saying. *The members have a demanding itinerary before they reach Istanbul*, explained his fax. *Make sure they have some R&R before the long trip home.* In fact, while in Athens, the members had spent a day at the Acropolis and an evening at Delphi. In Israel, they'd floated in the Dead Sea, then viewed the fortress of Masada from the snack bar rather than tackle the long, stony path to the top of the hill. In Damascus, they'd cancelled their last two meetings to shop in the souk. Demanding itinerary indeed.

But George knew better than to argue. Nor did he complain when Colonel Ryan woke him up with a last minute request to collect the room keys in advance—a must if the bags were going to be tagged before the delegation's departure from Athens. At one o'clock in the morning, the logic of this request was lost on the hotel's duty manager, who took two hours to produce the keys. Mission finally accomplished, George stopped by the consulate to check for last-minute faxes, then made his way home through empty streets with first light only hours away.

No wonder he'd overslept—getting three hours of sleep instead of two – and arrived at the airport late.

George stares at the runway, accepts a cigarette from the guard, and waits for permission to pass through the gate. When it finally comes, George finds the congressmen already loading onto the bus. Priscilla is last up the steps. "Not the best morning to sleep in," she snaps, plucking the keys from his hand.

George can't blame her for being mad. It's not the first time I have let her down, he thinks to himself. Whatever happened to those once-a-week meetings? Somehow they had never quite happened. His stock with her had clearly crashed.

Frustrated, he scans the tarmac. The union baggage handlers are nowhere in sight. Sighing, he reports the news to Captain Holland, who grunts. When Holland grunts a second time the bags begin to move, courtesy of the U.S. Air Force. In ten minutes they are on their way to the city. There is no rain today, just a meager pall stinking of coal.

"Don't worry, the colonel doesn't dwell on screw-ups," says Holland. "What's done is done."

For the first time, George is worried. "Yes, well, it was my responsibility but..."

"Yes sir," he says.

At the hotel they get the luggage to the rooms, then turn to the heavy coolers. "We're going to need all the ice we can get," says Holland. "Got a lot of drinks here."

To George, this sounds a lot like an order. Does vice consul outrank captain? He wishes he knew. Lacking the energy to do otherwise, he dials room service.

Dawn is in the control room when they haul in the stuff. "How's it look?" she asks.

"Great," says George. The suite has two rooms, with office equipment in one and couches in the other. Mükrime, the cashier, sits quietly in the corner, ready to trade lira for dollars, or dollars for lira, whatever the congressmen prefer. The front desk does the same, but the consulate rate will save the congressmen two pennies for every dollar. Mükrime earns time-and-a-half for working on a Saturday.

"Looks like we're operational," declares Dawn, ignoring the fact that there are no pending operations to speak of. After the congressmen get settled into their rooms, they'll have lunch with Priscilla to talk about security; then it's off to the Grand Bazaar, before reassembling at six for transport to the Savarona.

"They're getting per diem, aren't they?" asks George. Under Holland's direction, a staff sergeant named Tucker is unloading an ice chest filled with Doritos and Twinkies and other delicacies. Nothing comes without a wrapper.

"Sure, but this stuff's gotta get eaten too. You want a drink?" He pulls the lid off the second cooler. "Help yourself. But keep the bottles in the bathroom."

George scans the booze; it's top-shelf stuff—*Stolys* instead of *Smirnoff*. A Bloody Mary sounds good, but there's no tomato juice in sight, much less a celery stalk. Anyway, it's too early even for that—not yet 10:00 a.m.

Suddenly Captain Holland is in the room, running to and fro like a man possessed. He ducks behind couches, whips open closets, disappears into the bathroom, then reappears rubbing his glasses so hard that George fears they might crack. "Any of the members' bags come in here by mistake? Only the coolers? You sure? Oh shit, Christ. Yeah, the chairman's. Oh Jesus..."

* * *

Listen up. Art Zimmerman's suitcase was gone—and with it any chance to derail the train I was on to its ill-fated destination—a gathering of congressmen aboard Atatürk's ship, and me among them, pointing a gun at Winston Craine's great bald head and applying gentle pressure to the trigger. It was a train powered by events that might have seemed random. But as with trains everywhere, once the tracks were laid there was no plausible chance of the train going elsewhere. That was the thing about trains.

Most of the stops were now in the past—Australia, Iran, Ararat. But the present was equally cruel: Bakirköy Psychiatric Hospital, where I awoke to Winston Craine's head swinging above me like a ceiling lamp. No, I take that back, not like a lamp at all since his head, as I said long ago, was like a shade tree in the burning sun.

Winston looked no more impressive than when I'd last seen him in Australia. His bald, flaky scalp still fell apart and got stuck in his ears, while beads of sweat anchored the hairs he had left which, unfortunately, he'd permitted to grow long, then combed sideways—well, you've heard all that before.

Bakirköy was one of the few buildings in Istanbul with a proper lawn out front, fields of green where a brown expanse of dirt should have been. To maintain the grass, they must have needed a bonafide lawn mower, maybe even a lawn-cutting service—not that such a thing existed in Turkey. The grass was wasted on the inmates; they were always indoors, babbling and hugging themselves, shrieking and hallucinating, urinating where they weren't supposed to, inside whatever building corresponded to their mental dysfunction. Billy Hayes of *Midnight Express* fame served his time in section thirteen. Me, I was in the less notorious section four.

My God, what had they given me? My head was so heavy that I needed both hands to raise it from the pillow; thankfully, they had unstrapped my wrists. After thinking a while I said, "Yes, I have money to pay..." But it was a sentence not worth finishing and, anyway, the strain was too great. "Where have you been?" I asked Craine as the men in white backed off. I let my head drop.

"Why, I've been here all along," he said, running his hand over his sweaty head. "I came as soon as I heard, Mister…" With no evident embarrassment, he flipped through his notebook.

"You don't… you don't…" It was a struggle to form the words. What *had* they given me? "…You don't remember me?"

Craine stopped flipping and looked up.

"It was three or four months ago…"

"Ah, yes," said Craine. "Ashgabat! You had your appendix removed, and when your children came to visit, I…"

Ashgabat? Ashgabat? Yes, I seemed to recall being there. Or was that Azerbaijan? But didn't I still have my appendix? An appendix yes, but no children… "I don't think that was me," I concluded. Then, with all the strength I could muster, "No, in Australia! You were dead… the shark… but, no, you were not dead. The file… you remember? I'm a writer… yes, that's it. Vietnamese food… don't you remember?"

"Is there a… chair, or… or something for me to sit on?"

Good God, why was he asking me? I glanced at my tethered ankles and he chuckled with embarrassment. A moment later he had found himself a seat.

"Well, then," he said. "Why don't we see about getting you out of here?"

Merely downloading his words took all the energy I could muster. What drugs had they given me, I wondered. And so I asked, "What drugs have they given me?"

"Sedatives," he said.

"Of course," I said. "But what kind?"

He considered the question for a moment, then shrugged. "This… was not precisely *elucidated.*"

I ran my tongue across the back of my mouth, and identified the vague bouquet of lithium. And my vision was… yes, blurry. But there was something else, too… my hands never trembled so fiercely from Lithium alone… and the dead weight in my skull… an anti-psychotic it must have been. God, not Haldol… leave it to the Turks to prescribe Haldol! Once in a supermarket I got such a seizure from Haldol that all my muscles locked up and I had to be carried from the deli section and injected with Congentin… Cogentin, ah, now that was a top-shelf drug.

"Do you know why you are here?"

I said nothing.

"You were directing traffic below Mihatpasha Stadium on the Sahil Yolu."

"Hmm?"

"Without any clothes on." He leaned forward in his seat.

"Oh," I said. That certainly sounded like me. Once in Rangoon, twice in Budapest, I had stripped to nothing and found myself an intersection. Why, I don't know. I always seemed to be taking my clothes off at the worst possible times. I liked historic crossroads. In Belgium I'd found myself at the Quatre Bras in Waterloo; in Budapest the Deak Ter. In Burma, God knew where I was.

"I have to pee," I announced, though I doubted my strength to follow through with this plan.

Winston ignored me. "The doctors say your condition has improved. You'll be out soon."

"When?"

"Now, tomorrow, next week. It's not easy to get a straight answer here." He leaned in confidentially, so close I could smell the simit on his breath. "I think the lunatics have taken over the asylum." He chuckled.

This was reassuring. "How long have I been—"

"Three days."

"Three days?" Three days was a lot of time to lose from writing. On the other hand, one could receive a lot of faxes in seventy-two hours, and one didn't even need to be conscious. Four thousand three hundred and twenty minutes. Hopefully, the little lady with the bee-bee-bee voice had kept them in order.

"I have to go." I tried to sit upright but found I lacked the strength.

"Ah, well, your release is rather… *conditional*," said Craine.

"Where is the file?" I asked.

"The file—"

"You really don't remember…" My mouth was so dry I could barely form the words. Yes, it was definitely Haldol. No doubt about it.

There was something different in the way he stared at me now.

"You do remember!"

"Australia," he said simply.

I closed my eyes. "The file," I breathed.

He put his finger to his lips and for a long time we were silent. When I heard his voice again, it seemed to come from a million miles away "As I said your release is conditional. They'll discharge you to the police, who will drive you to the border."

"The file. What about…" I was too exhausted to finish.

He looked away, as if surveying a great landscape; but there was no window in the room, only walls the color of model glue. "You traveled all the way here from Australia? Half way around the world?" Absently, he stroked his great bald head, front to back then back to front, over and over like a vacuum cleaner trying to swallow something too large. "You followed me here? For that?"

I suppose I nodded with my eyes.

"Why, that's..." He stared at me long and hard, then broke into a smile. "Just crazy."

A chill shot through me; it rested at the back of my throat, a lump that was fully physical, a lump like a tumor. Until that very moment I could still see the faxes in my mind—from Dell, Simon and Schuster, Random House. Now they were gone, replaced by chattering doctors and nurses, the whir of the lights above my sterile bed. There would be no faxes, no replies, as there had been none the week before and the week before that. My e-mail box was empty too; deep in my bones I knew it.

What born-again Christians felt at the touch of their Savior, at the moment of rapture when they accepted Jesus Christ, the big Halleluiah, when a hundred and forty-four thousand souls raced to the heavens, I now felt in reverse. Without purpose, agnostic, afraid. And so it was, Haldol or not, that I became unstuck.

"There, there. Gently, gently. Lay back," said Winston Craine. "What? What's that you said?"

But I couldn't answer. I was gone, drifting, first to vapid Australia, surrounded by track suits, then to snowy Kars, the end of my flight. I saw a stewardess standing on the tarmac, returning handguns to the passengers who'd surrendered them before boarding. Taxis were standing by but we mounted horses instead, riding beyond the city limits and onto the steppe, long and hard like cowboys, a hundred miles and then a hundred more, away from Ararat, away from the Kurds who had robbed me, to the shores of Lake Gölchük, a great place for camping, the water flat and amber-green, the sky lasting forever. Now, beneath the shade trees on the bank, a perfect place to pitch a tent, pluck a saz and sing *American Pie*, but for the heads sticking out of the sand. The ignorant Kurds buried the bodies too close to the water and of course the lake is always dry this time of year. Goddamit, I thought, the smell.

Armenians everywhere. Death. Murder. Genocide?

"What? What's that you said?

I jerked awake, catching myself in dream-fall; my hands clenched the armrests that held me upright. Was I sleeping? I stared at Nazan, then at Vram's father and back to Nazan. My heart thumped out of my chest. I heard tea boiling and glanced about the room, taking in the crucifixes, the porcelain figurines, the Virgin Mary shrine.

My feet wore slippers, not the Muslim kind, but a plastic pair that might have come from a wrapper. My toes were numb where they hung over the ends, and between them blades of grass from a manicured lawn. I ran my hands over my jeans and sweater; they were soiled but intact. How did I get here, I wondered.

"What did you say?" Nazan asked me again.

"What?" I replied.

"You're talking! He's talking," she shouted. Vram hurried in and sat down, joining his father in the room.

I tried my feet, and felt the blisters sting. "It wasn't important," I said.

The old man resumed reading from a book in his lap. Vram shushed him but it did no good. *"The bodies had been burned in the meantime, probably in the search for gold. We estimated that in the course of our ride around the lake, and actually within the space of twenty-four hours, we had seen the remains of not less than ten thousand Armenians who had been killed around Lake Gölchük. This, of course, is appro—"*

"Approck... approck..." said Vram's father, refusing to carry on until he'd mastered the word. Nazan made no effort to help. Until now his pronunciation had been admirable, but did he really comprehend the words? "Approck..."

I stood and tested my feet; they worked, but just barely. "What day is today?"

"Thursday," said Nazan. The information didn't help. How the hell had I gotten out of the hospital? Nazan's eyes followed me to the table, where I spotted Vram's passport and omnipresent visa documents, right where we had left them. How many days ago was that?

"Would you... like some tea?"

"Scotch, perhaps? No? Yes, of course, raki will do." I glanced at my damaged feet. Had the doctors released me, and Vram picked me up? Or had I succeeded where Billy Hayes had failed, escaping from Bakirköy with only the clothes on my back? I thought of my faxes. "May I use the telephone?"

"Please," said Nazan. "Do not ring the Marmara again. If you threaten them they will only... Please," she pleaded. "They are hiding nothing. If they trace your calls? You will only bring more trouble on this family."

This was a lot to digest. I sat down. What was the point anyway? There were no faxes waiting for me at the Marmara. I knew that. I think I had always known that. "You helped me escape?"

Nazan and Vram exchanged worried looks. "No, of course not. You don't remember? You rang us from the Aya Sofya? And we came for you? We don't know how you got out, but it does not seem possible that you walked from Bakirköy to Sultanahmet."

I followed her eyes to my troubled feet and decided that they were wrong—it was possible. Now I noticed pockmarks on my hands, as if I'd recently scaled a fence. I rather liked the idea, and felt my mood improve.

We might have pondered it further, but at that moment the front door opened and Uncle Hikmet came in. When he saw me sitting there his mouth fell open.

"He is better," said Nazan.

Hikmet unslung his camera and deposited it on the table, then emptied his pockets next to it. When he took off his jacket I saw yellow rings; his eyes were bloodshot. He went to Vram's father and kissed both cheeks. He turned to me. "You left the Swiss Hotel in a big hurry. I worried for you."

I nodded. "Where have you been?"

"Embassy of China. Very dull," he said. "And the food, every time the same." He pulled an hors d' oeuvre from his pocket. "Last week at the Bulgaria embassy I didn't eat. Then, ishte, the Chinli serve tonight. Look, I will leave it on the tray tomorrow for next time." He laughed nervously, then coughed and called out to Vram's sisters, who brought him a raki too.

"Tomorrow? What event is tomorrow?"

His eyes rested on me, then he shrugged. "Is nothing. Nasilsin? How are you?"

"What is your event tomorrow?" I persisted.

Nazan broke in. "You seem so... so much better. But are you well enough to go to the consulate? You see, Monday starts the Bayram, the holiday, so there will be no visas for a week."

Vram wouldn't meet my eyes. I took a gulp of milky swill, all but tasting the bacteria. I supposed that she meant the Kurban Bayrami, the slaughtering of sheep to be fed to the poor. It was a tradition that had held up well, even in modern Istanbul, where once a year the streets ran red with blood. But my mind was on Hikmet's event; I looked at him eagerly.

"There is nothing I can do," said Hikmet. "Bak." He searched his wallet, found what he was looking for. "There too many security, and only I have one ticket."

I put out my hand. He hesitated, then handed it to me. I recognized just one of the Turkish words, *Savarona.*

Hikmet looked relieved when I gave it back. "This is very big, very special. Atatürk's ship. Anladin mi? Do you understand? Usually 50,000 marks it costs. It will go all the ways to Ali Iskender's island. I will not miss for everything. There will be ministers from the national assembly. And members of your Parliament!

And diplomats, I thought to myself. Perhaps Winston would be there too—Winston, who had eluded me all these months but for a few narcotic moments at the asylum. "My press pass will get me in," I said. By this, I meant my expired *City Paper* ID.

Hikmet lifted his chin and nodded, no.

I rose and walked to the family shrine, to the bundle of crucifixes and tacky figurines, in three quick steps. "What do I have to do to convince you to take me?" Nazan inhaled as I inspected the icons, one by one. My hands trembled with the urge to destroy. A saint on horseback impaled a dragon with a very long pole; in the glossy reflection I saw my face, the face that would never grace a book jacket. I saw that I looked angry. All these months, all these years, for nothing. Thousands of pages written, twice as many miles traveled. Eighteen thousand dollars missing from my sock. No answer to my faxes. No file.

I studied the saint and saw myself in the image, just as passionate and idealistic, out slaying dragons whatever the cost. While Saint Michael did his thing, his contemporaries were probably back home tending the lawn, working nine to five and watching HBO. Throughout the ages, there have always been a select few, discontent and determined to rise beyond the banalities, the mediocrities, of everyday life. But unlike Saint Michael, my dragon was not dead.

"I want to go with you."

"Then you should have a ticket," said Hikmet.

Nazan rose. "Don't go," she said.

"Why not?"

"The embassy. Vram. You said you would help him. You..."

"No!" said Vram suddenly. "Istemiyorum. I don't want." Nazan tried to object, but Vram cut her off. He pointed at my feet. "Consulate. Tomorrow. Okay. No problem. But for visa, no. For you. For the doctor. Because." he struggled for the right word. Failing, he said, "Sick."

I gripped the icon tighter, felt it go to pieces in my hand. "I'm going to the Savarona."

"It's quite possible to do both, now isn't it?" said Nazan. She grabbed the glass from Hikmet's hand and drank until the ice rattled. Her voice steadied. "Though I don't know what you want with that party. All chock-a-block with politicians getting pissed. What kind of story is that?"

"No more stories," I said.

This silenced her. Perhaps in that moment she caught a glimpse of me, standing aboard the Savarona, cold metal in my hand, my life racing to its natural conclusion. But, no, how could that be? She could not see the future, not when I couldn't see it myself, not when even the past was a blur to me, when even the past few days had been misplaced.

"Do you think that Hikmet goes so that he can take pictures? Bloody hell. He goes for the liquor and the ladies in their fancy dress! But you are a serious journalist."

"Journalist!" said Vram's father. We turned to him in surprise. They, because the old man had never spoken a word of English except when reading from a book; me, because it was the first time I had ever heard sarcasm from a Turk.

"What did you say?"

"Ah," said the old man, and returned to his thoughts. There was soccer on the television, and a cheering crowd. I stood at the altar, fists clenched, staring down my attackers, but they only looked away. I crossed the room and found my raki, then drifted to the window. Headlights played like lightning down the avenue, too much for my eyes.

Why resist? I let the colors come, let them wash over me, let them seek every orifice, every opening in my porous body and mind. Let them come. Let them swallow me up.

Nazan was interpreting for Vram. "He says you do not have to do this. Canim, dear, are you alright?

"Where is my jacket?"

"But the embassy…" said Nazan.

"Right, Vram's visa."

Vram struggled to say something, but his English failed. He gave up and rifled through the documents until he found a letter that I'd done for him, something about university plans in California, something I'd written up and forgotten many days ago. He held it like a priest serving communion. He ripped it in two.

Nazan watched in horror, then looked down at her shoes. "Vram is saying go to the consulate. Not for the visa. Go and let them help *you*."

"My jacket—"

"Vram is saying you are welcome to stay." But no sooner had she said this than she was off to locate my meager belongings, leaving Vram hopelessly tongue-tied. Hikmet and the old man avoided my eyes, moved to the other room to take refuge in the soccer game. That left only Vram to foil me.

"May I have a glass of water, please?" I made a drinking motion with my hand.

The ticket was easy enough to find, shimmering like a jewel in Hikmet's wallet. Mission accomplished, I returned the wallet to Hikmet's jacket, thought twice, then pocketed the wallet too. I was already sitting down when Vram returned. Still holding my water, he glanced at the jacket and back at me. "Güle, güle," he said with a nod. The standard Turkish farewell. Go smiling.

But I found that I could only go.

The rain was falling hard, too hard to stop and inspect my stolen goods. I found a bar and ordered a whisky with Hikmet's money, my money now, and counted some 8 million lira—well over a hundred dollars—plus a credit card from an American bank. Hikmet's signature was easy enough to forge, and the boutiques in Shisli open late, so when I checked into the Hyatt that night I was wearing an Armani suit and wingtips made from alligator skin. Smooth, I said to myself. Smooth.

I tried to go to sleep, but when that proved impossible I put my suit back on, and my alligator shoes, and hailed a taxi to the spot where I'd once directed traffic in the nude, and from there it was not at all difficult to find the park. The rain had turned to a fine drizzle when I approached the merry-go-round and stuck my hand inside the muddy hole and felt something furry brush past; then the gun bumped against my skin and I pulled it clear. Funny how I could remember putting it there, but very, very little else. I rose and corrected my tie. If I were meant to go down, then I would do it in style.

* * *

In the warm summer months, a little boat called the Hiawatha cruises up one side of the Bosphorous and down the other, in a long arc between the Black Sea and the Golden Horn. For half a century it has plied these waters, carrying the likes of Douglas MacArthur, Eleanor Roosevelt, George Bush Senior, and too many congressmen to count. The boat is U.S. Government property and flies the flag proudly, a security officer's nightmare. No wonder it's as familiar to the fishermen as the bridges overhead, the eddies where the garbage swirls, or the docks in Asia where they stop to drink tea.

During the long wet winter, the Hiawatha rests in a boatyard north of the city. Few people know where, and it's unwise to advertise; only a few years back, Dev Sol fire-bombed the vessel as it sat unattended. No one was hurt, but the damage required a full restoration; with care the elongated wood strips were replaced and re-painted orange and maroon, until the great banana-shaped craft again resembled a 1970s station wagon, all panels and passengers.

The captain then was as famous as the boat itself. For twenty years he tooted the horn proudly and waved at the little people, until one day he was undone by a fender bender with a fisherman. The problem was not so much the accident itself, but the captain's failure to report it. Taking his queue from the motor-pool drivers who collected annual awards for allegedly going nine, twelve, fifteen years without an accident—and whose cousins all ran body shops—the captain contracted to fix the damage himself.

When things came to light, there was talk of liability and lawsuits, and he was unceremoniously dismissed. A succession of less famous captains replaced him, coming and going like so many bad visa cases.

The latest of these was a former navy man named Boray. On the job only a month, he was yet to see the Hiawatha in the water. Boray spent his days at the dry dock, overseeing minor repairs and renovations, pacing the work to last the full length of the winter. Having already conditioned his family to long absences, he was prone to sit for hours atop the grounded vessel, long after the day's modest work was done, his mind wandering in the solitude.

Today is such a day. Boray sits on the deck, holding his jacket tight against the chill. The tea has gone cold. Fog fills the straits like mud.

He lights a cigarette. Amazing how far sound travels across the water. Familiar music drifts in waves across the Bosphorous; one moment he hears it and the next it is gone. Oynama Shikidim shikidim, Ah yanar döner, a-achiipsin. Kids' music. The song has dominated the radio for months, the Turkish play lists are so narrow that the term "top forty" is a stretch; top ten is more like it.

He draws from his cigarette and contemplates a shot from the bottle of Russian vodka left behind by his predecessor. For weeks he has studied it, kept it hidden. But now the air is crisp and the music fills him with the sadness of the truly happy; only one swallow, he thinks, maybe two, and then he will throw it away. Oynama Shikidim shikidim. No question, the song is catchy.

A moment later, Boray's career as captain of the Hiawatha is over.

"Buyrun," says Gazi.

Red accepts his orders and hits him again, the lead pipe landing with more of a plop than a thud on the captain's head. This time there is no reaction, no cry or quiver; the blow is inconsequential, as mundane as striking a sack of potatoes but for the blood and gunk that creeps onto the floorboards of the boat.

Gazi stares at the mess in disgust. "Here," he says, "and here," pointing to his own head to show where the blows should have fallen.

Red takes a step back and shivers. Isn't it enough that he killed him? Must he now endure a lecture? The pipe rattles on the Hiawatha's stern; he follows the action to his gloved hand and sees it shaking violently. He lets the pipe fall. He is angry, but what did he expect from this little gnome? When he killed the drunk Australian—a lifetime ago, it seems to him now—Zakho and the others had all but swept him away on their shoulders. And now he has killed again, with all the ceremony of a supermarket checkout. He stares at the body, frozen. Must he now haul him away? Gazi sighs and motions to Galip, who lifts the corpse from the deck and chucks it easily to the ground. There it stays.

They do a sloppy job, getting the boat into the water. When it finally floats there are dents in the hull, long gashes where wood and metal disagreed. The Hiawatha pitches unsteadily in the waves. Gazi searches the boatyard for the proper key, returns and starts the engine, then shuts it off again. It is all much easier than he expected. He looks at his watch and sits down. They are ahead of schedule. They light cigarettes; Red is not a smoker, but the motion is satisfying.

A stain is visible on the captain's backside; when the breeze shifts, Red turns away from the smell. He holds his cigarette like a joint and blows the smoke quickly. No one speaks. Red looks again at the captain; his expression is oddly neutral, as if death, when it came, was like taking a phone call. He looks like a simple man, rather short on malice, with a face that's difficult to hate. Thankfully hate isn't necessary, not even desired. It's enough to know that he was a tool of the Americans. When he signed on to this job, he enlisted in their army; he traded his soul. Red drags from his cigarette, swishes the smoke around in his mouth. When one takes such a job, of course he knows he has joined a war.

The suits are brought out, and Gazi orders them on. Would he also tell them how to put on their pants, one leg at a time? Galip has his shirt on quickly, but the gaudy polyester tie brings him to an impasse; he holds it by one end, then the other, as if searching for instructions.

"I'm not wearing this," says Red. The pant legs are so short they leave his ankles bare.

Gazi ignores him. The outfits are a sore spot; five sets of suits, shirts, ties, belts and shoes had not been easy to procure. Red didn't know where they came from—it was Gazi, and Gazi alone, who spoke to the next cell above—but he had the vague notion that they'd never been officially approved. Nor had any new weapons been granted. Perhaps not even the PKK was immune to bureaucracy.

Red fingers the sidearm in his pocket, jogging a memory of the moments before he killed the young Australian, bringing one life—no, two lives—to an end. Though his parents and the rest believed otherwise, he is indeed dead, and there is no going back. All he has now is his gun. As usual, it's old and a little rusty, the kind of weapon best fired at close range and with accuracy to avoid the need for a second shot.

He resolves to challenge Gazi on the suit. "If Galip is going to be the best-dressed here, I suggest you have him do the talking when we reach the ship."

They stare at the big man, who still looks stumped, holding the tie at both ends like a clothesline. Gazi sighs and barks an order; the big man complies by stripping. Red takes the bigger suit and slips it on, then helps the others with their ties, keeping the best for himself. Then they are off, the boat slipping like a phantom into the current.

Out on the water, stealth is no longer an object, but still no one speaks as they putter south between the continents. The current is strong. In five minutes they pass the fortress called Rumeli Hisari, where the straits diminish to their narrowest point. Some say that when Mehmet the Conqueror laid siege to Constantinople, he blocked the Bosphorous with an iron chain at this spot to cut off reinforcements. Perhaps it also was here that in the time of Noah an inlet leapt its banks and fled north across a vast plain of scattered towns, half-emptying the Mediterranean to create the new Black Sea—for forty days and forty nights, an apocalypse of water, the map of the world changed forever.

"Louder," says Gazi. "Make more louder." He orders the flag mounted and unfurled, then slips a cassette into the stereo—Madonna's "Like a Virgin," the only tape he can find in the boat. Taylor chews his lip and stares at the oily blackness rushing by. He doesn't feel like talking, let alone celebrating; the event doesn't seem worth it.

To die in battle or to live alone—which is worse? He fingers the weapon again, clicking the safety to the off position, then on and off again. He wonders if he should pray. But to whom? Karl Marx? There is no God, no one up above, yet still he feels watched. Zakho? Comradeship is all that counts. Fraternity. He stares into the distance and sees the lights take shape. For his memory, I will be strong. In time he adds his voice to the others, and when they finally see the Savarona, translucent and glittering in the twilight, the Hiawatha is a rolling, rollicking feast, all cheers and laughter and full of purpose.

* * *

One of Atatürk's additions to the German-built Savarona was a hamam, a Turkish bath, carved from sixty tons of hand-finished marble from the Bursa quarries. It was one of Atatürk's few pleasures in his final days, says the tour guide. She is small and pretty and wears a tight-fitting skirt and speaks too-perfect English in a sing-songy voice. *Bee-bee-bee-bee*. The congressmen seem to like her company.

Next stop is the mini-museum, the ultimate redundancy on a ship where even the plumbing is sacred. The Father of Turkey's personal items—a comb, a timepiece, a razor, a letter opener—are there under glass, along with a plate of uneaten chick peas. "Well, doesn't that take all," says Zimmerman. "What are they going to do with our leftovers? Put them in Dolmy-Bachy Palace?"

The tour guide looks wounded. Zimmerman recovers with the natural instincts of the politician. "Miss, you're doing a wonderful job. Thank you," he says. With excessive enthusiasm, his colleagues concur.

George hangs back as they squeeze into Atatürk's old cabin, then slips away to relieve himself in a toilet so immaculate he is reluctant to pee. He takes a cloth towel from a pile on the marble counter, dries his hands, then picks the droplets off the sink before depositing it in the hamper. Ottoman muzak pipes in from the ceiling. As he leaves, he unclasps a cell phone from his belt and dials Truman.

"Where are they?" his friend asks.

"Getting the full tour."

"Everything okay?"

"They're happy," says George. "Priscilla's with them. When are you coming aboard?"

"I wish I knew! Ambassador's twenty-five minutes late. Is the party going?"

"No, too early yet," he lies, entering the main ballroom and poking his way through the crowd. Everyone has a drink, and the saz band is starting up. At the bar he cups his hand over the phone and orders a Chivas.

"Damn it," says Truman. "If he makes me miss... Oh, sorry, now you're screwed too. The truck is here."

George drains the better part of his drink, leaves the glass and heads outside. The truck is full of congressional luggage, they being the only guests who packed their pajamas. Tonight they'll sleep on Ali Iskender's island, amid crumbling pillars and chunks of ancient temples from up and down the Aegean. In the morning, they'll go to the airport by boat, without stopping back at the Conrad. They've already checked out one night early, leaving the manager in a snit.

Outside, Colonel Ryan gives George a cursory glance, then suggests he tag along with the porters. "Fine," says George, happy to steer clear. In the storage room, he counts the surviving luggage, which includes three bags of golf clubs the congressmen bought duty-free at one of their previous stops. He checks them over and sighs; his own clubs are an off-brand. He heads upstairs.

At the bar, Harold is telling Dawn about the DEA's latest bust. Her dress is white with pink flowers and cut just above the ankles, obscenely prudish in this sea of skin-tight black and boisterous cleavage. She sips Turkish wine and scrunches her face. She has done something evangelical with her hair.

"You look nice," George tells her.

"Don't lie. I'm not dressed slutty enough." She catches him looking away. "Don't gawk, George."

"Just checking if Craine's here," he lies. "He wasn't at work today. You think he's pulled another one of his disappearing acts?"

"Anything's possible with our Winston," she sighs.

"When are they going to replace him?" asks Harold.

George shrugs. "The ambassador's here," he says. Hutchins pauses at the door for effect before making his entrance. Ali Iskender greets him with a kiss on both cheeks, leaving the ambassador's hand dangling. "I suppose we'd better start schmoozing."

Dawn nods and drifts away, freeing George to order a second drink. A Chivas buzz is rare on his salary, and a welcome antidote to the rote questions that pass as conversation between the giving and taking of business cards.

Truman joins him at the bar. "Would you just look at him," he says. "Isn't he delicious?"

"He's a bodyguard," says George.

"I… will always love you…" hums Truman, doing his best Whitney Houston.

"Look at me," says George. Truman's tux is from his junior officer days, more than a decade old. His paunch has forced it loose at the middle, and his bow tie is crooked. With care, George straightens it out.

"Careful," says Truman. "Phil might see."

"So?"

"You don't want anything to happen to your security clearance."

George steps back. "What are you talking about?"

"Why didn't you tell me?"

"What do you mean?" Then, more loudly, "What has Dawn told you?"

Truman looks away. "What I should have heard from you. I have my own clearance to worry about, George."

George pauses while a Turkish couple squeezes by. Maybe. Maybe he should have told him. But then he would have had to explain the thing about Taylor Moore—how the CIA had recruited him for information on the PKK, and how Taylor had played them for fools. But there was another reason to hold his tongue. The truth was, George blamed Truman just a little for the mess he was in, for ruining his good name. What did Truman expect when he practically shouted his orientation from the rooftops?

"What do you have to worry about, Truman? You're out of the closet. You've said it yourself. There's nothing they can do to you. But me, they think I'm in the closet, which would be a problem if it were true. Which it isn't! I mean, how could it be? But of course Phil doesn't really believe it. He knows I'm not... He's just using it for— "

"For what? What's he using it for?"

George sips anxiously and scans the room. He locates Dawn with Priscilla, Hutchins with the congressmen and Winston alone in a corner, juggling a drink in one hand and his omni-present writing pad in the other. Finally he locates Phil in an animated conversation with a Turk. Tim is with them.

"Jesus. Is anybody *not* here? You did pretty damn well with the tickets, Truman." He reaches in his breast pocket. At thirty-three thousand a year, he owns just two suits and a sports jacket; the latter he can wear with either khakis or blue trousers, which makes not quite one outfit for each day of the week. With such a limited wardrobe, the chances are pretty good that it's in his pocket. It is.

Truman takes the photo. "Who's that with Tim?"

"Taylor Moore. My famous Welfare and Whereabouts case. Remember?"

"The terrorist?"

George nods and glances about. "Phil called him one of their mistakes." He studies Truman, who looks puzzled. "Truman, he was on their payroll! He was an asset! And meanwhile he was out planting bombs at the Aya Sofya and killing that Australian kid, whose body I almost sent home to Taylor's parents by mistake. Don't you get it!"

Truman stares quietly at the photograph. He doesn't look up, even when the great ship shudders and moves. They have disembarked and are on their way.

"Who took the picture?"

"This woman, Nazan, who I told you about. She told me she's on MIT's payroll, an informer for the Turks, but Phil thinks she's real MIT, and trying to recruit me, which is possible, I guess, though I'm not sure I completely buy it...God, this sounds like a movie." He stares at the drink in his hand.

"So Taylor's what, PKK? And Phil's blackmailing you to stay quiet... Wait, I don't want to know."

"You don't know!" George hisses. He snatches back the photo and re-checks the room.

To their surprise, he sees Winston Craine approaching, pen and notebook in hand.

"Winston. Long time no see."

"George," Winston nods. "Truman." He strokes his head from back to front, then back again. His shirt is rumpled and missing a button at the top. His tie is loose; he puts two fingers through it and further widens the loop. Along with George, he is one of the few in the room not wearing a tux.

"Lots of visas today?" asks George.

Winston ignores the question. "I was just wondering if you happen to know *that individual* over there."

"Who? The Turk with..."

"No, no. By the ice sculpture. The American."

George spots him, makes eye contact, then looks away.

"Never seen him before," says Truman.

"Jesus," says George. "What the hell's he doing here? That's the American who got drugged on Mount Ararat and came here. Remember? He's a nut case. I was trying to repatriate him, but he wouldn't go. Owes the consulate about two hundred bucks. Last time I saw him was at that reception last week. He freaked out and wound up in Bakirköy. Winston, you visited him. I thought the Turks were going to drive him to the border!"

"Yes, well, hmm. Seems he escaped before they got around to doing it."

"Escaped?"

"Hmm, yes," says Winston, observing his feet. "Life does go on in the consular section while you're out playing spy games."

Truman speaks up before George can react. "Fabulous suit," he says. "Oh, but those shoes…" He puts his hand to his mouth.

"How did he get in here?"

"Why don't you ask him?" says Winston. "Here he comes."

"Winston, do you remember his name?"

Bill. The name is Bill.

I fail to see why this is so hard to remember. Travel half-way around the world, nearly drown in the south Pacific, climb Ararat, get drugged and robbed by Kurds, spend a week in a straight jacket—and still people won't take the requisite two minutes to commit your name to memory. It's hard on a man's ego, let me tell you.

And why the surprise to see me? Should I be somewhere else? Perhaps living a *normal* life in some American suburb? Early to bed and early to rise, so that I can make it to my piss-ant job on time, where the cup on my desk says *nineteenth hole*? What would be the point? To pine away for happy hour at day's end, so that I can mingle with the other pointless people? To talk, to be funny, to find something, anything, to say, if only to avoid the lapse that stalks all conversation, that moment of shared revelation when we know it's all for nothing, that there is no point, no meaning, and that the words are empty. I know it, and you know it, and he knows it, and she knows it, but still we won't acknowledge it, will only ignore it with widened eyes and bared teeth, faking it, frauds that we are, conspiring together to fill the air with words, and any words will do.

Am I so different now?

George, I know you understand. You wouldn't have joined the service if you didn't—would have gone into accounting, engineering, real estate instead. But, no, you dreamed of transcending the workaday world. You wanted to be part of something bigger—bigger than you—wanted to be part of history, or at least its witness, wanted to serve a higher purpose. No, don't deny it. Even now I can see it in your face. It's true. You also have a cause.

And why not? Haven't we established that man is doomed to live either in the convulsions of distress or in the lethargy of boredom? It's the curse of our age. A few thousand years ago, we had to fight to survive, like any animal. Now any idiot can feed himself and put a roof over his head. Life is too easy now. Our brains have made us freaks of nature. Progress has freed us to do what we want, but what is there to do?

No, don't look away. Listen up. I read something in the *Herald Tribune* the other day. A train in London crashed, and what did the survivors do? They got up and dusted themselves off and headed straight to the airport and bought one-way tickets to Hong Kong, Australia, Argentina. You see, they'd been handed the gift of being dead, the chance to start anew. And how quickly they were willing to dump everyone and everything, their entire lives, though there were no saber-tooth tigers stalking their caves, no threat that their crops would fail! They just wanted out. What does this say about our world? Maybe death is the problem. With each passing year, it comes at us faster. At seven years old, nine-tenths of our lives lie before us, and the clock ticks slowly. No, I'm serious, deadly serious. At twenty-seven, less than two-thirds of our lives remain; we plunge like stones from a building, gaining speed as we go. Today there are more dead people than at any time in human history. Did you know that? By the time I finish this sentence mankind will break the record again. And again.

Convulsions of distress or the lethargy of boredom. It's one or the other. Don't you see? It says so right here, in this book I keep in my pocket. The author spoke French, so mustn't it be true? Distress or boredom. To feel something, or to feel nothing. Take your choice. I've made mine. Now kindly take your hand from my shoulder.

"Bill," said George. "Of course. I'm sorry." He took his hand away. "I'm not so good at names. No excuse for that in my line of work."

Craine shuffled from one foot to the other.

Truman looked thoughtful. "I read about that train wreck in London. Some of the passengers disappeared for a few days, but eventually they all lost their nerve and went home. Interesting. I think you're on to something there."

"They went home," I went on, "because they realized their plan—well, not their plan, really, since it was spontaneous—their ruse hadn't worked. The authorities had no trouble at all identifying the bodies, even the most badly burned. Dental records and all that. Turns out in the twentieth century it's what's been done to our teeth that makes us unique."

George clenched his own teeth just then, recalling his foul-up with the Aussie's remains. He flinched again when Ambassador Hutchins' hand fell on his shoulder. "George, the chairman needs something from his duffel. Give us a hand, will you?"

"Your excellency," I said, giving him a little bow.

He took my hand in a Texas clench and shook it hard, a double pump, then let it go.

"Uh, Mister Ambassador, this is, uh…"

"You the new man from Proctor and Gamble?" Hutchins crossed his arms. He'd heard only bad things about the new man from Proctor and Gamble.

"No, Mister Ambassador, he's…"

"Bill Bigelow, your excellency. I'm a journalist, a writer."

"Mmm. Which paper?"

"Freelance, your excellency," I produced a card that he stuffed in his pocket. "I've been in all the major weeklies at one time or another."

"What kind of story you working on now?" His eyes shifted and I saw that I had lost him.

"Well, sir, your men here were thinking I should retire," I said. "Suggested that I go home. Had a good run and all that, but now the creative juices are dry. And so on an and so forth. But I think they're dead wrong." My hand slid inside my breast pocket. The pistol's grip felt cold and rough, like a tiny moonscape. I worked the weapon loose from the fabric. In the small of my back, three hundred double-sided hand-written pages pushed heavily against my dress shirt—my manuscript. I could feel the paper soaking up sweat, the ink coming off on my skin. A single fly alit on the end of my nose. With my free hand I waved it away, but it only lapped my head and settled down again. I waved it away. The ambassador stared at me, puzzled. I should have acted then. Yes, I should have acted then. But I wasn't ready. I had not chosen this moment and I would not let it choose me. And so I hoped for the ambassador to stay, to stay and not to go, to allow me more time to decide, decide.

"I feel the same way myself sometimes," said Hutchins. "But it goes away with a couple of drinks. Leak something good to this young man, would you, Truman? Sounds like he's desperate for a story. Just make sure you do me justice. Pleasure to meet you, Mister… Enjoy the party. George, let's you and I find the chairman."

Ambassador Hutchins ambled off, George in tow, and I knew that the moment had passed and would not come again. Relief turned to disappointment, to anger, to deep remorse. My plan had been this: Jump behind the ambassador. Wrap my arm around his thick neck. Pull the pistol from my pocket. Jab it into his side. Order him on stage. Guide him to the microphone. Warn everyone to step back and no one would get hurt. Take my left arm from around his neck. Keep the gun where it was. Pull the manuscript from my shirt. Give it to him. Make him read it aloud.

Yes, that was my plan. My whole plan. Beyond that, I would have to improvise.

The pages under my shirt had become a source of great discomfort; they were crumpling now, bunching up beneath my jacket. In George's absence, Truman had slipped away, leaving only Craine and me—the first time we'd been alone since Bakirköy, and this time without restraints. A dam inside me threatened to burst.

Craine was stoic as I poured out my venom. I begged to know how he could conspire with the rest to silence me, to send me home, when I knew that he, and he alone, understood. I railed against his betrayal, at the failures of a lifetime, everything that should have been but wasn't. My eyes welled with tears, snaring the flies as they hovered too near. I felt the flies in my nostrils, in my mouth, clinging to my lips. I blew, I choked, I gagged, I spit them out on the floor. The other guests left us alone.

With Craine in the lead we drifted to the doors that led to the deck and into the night, assaulted by fumes from the Straits. I collapsed on the railing, short of breath and gasping. My chest heaved. I thought about the ambassador again—how close he had been and how I had let him go. Craine raised his hand and the large men who had gathered cut short their approach. The cold night air was too much for the flies. I felt my head clear. When Craine turned to face me, his face was serene, back-lit by the lights of the party inside.

"You let me down."

"I know," said Winston.

We were elbow to elbow on the railing. "It's over, isn't it? I have to go back."

He nodded.

"I've failed. I have to admit that."

"We all fail sometimes," said Winston.

"I have to go back. I have to go back and be normal. I have to swallow the pills they give me, tranquilize myself, be as docile as a zoo animal."

"Umm," he said. "Zoloft?"

"Serzone."

"Ah. Better," said Winston.

I saw him as if for the first time. "Better, yes. But still it makes you ordinary."

You can't make a revolution every day," he said. "It's too exhausting."

"Yes, but..." I stared out at the inky blackness, feeling jumpy, anything but exhausted now. On the far shore of the Bosphorous, the lights of Asia slipped by at a fast clip. The Savarona was riding five knots faster than the current, wasting no time to reach the island. It was bitterly cold on the water, but my psychosis kept me warm.

"It would be a lot less exhausting if you'd just give me the file," I said.

He shivered, then looked at me sternly. "Don't bother with the file. The file's not important. I regret ever suggesting that it was."

"I don't believe you. You showed me the pages. You stamped them CONFIDENTIAL. There are government secrets in there."

He smiled. "There are only my secrets in there. And those of this consulate."

"But in Australia you said… I remember. It's a house of cards. To bring it down, all I have to do is exhale."

He turned to me abruptly. "This is the house of cards, Bill," he said, tapping a finger to his head. "This is what I meant. The house of cards is here. And so every day I hold my breath."

He turned away and again observed the water. It was black and deep, impenetrable. Matter-of-factly he said, "Well, what's this? It's the Hiawatha."

But I didn't hear him, barely even noticed as the little boat pulled alongside our yacht. Bill, he had called me. Bill, with such ease and inevitability, it was clear that all along he'd known my name. At last I had arrived.

* * *

When the first gunshot sounded, Zimmerman kept right on talking, so focused was he on the problem of financing 3.5 billion dollars worth of attack helicopters for Turkey. But Hutchins was no longer listening. The ex-marine was waiting for the second report, which came quickly, followed by a third and a fourth. The shots seemed to come from the ballroom, where the guests were gathered.

"Is that a gun?" asked George. He looked at Hutchins.

"Go," said the ambassador. They picked up their pace down the hall to the storage room. George struggled to lock the flimsy door behind them. There were no windows, just mountains of congressional luggage. George felt for his cell phone. It was there. But whom to call?

"What the hell's going on?" asked Zimmerman.

"We'll find out soon enough, Art. You sit tight."

"Wait sir," said George. "You could be a target. You can't go out."

They heard another gunshot. "Shut the light off and open that door," said Hutchins. "Just a crack."

George peeked through.

"What do you see?"

The hall was empty. Yet from everywhere and nowhere came sounds of movement, people going up the stairs and down them again, opening and closing doors and panicking in multiple languages. The ceiling shook beneath heavy steps. Suddenly George found himself staring at someone's back, just inches away; he sucked in air. The figure continued down the hallway, his face still turned away. He was huge for a Turk, thick and clumsy, the matted hair on his neck making a joke of his suit, which was stretched to the breaking point anyway. A gun dangled from his hand.

George backed off, not daring to seal the door and lose the sliver of light. His eyes struggled to adjust. "Hide," he whispered, but Hutchins and Zimmerman were already down behind the bags. George tiptoed from the door, maneuvering blind in the dark. He bumped a suitcase and gasped as it fell to the floor; the thump was jarring.

He heard movement at the door and ducked as the sliver of light became a flood. Dropping to his hands and knees, he found a gap between two Samsonites. He heard the ambassador's joints creak several suitcases away—bad knees, he recalled from their day on the golf course. A shadow swept over the room. George felt his heart pound, up near his throat. To speak would be impossible; perhaps to scream was an option.

Heavy footsteps. It was impossible not to look. Galip plodded across the room, his gun leading the way. He hadn't bothered with the switch, or perhaps he couldn't find it. He bumped a suitcase and it too tumbled to the floor, threatening to trip him up. He froze momentarily. Then he was on the move again, closing in on where the congressman crouched, just a few feet away.

For George, the urge to do something and the urge to do nothing cancelled each other out. Decide, decide, decide, he thought. But then his cell phone decided for him. It rang.

George let it ring again, tried to will it away, pretend it wasn't there. It could be an unmanned phone in any bag, he told himself. He reared back on his knees, instinctively drawing his hands to his face. The cell phone rang a third time, then a fourth. The caller didn't know when to stop. George waited for the fifth. Entire minutes seemed to pass. Chivas and hors d'oeuvres bubbled up in his throat as he watched a head rise above the luggage. Do something, he thought. But he found he couldn't move.

George barely registered Galip's grunt as the Turk was hit from behind. Body and luggage tumbled toward him in the same motion. George rolled and came to his feet, his fists clenched. Galip rose, then dropped to his knees, one hand on his head, the other sweeping the floor for his lost gun. Giving up, he turned on Hutchins who still held the flashlight, industrial-sized, long and heavy with size-D batteries, poised to hit him again.

George got his left arm around Galip's neck before the big Turk knew he was there, but then his lungs were emptied by an elbow in his gut. Sucking air, he saw Hutchins swing again. This time the Turk was ready. He caught the flashlight on his forearm, lurched forward and found a handful of shirt, then drove Hutchins to the wall where they grappled for advantage. Still breathless, George resumed his attack, punching toward the kidney. The big Turk flinched. Emboldened, George threw a high right as the Turk's face came around, but found only forehead instead, hard as cement. George fell back as Galip lunged, but now Hutchins had him around the neck, forearms rippling. The Turk's face bulged. Pulling in his throbbing right hand, George jabbed pathetically with his left, peppering the Turk with blows that embarrassed them both. Suddenly desperate, Galip plunged backward, taking the ambassador to the floor where he lost his grip and rolled away.

When Galip came to his feet he was sucking air, red-faced and panting. He doubled over, one hand on his knee, the other raised. Time out, he seemed to say.

For a moment, Hutchins obliged. Then, breathing heavily, the ambassador crossed the room and sifted through the golf bags until he found what he was looking for. Successful, he returned to the Turk, steadied himself, then swung the five-iron like an axe. The club broke at the shaft. The big Turk toppled over.

"Nice shot, Mister Ambassador," said George, turning away. He felt a little ill.

This time, Hutchins accepted the compliment.

Incompetent Galip. The big Turk wasn't supposed to be brawling in the luggage room. He was supposed to be on the bridge, making sure the captain stayed on course to Ali Iskender's Island. There, they would have a defensible position to conduct their negotiations with the police. How many imprisoned guerrillas would the government exchange for the cream of Istanbul society? Ten for each hostage, they figured.

Gazi had expected bodyguards, but none foolish enough to draw their guns in the face of such odds, as Iskender's bodyguard had in those first frantic minutes, hitting his mark before taking bullets to the chest, leg, and groin, and finally to the head, execution style. Never send Galip anywhere alone was the rule, but now there was no choice—the cell was one man short. And so off he had gone to secure the bridge.

Of course, he'd gotten lost on the way, gone downstairs when he should have gone up, let himself be distracted by noise in the luggage room. All the while, the captain and his first mate had watched the shootout on the bridge, on the Savarona's state-of-the-art closed-circuit television system, where even the color of the blood was manifest, until enough was enough and they'd jumped into the Bosphorous and started to swim. *Abandon ship.* Their sole nod to duty had been shutting down the engines, leaving the Savarona to rotate slowly starboard as the current hauled it downstream. Soon the captain and his first mate were ashore, telling their story to a traffic cop as the great yacht faded in the distance.

The Savarona drifted with the current, bobbing in the waves like an expensive cork, no one at the helm, no one in control. Between Europe and Asia, east and west, it drifted south, neither near nor far from either shore.

Listen up. Gazi was making announcements in Turkish, which Taylor was translating to English in a shrill, nervous voice. "Anyone holding a gun will raise his hand and step over here. Anyone found with a gun later will be executed without question." A half dozen men laid down their weapons. Of course I did not. In the middle of the banquet room, the slain bodyguard lay where he had fallen, the blood turning to taffy beneath his head. People did everything they could not to look at him, turning their backs or studying their shoes. But I just stared. It was fascinating, like beholding a crystal ball, a vision of the future conjured by an oracle. I was hypnotized.

The two terrorists held their guns stiffly, clicking and unclicking the safeties and hopping little hops like joggers at a stop light. Perspiration and spit dampened their ski masks around the slits of their mouths. Thanks to Taylor, Gazi's instructions were easy enough to follow, the main point being to stand still and listen. Being a hostage was almost too easy, I decided, demanding little in the way of initiative, like being on Serzone I supposed.

The room was unbearably hot; the air conditioners had ceased with the engines and each passenger was his own little stove. Through the windows we watched Asia pass by, replaced by waves, then Europe and waves and Asia again. The ship slowly spun as if caught in an eddy, but I knew we were moving downstream at a fast clip, making vast concentric circles in the waves. Where would we come ashore? I hoped it would be at a seafood restaurant, and that we'd be permitted to move to the windows and watch the startled faces of the diners.

A woman made a sound like a whimper; I stared at her and smiled. I felt no fear, only annoyance that this motley band of freedom fighters had upstaged me, had robbed me of the limelight. It should have been me. Look what my hesitation had cost. Still, I couldn't keep the smile from my face. It was all too exciting. Finally, a crisis bigger than the one in my head!

George could hear it all over the cell phone, a single Turk bullying the hostages, mindlessly separating them into three groups—foreigners, wealthy Turks, and finally the bodyguards and waiters and other rabble who were there to serve them. The organizing seemed gratuitous, as if they were merely killing time.

He held the cell phone to his ear, the cell phone that wouldn't stop ringing before. Now it was working well as a microphone.

"Whoever called us left the phone open on his end," said George. To let us hear everything." He knew it was Truman who had done it.

"Clever," said the ambassador. "But it almost got us killed. Anyway, we need that phone to call for help."

"We can't give up this connection."

"There has to be another phone around here somewhere."

The crew had its own baggage in the room, filled with private pleasures—cigarettes and dirty magazines and condoms and flasks of raki and stuff to make tea. Finally, in the pocket of a leather jacket in the closet, they found what they were looking for.

Zimmerman spoke in a daze. "My wife told me why do I want to make this trip so soon after session. She had tickets for Florida. Give me the phone."

"No, sir," snapped Hutchins. "George, what's the number for the Ops Center?"

George poked at the buttons. A young lady answered, buoyant with caffeine and ambition. A conference call with the White House, the state department, the Pentagon and the FBI was set in motion. George passed the phone to Hutchins.

George put the other phone back to his ear. The Turk was still shouting instructions. Now he heard an American shouting too. Crazy bastard, he thought. Don't get yourself killed. But no, the American wasn't challenging anyone; he was interpreting. Yes, he was; and with a Boston accent at that. George jerked upright, astonished.

"What?" asked a worried Zimmerman. "What do you hear?"

George's reply was a raised index finger. He listened again. What was the game that Phil's son liked to play? The one where you hammer all the little people who pop up, but every time you hit one, they just pop up somewhere else?

Bastard. Maybe he'd been too concerned, after all, for this particular American. Maybe he'd been wrong all along. Maybe the Agency *should* have killed him.

The Savarona first touched ground near Ortaköy, lodging its stern between two fishing boats then, in a long and slow rotation, squeezing like a vice until the boat frames yielded in a sudden, violent fury. As kindling rained and splashed about, a mystified crowd looked on from the banks. Free again, the yacht retreated to the waves and lumbered back towards Asia, forcing a cargo ship to reverse its engines, then into the shallows where it tore through a fishing net and splintered the wooden deck of an old historic river house before it was again seized by the current.

Inside, the hostages gasped and held on where they could. Wine glasses toppled and trays of half-cold börek slid to the floor; the air reeked of sweat and hors d'ouvres. The hostages finished what remained in their glasses, then became impatient. What were the terrorists waiting for? They seemed as rudderless as the ship, arguing with each other in furtive whispers.

"Killing everyone wasn't our plan," said Taylor.

"To kill everyone, not possible," said Gazi. "But ten, twenty, before also we are killed."

"No. Let me go look for Galip!"

Gazi ignored him. "When the police are coming, you will shoot to the people only. If you shoot to the police, maybe you kill one. Maybe you kill two. One and two police. What does it care? Watch only the people you will shoot. Anladin mi? Do you understand? There," he said, pointing at the Americans. "And I will shoot to here."

"No. Let me find a passenger who can sail this ship!"

Gazi threw his head back, no. "The ship will goes to where it goes. We only are three now. Metin must to stay outside. Galip yok. Gone. Chikmish. We never going to see the island. I cannot to watch every person alone. Do not make low your gun!"

Taylor looked from face to face. Now some of them stared back, less fearful now, more assertive, an untrustworthy bunch, as if they understood that three could not hope to manage them all, plus the ship, when the police showed up, as of course they would eventually. In Turkey, terrorists could expect no quarter. His right hand felt the chill of the lead pipe he'd swung earlier in the night.

"Why are we making no demands?"

"Let the police come," said Gazi. "We will not negotiate. Let them come. Let them make the incident. Let the blood be on their hands. Bak! Your gun!"

Taylor grimaced as he leveled his weapon. Who would have thought a pistol could be so heavy? His forearm ached with pain, threatened to cramp. He was holding it too hard. He tried easing his grip, but feared it would fall from his trembling hand. Defiantly, he let it droop to the floor. He glanced at Gazi and felt no comradeship—only hate and horror. This was not as it was meant to be. Why was he here? What was the point? The cause had never before seemed so remote, so abstract. He felt the panic rise, and looked to the door where Metin had gone, tried to spot him on the deck. How far away was he? Could he hear or see them where he stood? Outside the windows, the Ciragan Palace hotel passed slowly by, phosphorescent through the smog; a man and a woman waved tentatively from their five-hundred-dollar-a-night room.

"These are not our orders, to kill everyone." He squared to face Gazi, his gun still lowered. Defiantly he whispered, "Apo didn't order this."

Gazi cocked his head, said nothing, waited for Taylor to go on. The trace of a smile, an unfamiliar expression, crossed his lips.

"Maybe one tourist, or two, or a judge or a teacher to make a political point. Killing one is more powerful than killing twenty. I have read the minutes of the seventh congress. Our orders would not..."

Gazi's smile was gone; he jerked his chin. "The seventh congress! Those said to lay down our arms, said us to surrender, Apo betrayed us, esek. On a safe island in the middle of the sea he commands us stop fighting and have a political discussion. Neden? Why? Are the tortures stopped? Do they tell us come down from the mountains? Is there amnesty? A free Kurdistan? No! Apo, when he is captured, he begged for mercy, he cried like a baby, do not kill me, he said, the PKK is wanting peace, we are not fighting for a free Kurdistan, only for the right to have a political discussion, a political discussion!" Gazi nearly choked on the words. He waved his AK-47 about. All eyes in the room zeroed in on his gun.

Taylor drew back, forced his weapon upward. It all made sense—the trouble with the suits, having to use their old guns. "Why must we kill everyone?" But of course he knew. His voice cracked with knowledge. The truth made him sick. This was a7 rogue operation, completely unapproved. He had joined a breakaway faction. Why hadn't he seen it before? Was there any way to make it right?

Perhaps there was—both for Gazi and for himself. "Let's concentrate on the worst of them," he said weakly. "Let's kill the CIA."

This gave Gazi pause. His eyes swept the hostages, as if seeing them for the first time. "Tamam. But who the CIA are?"

Taylor said nothing, just walked to the center of the room and cleared his throat. "Any employees of the Central Intelligence Agency should come forward now," he said. From the corner of his eye he saw Tim, just one face out of many. He laughed inside at how he stared away, refused to meet his eyes. Tim would never reveal their secret and, ironically, nor would he. Their relationship—what it was and what it wasn't—he couldn't possibly explain now to Gazi—not with so many nervous guns in the room. No doubt Tim had his own taskmasters to call him to account. Let it be a permanent pact between them. Let the secret go to their graves.

"For every agent who does not step forward, two innocent hostages will be killed," said Taylor. He trained his weapon on one of the congressmen, a

Republican from California, the only woman in the delegation. You have ten seconds, he shouted.

Gazi seemed to approve. He stepped around the hostages, circled them like livestock. He came up from behind, near the bar, listening to his comrade count. The hostages murmured in fear, shuffled this way and that, glanced about; the important thing was to steer clear of the Republican from California who gamely stood her ground, her face ashen.

Seven. Six. Five. But Gazi had stopped listening. A red light shone at the foot of the bar, mocking him. Four. How casually placed it was, as if someone had accidentally dropped it there. But Gazi knew better. Three. And for the first time, he knew that Red Halabja was right—the CIA *was* in the room. Two.

"Stop," he shouted. He picked up the cell phone and held it high in one hand, his AK-47 in the other. "Who?" His voice shook. "Who is this telephone?"

George was half way to the banquet hall when the shots rang out, short and crisp, execution-style. He had no way of knowing they were only warning shots, fired harmlessly into the ceiling. He felt woozy, dizzy; and had to stop to catch his breath. Another turn and he would be upon them; it was that simple. He put his hand to his breast pocket; yes, it was there; he pulled out the photo and held it out front, as if it might somehow shield him. He couldn't stop now. His movements were no longer voluntary, but a matter of fate. All his life he had been a spectator, and for what? Certainty swept him up, carried him along, set his head straight. For the first time all day, maybe the first time all year, he felt no fear. He put one foot in front of the other and repeated the motion. The body in Gelibolu, his near miss with Nazan—all roads led here.

He paused at the end of the corridor, choosing his moment. He could see the banquet room now; some of the hostages could see him. There was nothing left to hide. It was chaos now, a full room in motion. Gazi wanted the owner of the cell phone. Truman stepped forward. Then Phil and Tim stepped forward too. Priscilla stepped between the men, shouting words that meant nothing, was shoved back, hurled herself forward again. "I'm responsible here," she said. You couldn't hear her above the screams. Taylor lifted the gun at her, brought it to her face, yelled as she stood her ground. Phil pulled her away. Taylor's eyes darted in all directions at once.

Then the motion stopped. George found himself studying the room, the center of attention. He heard himself speak and was surprised at the authority in his voice, the calm. He looked directly at Gazi, as if only he mattered. *"It's over,"* he said firmly. *"Halabja has played you for a fool. Don't you see?"* He spoke rapidly, deliberately slurring the words, grinding them together, as semi-literate as a kebapci from Kars. Taylor flashed from face to face. *"Yes, of course these men are CIA. Ask Halabja. He can tell you everything. What kind of information they got from him, and how much they paid him for it."*

"English!" shouted Taylor. "Speak English!"

George ignored him, persisting in his most colloquial Turkish, spilling it all—everything the photo revealed, everything Phil wanted hidden, everything the Agency might have killed to conceal. And only those who were not cleared to hear it—every Turk in the room—understood.

George held the photo high. Now Phil looked afraid.

Taylor bolted across the room, his pistol thrust out at eye-level. But Gazi was the first one to George. He snatched the photo from his hand. "Metin," he cried, turning toward the outer deck. "Metin!"

"What is it?" Taylor demanded, trying to get in close enough to see. But Gazi only turned his back.

"Show me!"

The little troll was more nimble than he looked. He danced to the side as Taylor lunged, then buried the butt of his weapon in Taylor's face, sending him to the floor. He spun full circle, ready for an attack that didn't come, then steadied himself, studied the photo again, looked at Tim, then back at the photo. Why didn't Metin come? Taylor writhed on the floor, clawing in the wrong place for his gun, his eye already swelling above his caved-in jaw. Gazi approached slowly, speaking in low tones, his left hand clenching the photo, his AK-47 trained at Taylor's head.

George shrank back against the crowd. His speaking part was over. He was happy to leave the stage. Then, all at once—the pop so loud and close it might just as well have been inside his head, the splash of blood like a pebble hitting water, icy wind in his ear—not a breeze but a gale. He felt his bladder start, and with a conscious effort shut it down. The little troll had no time to register surprise; like a puppet with his strings cut, Gazi withered to the floor, purple-red spreading on his temple.

When George turned, he saw the gun and knew that it was true indeed; all roads led to this spot. He felt a sort of catharsis, a bureaucrat's epiphany. Two of his case files could now be merged.

Bill, yes, Bill, that was his name. *My* name! For there *I* was, poised to fire a second round, the revolver steady in my right hand, my left thrust behind me like some comic book action figure. Fancy shooting, if I do say so myself, a hell of a shot, one-handed as it was, and with an old pistol that on any other day might have sprayed wide and buried its cargo deep in George's skull, instead of merely passing through an ear en route to its intended destination.

George sensed Taylor rising up behind him but couldn't turn, not while his ear exploded with sound, not while I still aimed the gun, no more life-like than a wax figure, my eyes too big for my head.

George's ear throbbed, sending shockwaves through his body. A chill washed over him, buckling his knees, but Craine's strong hands were there to prop him up. His boss, the consul. Now it was Craine who stared down the barrel of my gun, his lips moving without effect, like an angry mime, for my ears were ringing too. As he advanced on me, my gun moved with him, the slightest of adjustments, impossible to confirm.

Don't shoot, he seemed to be saying. In his arms he held a slumping George. Behind him staggered Taylor with his hands to his face, holding the bones in place.

I stood my ground.

Then someone did shoot, again and again, a roar of gunfire, bullets flying in all directions, a good-old fashioned gun fight, as Turkish anti-terrorist police rather belatedly stormed the ship.

* * *

The cars on Burnside edged slowly past, well within the speed limit and sticking to their lanes, or announcing their intent to do otherwise with bright red flashes from their tail lights. Silently they moved, their horns dormant, to be employed only in emergencies, like flares kept in the trunk. I smelled beer, or at least its components, from the Henry Weinhard Brewery. The side of the old brick building was overgrown with hops. This was industry, Oregon-style.

I walked uphill. The air was cool and wet, but ever so clean above the hillside homes that went for a million, a million and a half, these days. Perhaps it helped that there weren't cardboard shanties wedged between them, with coal fires lit by refugees of poverty, war, and worse. The power lines suggested ample supplies of electricity for all. The landscape was fungus-green, a saturated sponge.

I found a Thriftway. The novelty would wear off soon enough, but as long as it lasted I would stroll the aisles, losing myself in the bounty, the sheer abundance. The cans and boxes and plastic bottles were stacked in sacred pyramids, like temples to the Gods, their labels praying in the same direction. There were a hundred different kinds of cereal. A girl sold something called Frapuccino from a mobile unit; in her matching hat and apron she seemed at peace with the world. The checkout girl and I spoke English to each other, not snippets of easy words but full sentences, while I paid for ready-to-eat sushi and a Snapple and a *Time* magazine. We had an actual conversation, all friendly-like, and then she said in conclusion, "You have a good one, sir," which I took as my cue to leave.

To call it fun might be a stretch, for no real fun was possible on my present cocktail of pills. But satisfaction was not too strong a word, albeit of a rather workmanlike variety.

I found 23rd street and turned left. There were more shops than I remembered, little smoke-free places with tie-dyed twenty-somethings sipping from cups with lids. In America, the smallest size was a *tall*. I continued my nostalgia tour by finding the Nob Hill Bar and Grill, where I was once eighty-sixed for spitting on a waitress. So much time had passed that I now went unrecognized, or perhaps the statute of limitations for expectorating on the help had expired. In any case I went unmolested as I found my seat and ordered a Chivas. After ten minutes the bartender brought a dusty bottle. He poured it with no small hesitation—perhaps it was reverence—and gave me a napkin with my glass. I threw the ice against my teeth.

The faces of the strangers disappointed, but I was no more capable of deep lows anymore than I was of manic highs, so I only took another sip and settled back in my chair and thought about my failure. *Fight the Power* was no more, if indeed it ever was. I tried to summon some grief for my moribund book, some appropriate heartache, but the Xanax got in the way and I succeeded only in feeling vaguely thirsty. So I finished my drink and ordered two more.

When the waitress brought my drinks, I tried to hand one back. "Drink to new beginnings?" I asked her.

"Ten-fifty," she replied, extending her hand.

When I had finished both drinks, I stumbled outside. A light rain was falling. I shoved my hands in my pockets and let the rain come down and wondered if I would ever feel again. Anything at all. Scenes from the Savarona flooded back. Perhaps a smile came to my face. When I pulled the trigger… Yes, when I pulled the trigger and I saw the splash of blood, then stood there, considering whom to shoot next, my arm as steady as a marksman—in that moment I was God. But not a benevolent God, not a loving, forgiving, merciful God. No, I was an angry, vengeful God, a Leviticus in-your-face kind of God, ready to give someone a good smiting for eating shellfish or touching the skin of a pig or working on the Sabbath day.

But then the moment passed and I was just a man, and not a particularly impressive one at that, deeply ashamed and, I dare say, as disgraced as Adam in the garden. A moment later my gun was bouncing on the floor, alerting me to the fact that I had dropped it. Then came the roar of gunfire from every direction. Amid the chaos, only I remained standing, frozen—for I had killed and I would never be the same again.

Phil's was the first face that George saw when he awoke. He rolled over and threw up. A nurse entered the room and placed a bucket on the floor.

"Nice to see you too."

"It's the anesthesia, I guess."

"How are you feeling?"

George nodded and touched his ear. Then his hand went to the pile of bandages on his stomach.

"They found the bullet. Next to your pancreas." Phil looked away. "They say there's no permanent damage."

"I don't remember getting shot in the gut. Jesus. My ear, yes, but not my stomach."

Phil shrugged. "It was a Turkish slug. One of the special ops guys. An accident, probably a ricochet. If it'd been a direct hit, I suppose it would have gone right through you."

"I feel like shit."

"Can I do anything?"

"You've done enough, thanks." This was as much as he would say—and this, only because he could chalk it up to the medication.

The nurse used a torn rag to mop up the puddle of barf. When she was finished, she fluffed up his pillow. There was an awkward silence until she was gone. Then Phil said, "You're going home."

"Am I?" George had thought this might be coming. But still he hadn't fully anticipated the flood of mixed emotions, the clashing sense of failure and relief.

"We found quite a haul at their safehouse. They had half the consulate under surveillance. You especially. A diagram of your apartment. Maps. Admin doesn't want to get rid of your place, too good a lease they say, but we'll make sure they do." He drifted to the window and lifted the shade, squinted into the sunlight.

It occurred to George that the smog was gone. How long had he been out?

"You left your apartment every day at seven o'clock, George. Seven-ten at the latest. You took the shore road almost every day. If they hadn't gone after the Savarona, chances are they would have gone after you."

George considered this carefully, and decided to believe him.

"Between that and the girl, what was her name…"

"Nazan."

"Nazan. And what you did on the ship. And…" He took a breath. "And your involvement with Taylor. Well, let's just say you're up to your neck in it."

"Is this going to—"

"Show up in your performance file? Tell me, George. Was that the last of the photos? The one you showed everyone on the ship?"

George hesitated. "No," he said. "I've got two more. Just two. They're at home. They're in my—"

"Sock drawer? Okay, we got those. Had to pack you out, you know. That's all? Good. Listen, this is an operational decision, nothing more. None of this is going to hurt your career. I'll see to that."

George let his surprise show. Pleasant surprise. He had expected Phil to be in a rage after all that happened on the ship. "What about Truman?"

"What about him?" Phil's eyes followed George's to the flowers on the credenza; the arrangement was flamboyant, much like the sender. "The department hired him with its eyes open. Truman's not our problem."

They were quiet for a while. Then George said, "Would you really have killed Taylor?"

Phil laughed, a bit too heartily. "You've seen too many movies, George." He turned again and studied the sunlight. "Look, George, we made some mistakes. Taylor, that little… He took us for a ride. But don't misunderstand, George. We've got other assets out there, good ones, giving us good information, saving lives. Just one bad apple, George, that's all he was. But that's the trouble, you know? People only see our failures. People only know about it when we screw up. They don't see our successes, *our wins.* That's the nature of clandestine work. And so people get mad when we break the rules. But they don't know anything. They don't know about all the good stuff."

"Look at it this way, George. When some psycho walks into Washington with a nuke in his suitcase, will they still be mad? Will they still care about the rules? I don't think so."

He crossed the room and put a hand on George's shoulder, a gesture so wildly out of character that George had to flinch. "Your file is clean, George. You have my word." Then, too smooth to be an afterthought: "So long as you keep our little secrets, we'll keep yours."

"But I don't—" He bit his tongue. Truth be damned, the important thing was that it was over, both of their files were closed. And so he was already forgetting, already flying to America, when he hung out his hand and allowed Phil to shake it goodbye.

Listen up. I would have liked to pay George a visit too, if for no other reason than for once to chat with a diplomat as he lay recuperating in a hospital bed and not the other way around. But the Turks seemed to prefer that I proceed directly to the airport, without any stops en route, and even dispatched a follow car to ensure that I did.

My sense was that the police didn't know quite what to make of me. I had escaped from a psychiatric hospital, and had broken locks and doors in the process (this was news to me). I had impersonated a journalist to sneak aboard a ship full of dignitaries. I had placed another man's wallet in my pocket, and used his cash and credit cards. I had brought a concealed weapon on board

Atatürk's ship, an unregistered one whose origins were murky. I had fired it, taking off a goodly portion of a diplomat's ear. I had failed to settle my debts at a half-dozen local establishments, some of them reputable. My visa had expired.

On the plus side, I had killed a terrorist and some former hostages were calling me a hero. I had an American passport—a new one thanks to Winston—and a courteous manner under interrogation. The cop had shown interest when I told him how the government had opened my head when I was a child, and had done fancy things inside. Ever since then, I said, I had wanted to fight the power, but since killing a man, I wasn't sure I felt that way any longer. I had had a good run, but now I was leaning toward resuming my medication. The cop said nothing, just listened in silence and tugged his mustache from time to time. At last he stood and laid his hand on my shoulder. "You think such very big thoughts," he said. "You have to stop these thinkings, and only just take care of yourself."

"You're right," I told him. He was a wise Turk indeed. "I should have listened to you from the very beginning. The important thing is to cultivate one's garden."

And so it was that the local authorities settled on deportation as the only sensible solution, with the strong admonition that I never return to Turkey. Meanwhile, the consulate had decided that Winston should accompany me all the way to America, door to door as it were, to ensure a smooth voyage.

The police were with us all the way to passport control, where they dropped back and let Winston pay the fines from his pocket.

Nazan had no such restrictions on her movements. While I was at the airport she was at the hospital, where George was packing his things, moving gingerly about the room. He nodded as she entered, as if he'd been waiting for her all along.

"I wanted to say goodbye."

"Well," he said. "Goodbye."

This seemed to sting, but she ignored it and pressed on, talking about everything except what was on their minds. The government had failed to secure a vote of confidence, so there would be yet more elections; Galatasaray had won the European Cup and their supporters were dancing in the streets again; spring had arrived and the smog was gone—why not open the shades? George barely listened. In a matter of hours, he would be flying home; Turkey had already taken its place among the Monrovias of his mind—to be remembered as one remembers a bad book, populated by characters instead of people.

She grew more anxious as the time ran short. When he told her he had a car waiting, she insisted he take a seat. "George, why did you never recruit me? I gave you those snap shots, I showed you how useful I could be. Really, George, must I beg to be an informant? Was it so difficult for Taylor to be hired?"

"You've got it all wrong, Nazan."

"I want to work for the best."

"You want to work for the best pay."

"Is that a crime?"

"You should have come yesterday," said George. "You have the wrong guy." He was relieved when his driver appeared at the door. "I'm sorry, I have to go." The driver took his bag and for a moment they were alone again.

"It doesn't matter," she smiled weakly. Her eyes glistened as she crossed her arms. "I am not in the habit of begging for visas for my friends. But with Vram, you see, I'm responsible for his brother being in prison. I collected the evidence. I led them to Rabo, just as I led you to Taylor." She paused. "They are both terrorists, but still I feel guilty, because of the money. Is that why? I must be daft for telling you this. Do you think that I'm too sentimental? That I don't have enough *sang froid* to be your agent?"

No, that wasn't what he felt. She was still a mercenary in his eyes, though her admission of guilt for deceiving Vram's family redeemed her a little.

"Never mind," she said. "I really just came here to thank you. For what you did for Vram. So…" she stumbled. "Thank you." With that she was gone.

George listened to her footsteps in the hall, listened until he could hear them no more, until the room was silent again. He had no idea what she was talking about, no idea what he had done for Vram, no idea what she had thanked him for. But nor did he care. He was tired of understanding.

His driver stood again at the door. Just one second, he motioned with a raised hand. He returned to the window and pulled up the shade, and as the sun poured in he covered his eyes.

Of course, he had done nothing special for Vram. It was Dawn who Nazan should have thanked, for it was Dawn who had cut a deal with God aboard the Savarona, Dawn the hostage who had promised never again to deny aid to a Christian if only her life would be spared. Who's to say it was a bad idea? Perhaps the other hostages cut their own deals as well. After all, most of them emerged unscathed. George, on the other hand, hadn't prayed, and look what happened to him—a bullet through his ear and one near his pancreas, bullets that had not been meant for him, but for others. One wide shot and a ricochet—what were the odds? Are there really such things as accidents?

By Tuesday morning Dawn had come to her senses, and had stopped issuing visas to all Christians who applied. Three Syrians and a little old Greek were summarily sent packing. Perhaps she'd had a second conversation with God the night before, and He had agreed to let her off the hook. No matter—Vram had been lucky enough to apply on Monday and was already packing his bags. In the Hurtuoğlu family, the mood was bittersweet.

And so I supposed that Vram and his Uncle Hikmet had booked themselves on United, same as me. Hikmet liked a drink as much as the next guy, and even in coach class the liquor was free. The stewardess avoided my attempts at eye contact but I was persistent, and soon I had another Chivas on my retractable tray. Winston smiled and wagged his finger.

"Tut, tut," he said, one of his many useless expressions.

"One last hurrah."

"With you, my friend, I'm afraid there's no such thing." Winston had long since raised his tray to make room for the briefcase on his lap. Now he drummed it anxiously with all ten fingers. Inside, I knew, was his CONFIDENTIAL file. At the gate, he had allowed me to look but not touch. But that was quite enough for now. The three of us were together at last—I felt immensely satisfied.

I eased the seat back and lost myself in the droning of the engine. The Serzone coursed through my veins; the Congentin made for a pleasant mix. Finally the Turks had gotten it right. I opened my eyes and heard myself speak. "What happens next?"

"Health and Human Resources will meet us at JFK. They'll help you get back on your feet." He paused thoughtfully and added, "This may sound, well, crazy, but back there, on the ship, for the briefest of moments..." He drummed his fingers on the brief case some more. "Well, back there, I had the vaguest notion that you really might shoot me." At that, he chuckled and stared at the seat in front of him, as if he'd unraveled a great mystery in the little slot where they kept the barf bag and the in-flight magazine.

The stewardess came from the other direction, and I intercepted her with my cup of melted ice. With newfound restraint I let her take it away without asking for another. A moment later we were descending through piles of fluffy nimbus. Winston had fallen asleep, his head toppled sideways, a trace of spittle on his lips. I watched him and wondered where they would come for me. Would it be at the gate or at the baggage claim? Either way it was okay, I told myself. The time had come. I would accept their help; I would turn in my passport; I would swallow their daily pills. Hallelujah, throw me in the river. I needed a rest. Free will was such a burden.

I looked at Winston sleeping peacefully and remembered his question. "No," I said aloud. "That doesn't sound crazy at all."

They had intended to meet us at the gate, but running late, failed to spot us before we made a stop at the bathroom. "I must use the little boy's room," said Winston, handing me his briefcase and obliging me to stand idly by as he stood forever at the urinal, reading clippings of *Calvin and Hobbs* that some genius had scotch-taped to the wall. As it happened, I was still holding the briefcase when we walked back out into the corridor and followed the first sign toward ground transportation. A man and a woman in suits stopped us well before we got there.

"I'm Bill Bigelow," I said, shaking their hands.

But they only had eyes for Winston. "We're from the Office of Medical Services," they explained. "No, the State Department's. Yes, that's right. You have an appointment in Med this afternoon. You weren't informed? Well that's not right, but I can assure you it's not our fault. We've spoken to the embassy. Yes. Yes. Your admin officer will hear from us, I can tell you that. But come, we can catch the next Washington shuttle if we hurry. Your return tickets? It's all taken care of. Here are your new orders. Can we go now? Nice to meet you, young man. Health and Human Services? I don't know. Try waiting at the gate. No? I suppose you might try the white courtesy phones."

And with that they left me standing there, left me with the briefcase, left me watching Winston's stricken face as he glanced back at me every few steps down the long wide corridor. Was he waiting for me to intervene with his captors, to spring him loose with some daring stunt? Or did he simply want his briefcase back? This I pondered as he became smaller and smaller down the corridor. Soon, Winston and his handlers were out of sight and I was truly alone.

I looked around. There were no white courtesy phones in sight. In disbelief, I looked at the briefcase and my head cleared a little.

They weren't at the baggage claim, where I retrieved my backpack from the turnstile, nor did anyone approach as I sat outside, absently picking stones off the sidewalk. Every passing taxi honked my way. Free will—there was no escaping it! With a sigh of resignation, I rose and counted the money in my wallet then rode a cab downtown until the buildings towered above us and we passed a diner boasting breakfast for a dollar-ninety-nine. I ordered coffee and took a seat. There were butterflies in my stomach as I set the briefcase on my lap and undid the clasps. The paperwork was inches deep. I felt dizzy, almost panicky, and closed it up again. How many thousands of miles had I traveled so that I could have this moment? And now I felt the oddest urge not to read it at all.

A dream made real is a terrifying thing.

I decided that I would read the top page only, no more than that.

It is said that the Bosphorous Straits, the mighty waters which cut through Istanbul, flow at once in two directions: On the surface, the current is strong and true, spilling from the Black Sea south, driving untold tons of sewage first to the Sea of Marmara then on to the Aegean, where it clings to the bodies of unsuspecting bathers. But farther below, in the depths beneath the white caps, scouring the mud which holds the secrets of a millennium, a hidden current doubles back and flows north, ensuring that the city will taste its refuse twice.

Not bad, I thought to myself, though not so very good either. The metaphor annoyed me, the north-south thing. After all, this was Turkey, where everything was about East versus West—you know, the only country to sit astride two continents. The bridge. The crossroads. Orient and Occident. *The clash of civilizations*. So, you see, it didn't fit. Not for Turkey. No, not for Turkey.

But now my curiosity had gotten the best of me, and I read on without pause. Only when I had come to the end of twenty pages did I stop reading, and put it back in the briefcase, and closed it up tight. I finished my coffee in silence. There was nothing in those pages, I thought, that a little editing couldn't fix.

George's shirt hangs on the open bathroom door, a spit stain on his button-down collar. The window above the sink is foggy and wet. He lies back in the tub and shuts his eyes, enjoying his first bath without stitches. His bad ear slips underwater; he sits up with a start. "I'm sorry?"

"She was begging for you," says Margaret. His wife stands in the doorway with a glass of Chardonnay, reminding him of his own. He takes a sip, then lies back, crossing his legs to hide his groin. She looks him up and down and smiles. "Will you have that forever?"

He ponders the scar on his belly. "You should see the other guy."

"I can't. I'm married."

He splashes water on his face and rubs his eyes. "Maybe I should go in there," he says.

"No. She's asleep now. You read her too many stories already. She's usually in bed by eight. Just stay out now."

"Will she be in our bed again?"

"Not if I can help it." She looks at him coyly.

"I'm nice and clean."

"I noticed." She sets her wine down and crosses her arms, displacing her tank top so that her midriff shows. Stretch marks peek out from the top of her jeans and her breasts are lower than he remembered, but still she has never looked so beautiful. "What time are you going in tomorrow?"

"Early, for once. I need to go to the transportation office. Our household effects finally got to Istanbul. Truman told me when he called." He checks her face before going on. "The day after they shipped me out. The day after!" He glances at her anxiously. "Can you believe it? They even moved them into my apartment. So we're completely unpacked now, just in the wrong country."

He is relieved when she only smiles.

"And I'm meeting with Personnel. They've been treating me with kid gloves, these guys, telling me to take all this time off. Maybe they're afraid I've got some kind of post-traumatic stress disorder."

"Maybe they're afraid you'll sue."

He touches his belly scar again, then the missing part of his ear that they have promised to replace with skin from his ass. Miraculously his hearing has returned. "I think they're going to give me a choice between the China desk and the Ops Center. Or..." he hesitates. "There's this refugee job in Geneva. Getting shot may have been the best career move I ever made."

"Geneva?" She looks alarmed. "You said you were looking at Washington jobs."

"I am, I am. I was just saying—"

"I don't want to go overseas. We're all settled here. How can you even think of going overseas again? You need a break. You said..."

"I know, I'm sorry. I didn't mean I was interested..."

"What's wrong with the China desk? Or the Ops Center?"

"Nothing. Nothing at all. Let's stay. I agree. You decide. I promise. Okay?"

She looks at him warily, sits at the edge of the tub and lets her hand drag in the water. She gives him a squeeze that's playful, but also makes him gasp. "You better mean it."

And he does. In that tiny bathroom, and in the room next door, is all he'll ever need—of this and only this he can be sure of, at least for now. Whether it will still be true in the morning he doesn't know, but for the moment, the right answer is also the honest one—how rare. It seems a moment worth savoring.

"Come to bed," she says, standing and removing her top in a single motion. The water laps at his legs as he strains to pull himself out of the tub. Before he is out, Margaret returns and pokes her head in the doorway. Her arms shield her bare breasts. She looks thoughtful. "Geneva, huh?" she says.

Listen up. That's all I have to say about George. Tempted as I am to use words like *happily ever after*, I know that you wouldn't believe them, and I'd be lying if I said I knew what they meant. Let's just say that George's life has entered a phase too dull to record. What remains can be said by someone else—someone better versed in the ways of the human heart. My domain, you know, has always been the head, and the head has grown fuzzy thanks to the cocktail of pills I've taken to swallowing each morning, the pills that get me up and out to the workaday world. Without the pills, God knows how many McGregor woods and PING irons would go unsold. Good retail help is hard to find these days.

It's not so easy to write anymore. Gresham is roughly as inspiring as Australia was. But now, instead of flies and jogging suits, it's suburbs and meds that fog me in. Nevertheless I do my best, tapping away on a garage sale typewriter adjusted to my height by three hundred stained and crinkly pages of *Fight the Power*, exclamation mark. My new book, which still lacks a title, is slow going, even though my only distraction is a young Chinese man who sometimes appears at the dumpsters outside my window, hefty bags in hand. I dare say that we have struck up something of a friendship, though we've expressed it so far only in waves. The restaurant must do a decent business, for there seems an awful lot of garbage.

Only my sense of obligation keeps me writing—not to any person, certainly not to myself—but to this file, to this collection of facts that I inherited from Winston Craine, whether by accident or design I'll never know. But I do know that the file is all that stands between devastating boredom and me, my last defense against the sheer pointlessness of it all.

If I don't use it, it seems only fair that I should return it to Winston. Once, in a fit of self-doubt, I came close to doing just that, calling the switchboard at the State Department where I was transferred to an office identified by an acronym I don't recall, and heard Winston's somber voice before hanging up without a word, wondering if my number could be traced. After that I felt less guilty, maybe because Winston had sounded so officious, so in place, so very *State Department.* He certainly didn't sound like someone in the care of psychiatrists—so I thought hopefully that he wasn't, at least not during business hours.

What had he told me back in Australia, so many months ago? That if anything should happen to him, he wanted me to have the file? Well, something had happened to him—he'd been co-opted by the bureaucracy, dragged back into the fold, reclaimed by the system, absorbed by *It*. Wasn't I merely carrying out his wishes?

And so I settled down to business with the file, with Winston's file, *his* manuscript, *his* book. God knows how many hundreds of hours Winston had spent scribbling in his little spiral notebook out by the visa files, or pecking at his typewriter behind a closed office door; the result was quite substantial.

For the first few months I barely tinkered with his words. But in time, I became more daring and started working in my own thoughts, filling the gaps in Craine's narrative, perhaps embellishing on Winston's story just a bit, until the manuscript evolved into what you see now—not Winston's book, but ours.

As I read it back now, there's a *wholeness* that is satisfying. What I mean to say is that I can no longer distinguish Craine's parts from mine, between the contents of his file and the clutter of my brain. On paper, they have merged so completely that it is no longer possible to say which is which and whose is whose. The facts are a blur—yet facts they remain. For I can assure you that every word of this story is true. Every single word.

Well, perhaps not *literally* true. But certainly *politically* true—as Vram's father might have put it. And isn't that all that matters?

Hanging above my desk, that is to say above the slab of wood that sits atop twelve sturdy milk crates and holds up my typewriter, are some photos from Turkey, among them the portrait of Lahcen and me and the Doggy-beyazit Police Chief. Nearby are the faxes that I once dispatched from the Marmara Hotel, which remain, so far as I know, unanswered. In the morning they inspire me to write long and hard, but in the evening I do more sorting than writing—of my many pills, that is—so that when morning comes I won't confuse the red ones with the whites, or the white ones with the greens, or the blue ones with the yellows whose job it is to counter the side effects of the reds. This I do for the next day, and the next day only, to ensure that I will actually take them, with no grand promises for the next day after that.

A word about Taylor. Unlike Gazi and the other terrorists he survived the Savarona with only a broken jaw and was sentenced by a state security court to thirty years in prison for membership in a terrorist organization, among other crimes. His father was not pleased with the sentence, nor was Zimmerman, though I hear it didn't stop the Congressman from supporting that big helicopter sale he was always fretting about.

In prison, Taylor learned that he was no longer a member of the PKK—not after participating in Gazi's rogue operation. And so for many months he found himself among the outcasts, neither criminal nor freedom fighter, huddled in a distant corner of the ward, bait for the sexually predatory, seldom to stray from his cot.

When he was cut one day with a knife, there was sensible talk of moving him to the foreigners' ward to live among the drug traffickers. But Taylor refused. I suppose he still harbored dreams of reclaiming his place in the organization and was no more capable of cutting his losses, of turning his back on the cause that had sustained him so long, than I had been capable of abandoning my flights of manic folly. Taylor was no more willing to be tranquilized, to have the fire snuffed out, than I was, and I suppose I can't fault him for that.

And so, against the consulate's advice, Taylor got himself transferred to a different ward, filled with members of Dev Sol, the Revolutionary Left, a group with even less compunction than the PKK when it came to taking lives. With Dev Sol, idealism knew no boundaries. Last I heard, Taylor was on a hunger strike. He seemed happy enough.

That's really all I know, or at least all I have the energy to tell. In my little Gresham world, I have lost touch with the rest of them—though from time to time I'll be walking along and see a flash of face that looks like Winston, or George, or Truman, or Dawn, or Priscilla, but of course it never is. Once I even thought I saw Vram on 82nd Street with a sack full of groceries, but on closer inspection I saw that it was just some other new immigrant, ambling home at day's end to feed his family, his face drawn with determination, his hands worn by labor.

Not Vram at all—just someone else, making a better life for himself and his own, seeking the American dream, cultivating his garden.

Printed in the United States
30381LVS00004B/278

9 781413 714463